Praise for Mary Wine's

"A wonderful, sen... ...
Cleverly written, tou... ...
sible to put down."

—RT Book Reviews, 4.5 Stars

"One gripping plot twist follows another: dastardly English trickery, complex Scottish alliances, and kilt-tossing, sheet-incinerating lovemaking."

—*Publishers Weekly*

"Whenever I pick up a book by Mary Wine I know I'm going to be engrossed in the story for hours."

—*Night Owl Romance* Reviewer Top Pick

"Love in the Scottish Highlands has never looked so good... Great characters, thrilling drama, and smoldering passion make this a 'must read' novel."

—*Romance Reviews*

"Not to be missed."

—Lora Leigh, *New York Times* #1 bestselling author

"Mary Wine brings history to life with major sizzle factor."

—Lucy Monroe, *USA Today* bestselling author of *For Duty's Sake*

"Deeply romantic, scintillating, and absolutely delicious."

—Sylvia Day, national bestselling author of
Pride and Pleasure

"Hot enough to warm even the coldest Scottish nights… An addictive tale of betrayal, lust, power, and love with detail-rich descriptions."

—*Publishers Weekly* Starred Review

"[The characters] fight just as passionately as they love while intrigue abounds and readers turn the pages faster and faster!"

—*RT Book Reviews*, 4 Stars

"Fiery passion as elemental, raw, and beautiful as the Scottish Highlands… Details that intrigue, excite, and pull the reader into this time in Scottish history with characters that are breathtaking make this one a keeper."

—*Long and Short Reviews*

"Mary Wine takes the passion to a new level."

—*Romance Fiction on Suite101.com*

"If you like hot and sexy Scottish medieval books then this is the series for you!"

—*Queen of Happy Endings*

Also by Mary Wine

The
TROUBLE
with
HIGHLANDERS

MARY WINE

sourcebooks
casablanca

Published by Sourcebooks Casablanca, an imprint of Sourcebooks,
Inc.
P.O. Box 4410, Naperville, Illinois 60567-4410
(630) 961-3900
FAX: (630) 961-2168
www.sourcebooks.com

Printed and bound in Canada
WC 10 9 8 7 6 5 4 3 2 1

This one is for Sharon Robinson. A golden friend and a whole lot of fun too! You're a gem, and so is your camel-herding man!

One

MacLeod land, late summer 1488

"YE ARE NAE ME HUSBAND..."

"*Maybe I want it just that way, marriage is boring...*"

Daphne MacLeod kicked at her bedding, but the dream held her tight. Part of her was content, maybe even eager to sink down into the memory of being in Norris Sutherland's arms.

"*I want ye demanding and passionate, nae filled with duty, lass...*"

She twisted again, feeling his arms around her. His strength had been impressive and arousing. Never had she imagined how much she'd enjoy being pressed against a man, beneath him or when she decided to straddle his hips and take charge of their pace. Just as long as she felt his hands holding her as though letting her go might devastate him.

"*And I want ye to stop telling me what to do...*"

Need and yearning filled her. It traveled along her body, teasing parts of her she hadn't known could feel so good. The sensation was building, twisting tighter as her body neared the point where it would burst into a shower of pleasure.

Instead, she jerked out of her sleep, escaping the hold of the dream only to discover that her freedom was cold and dark. She pressed her fist against her mouth to silence her cry. The chamber was silent, and yet it felt as though Norris was in it. She could sense him, would swear she felt him close enough to reach out and touch.

But there was no need to light a candle. The wind rattled the window shutters, blowing inside through the broken glass to chill her arms. She lay back down and pulled the bedding up. Her thick comforter was a luxury, and she snuggled beneath it gratefully. But her belly growled, reminding her there had been little comfort set out at supper. The stew the cook produced had been more water than anything else, but it had needed to fill many bowls.

It was a sure bet Norris Sutherland, heir to the Earldom of Sutherland, wasn't awake in the dark hours of the morning with an empty belly. Even his accommodations in a military camp had been grand, the bed on which he'd taken her maidenhead a comfortable one.

Ye mean the one ye joined him on as his lover...

She closed her eyes and ordered herself to sleep while she might. The summer days were long, and there was much to do. Once winter closed its icy fist around the Highlands, there would be naught to do but seek out her bed for warmth.

She certainly wouldn't be seeking out Norris Sutherland. No. She might have enjoyed the time she spent in his bed, but she could not ever forget that she had gone there to avoid wedding a man who loved another. She must not forget, because a man such as Norris certainly did not lack for willing bed partners. She would not join the ranks of his mistresses.

Even if she did dream of the man.

❧

Dunrobin Castle, Sutherland

"Is there anything else ye desire, me laird?"

The serving girl was pretty, and she had curves in all the places Norris liked women to have them. Her dress was open enough to allow him a generous view of her breasts.

"Nae."

Disappointment flashed across her face, her gaze sweeping his chest before she picked up his empty mug and placed it on her serving tray. When she turned around, he was treated to a view of her backside as she descended the four steps leading down from the high-table landing to the floor of the great hall.

Yes, definitely curves in all the right places, and she moved with a sultry motion that should have sent heat through his veins. But his cock lay slack and uninterested beneath his kilt. He reached for the fresh mug of ale the serving lass had delivered but didn't lift it to his lips. This was becoming tiresome—exceedingly so.

He scanned the hall, catching the smiles of other lasses all watching him to see if he would summon them forward. There were dark-haired ones and blondes, even a redhead, but none of them sparked even a twitch from his cock. The thing had been useless for nearly three months.

"I'm growing worried about ye, me boy."

There was only one man who would call him boy and not get smashed in the face for it. Norris stood as his father appeared from the archway that led to his private study that was hidden behind the raised floor at the end of the great hall. Norris had helped outfit the room to give his father a sanctuary when he needed a few moments of rest. It would never do for the Highland earl to appear fatigued in front of his clan. The chamber had become the earl's favorite for business, but Norris did wonder if part of the appeal was being able to sneak up on his son.

Lytge Sutherland walked straight to his chair, even if he did it slowly. Norris didn't sit until his father was settled in the huge, ornately carved chair set at the center of the high table. Even so late at night, they showed respect to each other, for there were many watching.

"Ye have naught to worry about, Father."

Lytge reached for the mug of ale Norris had left untasted and drew off a long draught. He nodded then set it down. "Nonsense. Ye have nae been the same since returning from Sauchieburn." His father settled against the high back of the chair. "I went to so much trouble to secure ye that royal-blooded bride. Ye allowed her to ride out of here wearing the colors of the MacNicols."

"She was in love with Broen MacNicols…"

Lytge stroked his beard. "Ah yes. The same reason young Daphne MacLeod used to explain why she did nae wed Broen MacNicols as her father arranged. Ye seem to have helped Broen twice in the matter: once by taking Daphne to yer bed so she could be disgraced, and again when ye allowed yer own bride to escape the consummation of yer union."

Norris reached for the mug and took a swig. "I wondered how long it would take ye to hear of the part I played in helping Broen out of his betrothal with Daphne."

His father grinned, as arrogant as any man half his age, but his hair was completely gray now. "I've known, boy. Everything ye do is important to me."

There were men who would have bristled, but Norris returned his father's grin. "Sometimes helping out a friend is a pleasant duty."

His sire's eyebrows rose. "I imagine it was a fine bit of fun to help Daphne MacLeod lose her virtue so her betrothal might be broken, but what did ye gain from it? What did you bring home to yer clan, me boy?"

Norris felt the bite of his father's displeasure. It was there, glittering in the older man's eyes. What made it sting was that his father wasn't railing at him. The subtle stab was more wounding than a raised voice rich with insults, because his father was speaking to him like the future leader of the clan. A laird never forgot to weigh the benefits of any situation.

"Securing the loyalty of Laird MacNicols is worthy of note," Norris offered.

His father nodded. "Aye, it is."

"And Clarrisa may have been royal-blooded, but she did nae come with a dowry," Norris finished.

"True enough. But blood has its worth. Why do ye think I keep Gahan near? He's me bastard, and Sutherland blood is valuable. Yer bride may have cost me, but she was a York bastard, and yer offspring would have been kin to the King of England." His father tilted his head to one side and returned to stroking his beard. "The MacLeod lass, according to Gahan, she's a fair sight to behold."

"A fact she despises."

His father chuckled. "That's her youth blinding her. Time will steal her beauty soon enough. Ye learn that by my age. Best to enjoy what ye have when ye have it. I hear ye did that well enough when the lass was in yer keeping."

She'd been passionate too. Norris looked toward the hearth and signaled one of the serving girls forward to avoid having his father witness the flare of excitement that went through him. Daphne had blonde hair but dark eyes, which fascinated him. When he locked gazes with her, he had the sudden feeling he might lose himself in those dark orbs and be shielded from all life's travails. He'd never been one to shirk his duty, but he would not deny how tempting it was to seek her out again and lose himself in her enchanting embrace until dawn broke the spell.

"Gahan seems to have had a great deal to tell ye," Norris groused.

"As I said, he has his uses, and being the head of yer retainers is one of them," Lytge stated. "But he is nae the only source of information I have. In fact, Daphne MacLeod is the subject of interest at many a table in the Highlands. The rumor is that the lass has a fortune for a dowry, one nae discovered when the MacLeod land was raided by those clans who claimed victory at Sauchieburn."

"Who raided her lands?" Norris demanded.

"Comyn, Campbell, Lindsey. Does it matter? Her father fought on the losing side, and those who backed the young king took their pay out of the lands of those clans who did nae make so wise a choice."

Rage heated up inside Norris. It turned white-hot before becoming a rapid boil.

"Why do ye care, Son?"

His father was astute and too keen for Norris's mood. The serving girl delivered another mug of ale, and he lifted it to his lips. "It does nae matter."

"A fortune for a dowry matters. I hear her father had a bastard, and the man is set to inherit the MacLeod lairdship. Being wed to his only sister would be a good alliance." Lytge leaned forward and lowered his voice. "If there is a fortune involved, that is."

Norris sat up, the idea immediately taking root in his head. He realized he shouldn't, but still he couldn't seem to squash the urge to see Daphne again. No, he wanted to let that urge loose and follow it.

"Perhaps I'll ride out and see if it's true."

His father grinned. "And ye think she'll tell ye? Do nae be thinking one night between her thighs will endear her to ye."

His cock was hardening. His temper rose along with the organ. Still, he stood. Becoming a slave to his impulses was dangerous, but the opportunity was simply too tempting to ignore. He winked at his father. "Then maybe I'll have to charm me way into her bed again."

❧

"I do nae take orders from ye."

Daphne MacLeod had heard the same from more

than one of her father's retainers. She sweetened her expression, fighting back the urge to call the man a fool.

"I am suggesting ye recognize the logic in helping me round up the sheep before they stray too close to Comyn land. Their wool will be one of the few things we can harvest this season."

Keith MacLeod frowned. "Better that ye should have used those honey-coated looks on Broen MacNicols. If ye had wed him, we'd nae have suffered being raided after the battle of Sauchieburn. If ye were the wife of another Highland laird, no one would have dared even to think about taking what was ours."

"My father stood on the defeated side," Daphne argued, dropping all hints of sweetness. "We'd have been raided, have no doubt. My actions had naught to do with that."

"But we'd have a strong ally to protect us. One that might have made some of the smaller clans think twice before trifling with us. The MacNicols are vassals of Sutherland."

"So are we." Daphne lifted her head, drawing her back straight and glaring at the men standing before her. "I believe we are strong, and I will go after the sheep myself. I am not afraid, nor am I content to sit here and pity me plight. We were raided and have lost much—all the more reason to make sure we lose no more."

She turned her back on Keith. She could feel him and his men staring at her, but she never faltered. Her cousins were still seated at the tables that filled the great hall. All three of them claimed they were the rightful heir to the MacLeod lairdship, and they were using their blood ties to her father to spend the day doing nothing of value. She passed them, but not without shooting them a hard look. They might label her many things, but they would not call her a coward.

Gitta waited where the great hall ended and the hallway began.

"Ye are nae endearing yerself to the men."

Daphne didn't slow her pace. "If they cannae see the need for us to work together to pull in enough of a harvest to survive the coming winter, I have no time for them. Arrogance and pride will nae fill bellies. Me brother is nae here. I am."

Winter would close in on them too soon. Most of the seed grain had been stolen, and what fields were planted had been trampled. Some of the young plants were recovering, but time had been lost, and the yield would not be great.

"Ye should nae go riding. What if ye're carrying?" Gitta whispered, panting from the exertion of keeping up with her.

"I am nae with child." However, Daphne did slow her pace, and her cheeks heated with shame for making the older woman rush.

"Ye've nae bled," Gitta insisted. "A Sutherland bastard would give us an alliance—a great one, if it were a son. The Sutherlands keep their blood close." Gitta looked at Daphne's belly, reaching out to smooth the fabric of her skirt flat.

Daphne flinched, jumping back a step. "Enough. If I am with child, it will nae be a matter to worry about for many months. Today our sheep are happily on their way off our land with their winter coats still on their backs. We need that wool to buy seed for next year. I will return soon." She left Gitta at the tower steps and stalked toward the stable.

She couldn't think about a possible child. Norris Sutherland was wed. The news had traveled quickly. What bothered her most was how upset she was to know he was bound to another woman. Hadn't she suffered enough at the expense of fate? Everything she'd done had been for the right reasons. If she were shallow or greedy she'd happily have wed Broen MacNicols without a care for the fact that he was fighting with his best friend over her, or that when he discovered her still alive, the man was in love with another woman. Oh no, she would not have cared one bit how unhappy he was in their marriage. Legally, the man had been bound to wed her.

Yet she did not lament her actions to set him free of the contract her father had made with him.

Ye enjoyed the duty sure enough…

Her cheeks heated, and her pace quickened. She'd let Norris Sutherland seduce her so Broen MacNicols might renounce her and wed the woman he loved. Their night of passion had served a purpose. She had no reason to be upset over Norris Sutherland's taking a bride. The man owed her no affection.

Keith wasn't the only man wearing her father's colors who resented her choices. But a child? She didn't need the guilt of knowing she'd forced an inno-cent to wear the label of bastard. Even being the child of Norris Sutherland, heir to the earldom, wouldn't save it from scorn. She smoothed her hand over her belly, searching for proof that it wasn't rounding.

What she needed was for her courses to arrive and

silence the rumors, but they had never been predictable, so there was no way of knowing if she were late or not. If she bled, it would make her happy, but she feared it would be yet another reason for her people to resent her.

At least the horses greeted her kindly. She rubbed the velvet muzzle of one and muttered softly to it.

"Shall we go and sample some of the fine summer weather?"

As if understanding, the horse tossed its head, sending its mane flouncing. No one would help her saddle the animal, but she knew the way of it. The stable master was a good friend of Keith's and always sent his workers in the opposite direction when she appeared.

They thought she should be ashamed.

"Ye've a solid point about the sheep."

Keith startled her. She jumped and muffled a curse when the horse sidestepped nervously. Keith frowned, but she reached up and took the bit, controlling the animal with a steady hand.

His disapproval softened. "Even if I think ye should have been thinking of yer clan when ye broke yer betrothal with Laird MacNicols."

More retainers walked down the rows of stalls. Horses tossed their heads and snorted as the men began to saddle them. The stable was full of the scent of straw and leather.

"The first time I refused to wed him, I did it to prevent him fighting with Laird Chisholms. There would have been a feud."

Keith pulled a leather strap tight before granting her a grudging nod. "I agree ye did a good thing there, even if they be the ones who should be ashamed for acting like lads no higher than me waist. We do nae need a feud, especially one started over a woman, even a laird's daughter. I find meself liking that bit of action on yer part."

She used the stall rail to help her mount and suffered the harsh looks of some of the men. She bit back the tart response she would have liked to make. Pointing out that she was a foot shorter than any of them would serve only to remind them she was a female trying to take on the duties of a man.

"But the way I heard it…" Keith continued as he led his stallion out of the stable, "the second time, ye defied even the young king by refusing to take yer place as Laird MacNicols's bride."

Daphne flattened her body across the horse's neck to make it through the doorway of the stable and into the yard. "Which gained us Laird MacNicols's good will. The man is in love with another woman. He'd have wed me sure enough and resented me."

Keith mounted and reached up to adjust his knitted bonnet. He'd been her father's head of retainers and still wore one of his three feathers upward. By tradition, he should have lowered the feather, since the new laird would be the one deciding who claimed the privilege of serving in such a high position. It was just one more detail that screamed out the lack of respect her father's men had for her.

"The marriage contracts were agreed upon by yer father and Laird MacNicols. The man should have kept his word or at least made recompense to us, nae left it to you to disgrace yerself so he might be happy."

"He didn't. I made the choice." And she refused to regret it. "Enough. I know yer position on the matter. Ye've told me plainly enough. Let's get the sheep."

Keith surprised her by grinning. He was a fair-enough-looking man when he wasn't scowling at her. His hair was a dark sable, and his eyes a warm brown. There was a thin scar running along the right side of his cheek, but it served only to make him look capable.

"I do respect yer ability to recognize what we need to survive."

She turned her horse toward the gate and rode through it. A smile graced her lips even as she leaned low to flow more fluidly with the motions of the animal. She rode a mare, but a young one with plenty of spirit. The animal took to the uneven ground easily as Daphne guided her toward the border of her father's land. The wind was warm, and it tore at her blonde hair. She'd cut it off a year ago, and the strands were only a foot long now. They didn't want to stay in the braid Gitta had woven at sunrise, but slowly worked free.

Well, it suited her, for her hair wasn't the only part of her that didn't want to be contained. She'd grown up with Broen MacNicols and hadn't wanted to be his wife. The single kiss he'd pressed against her lips had left her cold.

Norris's kiss had sent her heart racing...

She might never have known the difference—or worse, learned of it after she was wed. Maybe the Church was wrong about infidelity. Maybe those who strayed from their wedded partners were to be pitied because they'd been locked into unions with the wrong person.

Ye're going to get locked in the stocks for thinking like that...

Well, only if she was foolish enough to voice such ideas. She raised her head and felt confidence rising inside her. Over the last year, she'd learned a thing or two about keeping her thoughts to herself.

Ye've also learned how to take a hand in yer own destiny...

Maybe she was meant to be alone in life. The Church also preached that women should remain humble and yield to a man's authority. Well, she was far past yielding. She wrapped the reins around her fists and urged the horse faster. Maybe she wasn't humble, but her father's people needed someone to take action now.

Maybe she was exactly what she needed to be.

⤵

"Was there something unclear in me orders?" Morrell Comyn asked in a low tone. His retainers eyed him hesitantly. He slammed his fist into the table, and dishes clattered. A mug turned over, but the serving wenches were all cowering in the kitchen.

"Damn fools! Why do I suffer ye wearing me colors?" He sat back in the huge throne-like chair that had belonged to his father. The back rose a full foot above his head, so the carved stag was clearly seen. "Get out of me sight."

The retainers tugged on the corners of their bonnets and hurried away.

"Ale!" Morrell roared. "And send it with someone pretty!"

He frowned when his second-in-command climbed the two steps to the high table with a mug for him.

"The lasses are all too afraid of young Katie to

serve ye," Ranald informed him before tugging on the corner of his bonnet.

Morrell snickered and grabbed the mug. He took a swig of the ale, wiped his mouth across the sleeve of his shirt, and pointed at the chair beside him.

"They should be. Katie is a little savage, but I like her wild ways." He slurped his next measure of ale and belched. "I wanted that MacLeod bitch caught. Why do ye think I lured her sheep onto me land?"

Ranald sipped his own ale. "Sure ye want her when ye just said Katie is a savage?"

"Oh, she is, I assure ye of that!" Morrell answered gleefully. "But I'm her master, sure enough. Katie will warm me cock no matter what bitch I bring here as me wife. I want that dowry, and I'll bed whom I fancy, as well. I am master here."

"Ye and half the Highland lairds sought that treasure, but not one could find it."

Morrell waved his hand. "No one breached the tower. It's there for certain. Why else would the MacLeod be willing to put up with a woman running the clan? They are doing it to keep the gold in their coffers."

"That makes sense. I hear there are three claims to the lairdship, but nothing has been settled as yet."

"Nae yet, but soon," Morrell grumbled. "Which is why I need to catch that bitch and make her me wife before any single man has the backing of the entire clan. It's nae as strong as it was before Sauchieburn, but there are still more MacLeods than Comyns."

"Well, she has her sheep," Ranald answered. "Ye'll need to think of another way to claim her before those MacLeod get finished fighting among themselves."

Morrell laughed. "Ye've hit the nail on the head, Ranald. The MacLeod are squabbling. A bit of action, and I'll have that dowry."

"She's still got a castle to take shelter inside of."

"I know that." Morrell shot his companion a hard look. "It's the only reason she still has her dowry. We're going to set another trap for her, and this time, I'm going to see to the deed meself."

Anticipation warmed his blood. His cock thickened with need, so he stood. "But tonight, I'm taking me cock to wild Katie."

❧

"Go on with ye." Daphne wiped her hair out of her eyes and tried not to let frustration get the better of her. The sheep were unruly and foul tempered. She guided her horse around the ram, who was trying to return to the Comyn land.

"They've got his attention for sure." Keith helped her block the animal. "Damn them for laying out feed for him. We'll have to pen them, or they'll return to Comyn land."

"I'm going to enjoy selling the fleece the Comyn fed me sheep to produce."

Keith's eyebrows rose, and he laughed. The other retainers looked on before relaxing their stern expressions. As the men became more accepting of her, the tension that had drawn Daphne's shoulders tight released. She wouldn't say they were happy, but at least they no longer sent her cutting looks. By the time they got the flock near the castle, sweat had soaked her. The summer was warm, and she envied the men their bare knees. The sun beat down on her, and her wool skirts were a torment.

But she was pleased when they herded the sheep into a makeshift holding pen for the night. The younger boys were set to hauling grass down from the hill for the penned animals. They used sickles to cut it and piled it high on lengths of MacLeod plaid.

"In a few days, they'll learn to stay on our land," Keith remarked.

"We can shear them while they are here too."

The wool should have been cut a month before, but the men had marched away at their king's command. So the summer had come and almost gone while everyone was dancing to the tune of politics. But it was over now, and time for the living to get on with preparing for winter.

Daphne smiled at the hundred or so sheep. It was not much, but it would be something. Her aching muscles didn't seem to hurt as much when she weighed the sting against the satisfaction of knowing she had been productive.

"Let's wash the sweat off our backs, lads!" Keith announced. The men cheered and set off for the river. It was a short ride, and several of the women doing laundry came running up the bank with smiles on their lips.

Daphne turned her horse toward the gates of the keep. Perhaps fate was ready to bestow some kindness on her at long last. But when she slid from the back of the horse and turned to look at the keep, she discovered herself facing the priest. Her happiness froze beneath the chilling look Father Peter gave her.

❧

"I had to heat the water again because Father Peter kept ye so long," Gitta said. She used a large iron hook to pull the kettle out of the hearth where it was being licked by flames. "He looked powerfully unhappy with ye."

As Gitta poured the water into the waiting tub, it sizzled. Daphne worked a brush through her hair then stepped into the bath.

"Father Peter doesn't share yer hope that I'm with child." The water felt wonderful against her skin. "In fact, he threatened to write to the bishop and tell him of my transgressions. The good father believes I'm setting a poor example for every woman in the clan."

As well as telling her straight that she was on a path to damnation.

Gitta made a harsh sound and lifted a cupful of water to wet Daphne's hair. The hearth was a small one, used mostly in the wintertime, when firewood was precious. It was set into the back of one of the towers, which allowed her privacy when she bathed. The tub was made of copper with a high back so she could relax while in it. Daphne tried to, but her shoulders were knotted again. Even the hot water washing over her skin wasn't enough to ease her.

"I can hear him saying such a thing, but there is more to this life than just the ways of the Church."

Daphne smothered a giggle behind her hand. "Ye're going to get us in trouble with talk such as that."

Gitta rinsed the soap from Daphne's hair, and went to retrieve a length of toweling. "I'm more concerned with what we'll fill our bellies with once Samhain comes and goes. It would be a blessing if yer brother would arrive and settle the matter of who will be laird. There will be bloodshed if Saer does nae show himself soon."

Daphne walked toward Gitta but had to reach for the toweling, because the older woman was busy looking at her belly.

"I understand why yer mother put his mother out. She was a savage from the isles and had no decency when it came to the fact that yer father was wed to yer mother. She thought to take that place for herself simply because ye were a girl babe." Gitta shook her head. "Yer father must have done something to displease fate, else his only son would nae have been a bastard born to a woman in exile."

Her father hadn't had a happy life. Daphne tried not to dwell on it, but it was true. She dried herself and picked up a clean chemise. Broen would never know just how much she'd dreaded following in her parents' footsteps. She'd have truly taken vows as a nun rather than live the way her mother had while watching Broen turn bitter as her father had.

Ye did nae mind yielding yer maidenhead to Norris Sutherland…

She yanked the brush through her hair a little too fast, and it snagged on a snarl. The last thing she needed to think about was Norris. The man was certainly not spending his time dreaming about her. He was the heir to the earldom; women spent endless hours trying to think of ways to catch his eye. Half the lairds in Scotland were trying to secure a marriage contract between him and their daughters. Her own father had done the same. But she did not have as much noble blood as some others, and the Sutherlands always wed with an eye on advancement.

Gitta helped her into a dress and began to braid her hair, when the bells at the gate began tolling.

"Where are ye going?"

Daphne didn't stop. "I have to see who is here."

"What if it's trouble? Better to leave it to the men."

"It's me duty, Gitta."

Even if half her clansmen didn't agree. She hurried around the outside of the keep and into the larger tower. As the bells continued to warn them of approaching riders, women and children were rushing into the great hall to take shelter. Daphne fought her way past them to reach the doorways. The walls surrounding the yard prevented her from seeing who was approaching. The MacLeod retainers were pulling on their helmets and climbing to the top of the curtain wall.

She took a deep breath and followed them. There was more than one curse as she threaded her way through the men. Her small frame allowed her to pass them on the narrow walkway at the top of the wall.

"What in the name of Christ are ye doing up here?" Keith demanded.

"Seeing who's approaching," she spat back. "Like it or not, I'm the head of this family until me brother arrives."

"Well I do nae like it, but I like it more than listening to yer cousins squabble over who has the better claim." He pointed down into the yard. "Nae a single one of those cowards is up here."

Keith didn't lower his voice. Several of her father's men looked at him and then scanned the yard. Daphne's three male cousins were taking shelter below because there was no one to tell them to take their positions. The wind whipped at her dress, chilling her legs, but when the men standing along the ramparts looked back toward her, there was respect in their eyes. She couldn't take time to enjoy knowing she'd impressed them. The curtain wall was topped with a facade to shield the men defending the keep from attack. She leaned around one to see the approaching riders.

Her belly knotted. Twin columns of riders were heading straight toward them. The lowered gate didn't seem to worry them at all. Their pace was even and their number impressive. There were sixty of them, and every one rode a full stallion.

"They're flying the standard of the Sutherlands," Keith announced.

"It cannae be." Daphne reached for the spyglass Keith held. He gave it to her, and she held it up to her eye. Once her vision adjusted, she aimed it toward the lead rider and the pennant he was holding: the rampant lions, denoting the nobility of the man riding with them.

"It is," Keith assured her. "At least that is good news."

"Until ye consider we'll be expected to feed them," Daphne muttered, dreading having to tell Norris how little they had. Her pride was suffering under the weight of the knowledge, but there was no help for it. He was their overlord. She could not refuse him entrance or shelter within the castle for the night.

The riders had made their way to the gate, and the man leading them held up one leather-gauntlet-clad hand. The horses were pulled to a stop, but the stallions pranced in spite of the tight hold their riders had on them. Full stallions didn't stand still easily.

Norris Sutherland wore a leather doublet with studs worked into it for protection. He looked like a Highlander sure enough, just as ready to defend himself as any man riding behind him. The setting sun illuminated the red in his blond hair, making him look as though he were some sort of fire god from the Highlands' pagan past. He raised his head and found her, his eyes narrowing.

"Lift the gate." His voice rang out clear and full of authority. But Keith delayed giving the order until she nodded. Her insides were quivering, and she bit her lower lip to try and distract herself from her emotions.

He is nae here for ye... Why would he be?

She hurried down the stairs as the gate groaned and began to be lifted up by the huge gears used to wind the chains. Someone pounded on the doors of the keep, and they opened to allow the women and children out. They hurried to claim a good spot to watch the arrival of their overlord.

Her lover...

She drew in a stiff breath and forced herself to stand still. She'd made her choice and had known she'd have to live with the consequences of her actions.

Norris didn't wait for the gate to rise completely. He leaned down across the neck of his stallion and rode into the yard the moment there was enough room. His men followed, their kilts flapping in the evening light.

"Are ye insane, woman?"

He was off his horse and standing in front of her in a flash. Somehow, her dreams hadn't recalled to her just how large a man he was. The top of her head came only to his shoulder, and he was easily twice her weight. There wasn't a hint of fat on him. His thighs were lean and cut with corded muscle, as were his forearms where he'd rolled up his sleeves.

"I asked ye a question, Daphne MacLeod."

"It sounded more like a demand." The women behind her gasped. Her belly did a little flip, but the words were spoken, so she lifted her chin and locked gazes with him. Father Peter could add being disrespectful to her overlord to the list of her sins.

She'd forgotten how intense his green eyes were too…

He frowned at her but scanned the men still up on the walls. "Who allowed a female onto the walls when ye had riders bearing down on ye?"

"No one allowed me," Daphne informed him. "I went up myself, since there is no one else here to see to this clan."

"So ye are insane." Norris delivered his opinion in a hard tone. He hooked her upper arm with one hand and swept her toward the keep. The people standing on the steps scrambled to clear a path for them.

They were inside the great hall and inside the chamber her father had used for meetings with his captains before she shook off her shock. The weapons and armor that hung on the walls seemed to suit her mood.

And Norris's, too, by the look of fury on his face.

"Enough, Norris Sutherland…" she sputtered softly, his name feeling foreign on her tongue. "I am not insane but seeing to the things that need doing until me brother arrives."

"Ye do nae belong on the wall, woman. An archer could take ye out in a heartbeat, since ye have nae been trained to protect yerself and ye had no protective clothing covering yer chest and neck."

"Well, that would please more than a few."

Her comment surprised him. For just a moment he stopped glowering at her, and she had a glimpse of the playful nature she had a dim memory of. It was fleeting, though, and he crossed his arms over his chest. His gaze was keen, and he swept her from head to toe. His leather doublet had dust on it from the road, but his chin was free of whiskers. On his head was a knitted bonnet, just like his men wore, only the three feathers adorning its side all pointed up. He was every bit the laird, even if his father still lived. As far as the Sutherlands went, they were solidly united. Norris had the authority to do whatever he pleased, but at the same time, all knew he was a loyal son.

She lowered her eyelashes for a moment, unwilling to let him see the hunger in her eyes. "What do ye want, Norris Sutherland? If ye are seeking shelter for the night, we've pitiful little to offer ye. I can barely feed me own kin."

"Is that why ye are so thin?" he asked with too much knowledge for her pride. She could see him tracing her exposed cheekbones. It irritated her because she didn't need everyone in the Highlands to know their plight. They'd bear the burden, and it would pass into memory soon enough.

"We're well enough."

"How much did they take?" he demanded softly.

"All they could," she admitted. "We'll survive. But as I said, we have little to offer yer men for supper."

"Gahan."

Norris Sutherland was an important man, and the huge retainer who stepped out of the doorway was no doubt charged with his safety. She recalled him, and he nodded to her and then aimed his attention at his laird. Gahan was Norris's half brother, born to his father's mistress. He was Norris's opposite, with dark hair and black eyes.

"Select one of the rams and set it to roasting," Norris instructed.

Gahan tugged on the corner of his bonnet before leaving.

"Ye'll be compensated for the animal," Norris informed her.

"We do nae need—"

"Yes ye do," he interrupted her. "The crops are not going to yield ye much this season. Why are the sheep penned?"

"Because me neighbor lured them away and set out feed to keep them on his land." She hated how weak her reply sounded. "But I retrieved them, so there is naught to worry about. Tomorrow they will be sheared, and we'll begin rebuilding. There is naught for ye to concern yerself with. Ye can be on yer way in the morning."

His lips rose, something glittering in his eyes. "Why, lass, I've only just arrived. What is yer reason to send me on me way at first light? It's been so long since I saw ye last."

"It has been mere weeks."

Triumph gleamed in his eyes. "'Tis nice to know ye are counting the days we are separated."

"I'd be a fool to do so. Besides, I heard ye wed."

He stepped closer, crowding her. She shivered and lost her nerve, stepping aside rather than allowing him to loom over her. "The terrible truth of the matter is that me fair bride, Clarrisa, decided to do very much the same as ye did and lie with another man rather than consummate her vows. She's wed to Broen MacNicols now."

She smiled, emotion taking control of her in a flash of white-hot happiness. But horror followed it, and she shook her head, trying to master her impulses.

"Just how did yer bride elude ye in yer own castle?" she inquired suspiciously.

Norris grinned, cocky and full of confidence. "I may have had a hand in making sure Broen could interrupt us. Be sporting enough to admit that was right kind of me, considering they were in love."

It had been, and for a moment, Daphne found herself liking Norris Sutherland a great deal more than she'd ever anticipated. The man could be compassionate.

"Well, it matters naught. Yer father will likely be well on his way to selecting another bride for ye, and I do nae need any rumors linking us."

"I rather enjoy the memory of the facts linking us." His voice had dipped low and deep, just as it had the night they…

"Ye should nae voice such things," she sputtered.

He was amused by her, his eyes twinkling with pleasure. "And why nae? Ye enjoyed making those memories—a great deal." Now there was a hint of pride in his tone.

Daphne fought the urge to shiver. Emotion wanted to wash away her sense and leave her helpless in front of him.

"Enough, Norris. The priest is already threatening to write to the bishop about me transgressions." She bit her lip, stunned by how easily she was sharing personal information with him. "I have enough to worry about."

"I see…" he muttered in a tone she recalled instantly from their more intimate moments. "Ye mean the man is threatening to write about our transgressions, do ye nae, lass?"

"No," she snapped and sidestepped once more to avoid him. "Father Peter would never accuse ye."

He paused for a moment, his expression turning pensive. "In that case, the man is a hypocrite. I recall being deeply involved in your transgressions. In fact, I'm very tempted to add to the list. If the man is going to carry tales to his superior, I believe we should make sure he has something unique to report. I know a few positions he's likely never heard of."

Her eyes widened. "Ye're going to end up locked in the stocks for saying things such as that."

Norris grinned, flashing his teeth at her. He shook his head, irritating her. She couldn't seem to shake the urge to argue with him. She stepped forward and pointed her finger at his wide chest.

"Don't think being the son of an earl will save you. The Church will no doubt double their efforts to make ye repent, so ye set a good example. Mind yer words, and do nae be grinning at me like that."

"I'm grinning because I assure ye, lass, if I get locked in the stocks for impious behavior, it will be for me actions, not just me words. Which means I would nae be alone." He caught her up against him in a motion that was almost too fast to see. One moment she was pointing at him, and the next moment his arms bound her against him. She had only a moment to inhale the warm scent of his skin and notice just how solid his body was before his mouth claimed hers.

His kiss was demanding. His lips pressed hers apart while he cupped her nape and angled her face upward for the assault. She struggled against him, trying to push him away, but he held her prisoner. It was a desperate attempt to maintain her sanity. A moment later, her discipline crumbled beneath the teasing motions of his lips. He wanted her mouth to open, and she had lost the will to deny him. What was worse was the fact that she wanted his kiss, needed it to be harder. She curled her hands into his doublet, holding him close as she kissed him back.

The kiss changed instantly. He became more demanding, and it fanned the flames smoldering inside her. Passion leapt to life between them, as though they hadn't parted for weeks. It twisted and bit into her, potent as a drug. But she wasn't its only victim. Norris growled softly, the savage sound one she recalled from the darkest hours of the night they'd spent together. He trailed his lips along her jawline and onto her neck, where he bit her gently. She shivered, the reaction instant and uncontrollable. His grip held her in place as he raised his head and locked stares with her. For a moment, he let her see what the darkness had prevented her from gazing upon the night they shared his bed. Hunger glittered in his green eyes, making them glow. She was mesmerized by the sight, because it echoed her own longings so closely.

"Since ye kissed me back so passionately, ye'll be in the stocks beside me."

His words were bold. She tried to shove him away and would have bitten the beast if he hadn't released her. Her skirt got caught beneath her feet, and she stumbled farther away.

"Ye insufferable marauder."

He tipped his head back and roared with amusement. Her temper sizzled, turning her cheeks scarlet.

"Take yer demands somewhere else, Norris Sutherland, for I do nae care whose son ye be or what title ye're set to inherit."

He smirked at her, but it was a very personal expression, one that reminded her he knew her... intimately.

"Since yer father is dead and yer brother has yet to arrive, ye'll face me demands, Daphne MacLeod, as a vassal should. I'm here to see what condition yer land is in." He closed the gap between them, gripping a handful of her skirt to keep her near so his last words could be shared only between them. "But if ye'd like me to run ye to ground, I will be happy to do so. So turn yer back on me, lass... I dare ye."

⸺⚬⸺

Insufferable brute. Dare her?

How could he suggest such a thing?

Daphne stormed into the storeroom and picked up a mortar. She used her frustration to grind the peppercorns into a fine dust. The grains tickled her nose, but she didn't take any pleasure in the scent of the costly spice.

Damn Norris for that, as well. She had precious few luxuries for her table. The man didn't need to irritate her so much she failed to enjoy the ones she had.

Gitta spoke softly. "It would help if ye softened yer heart." Daphne turned on her with a whirl of her skirts but froze at the look on her old nurse's face. There was the unmistakable sheen of desperation there.

"He's sought ye out, lass. Think before ye toss what fate offers ye out the window."

"To what end, Gitta? Father Peter is already threatening me with Church authority."

Her old nurse shook her head and grinned. "Ye are his vassal. 'Tis a tradition, which goes back to before the Church meddled so much in the doings of everyday life. Go to his bed, and yer child will bring us good fortune. Father Peter will baptize it sure enough, with the heir to the Earldom of Sutherland swearing it is his babe."

Gitta took the mortar from her and sniffed. "This will help light a fire in yer blood. I'll help the cook make ye a fine rabbit pie to share with his lairdship."

"I doubt he is accustomed to eating something so common as rabbit."

Gitta raised a hopeful look toward her. "Ye're right. I'll have one of the ducks brought in."

"Ye will nae," Daphne protested. "We need their eggs more than their meat, and we need every last one of them so there will be additions to the flock next year."

"But we must set a good supper for yer courtship. If Norris Sutherland is yer protector, he'll ensure we all have more than enough. I hear the tables groan under the weight of the plenty set upon them on Sutherland land."

"We can nae trust in gossip. Everyone likes to tell tales of how easy life is elsewhere."

Gitta offered her a blunt look. "It is certainly nae so grim as it is here, and the labor ye'd have to shoulder as a leman would be pleasurable. Stop talking like a bride of Christ. I never raised ye to detest the very flesh ye are made of. I saw the blush staining yer cheeks after he greeted ye."

Daphne had to resist the urge to rub her face. Gitta's gaze was too knowing for her comfort.

"Ye raised me to be respectful to the Church."

Yet she'd already fallen from grace when it came to Norris…

Something rippled down her spine that she refused to allow herself to acknowledge. She wouldn't admit he made her quiver. "Ye're a fine cook. He'll sing yer praises, no doubt."

She choked back the rest of what she wanted to say, because it was surly, and she had enough sins to answer for.

Like lusting after Norris Sutherland…

❧

"Ye must be getting old."

Norris eyed Gahan, and his captain chuckled at his sour humor. The remains of the duck sat in front of Norris, the scent of rosemary and pepper lingering. Daphne MacLeod had never joined him at the high table for the evening meal.

"The fair lass did nae show a single one of those

blond hairs tonight..." Gahan continued as he sat down and tore off a piece of remaining meat. "Ye must be getting old and ugly to prompt her to choose an empty belly over sharing supper with ye."

"Is that a fact?" Norris growled, balling his hand into a fist.

Gahan only smirked at his threat before popping the meat into his mouth and humming with enjoyment. He smacked his lips and pointed at Norris. "Well now, I suppose it could be on account that ye failed to impress her when she was in yer bed, but I did nae want to be overly harsh when I'm merely speculating."

"That would be a mistake," Norris retorted as he stood. He leaned over to make sure only Gahan heard him. "She was very well pleased, more than once."

"And still she is nae here when we've ridden so far to see her."

"Ye're an arse," Norris snarled.

"Aye, but nae a blind one."

Norris straightened. "Possibly a dead one before dawn if ye do nae cease to badger me."

Gahan considered him for a moment then reached for another piece of the duck. He drew a bone slowly from his lips once he'd sucked the tender meat from it. "If ye're staying here, do nae expect me to shine yer ego by ignoring the reason behind yer grumbling... Laird."

Norris stared at the look in his captain's eyes and left. Gahan was bold, but it was the very same quality that made him such an indispensable man. When Gahan told him something, it was the truth. The man had no use for ego polishing, and he was making a point by needling him.

He had come to see Daphne, and that was exactly what he was going to do.

❧

Her chamber was freezing.

Daphne snorted and rubbed her hands together, reminding herself this was nothing to the misery they'd feel in a few months when winter arrived. Better to keep herself from being dramatic; reality would be harsh enough.

Someone knocked on the door.

"Come in."

She turned around and felt her belly twist when Norris appeared in the doorway.

"No… ye stay out." She covered her mouth but not quickly enough, because her voice was high and squeaky, betraying her turbulent emotions.

"If ye are going to hide, the least I might do is chase ye to make it worth yer time." The door shut behind him with a soft thud.

"What audacity," she accused. "I did nae invite ye to me chamber, ye rogue. Ye knew me reasons for allowing ye… intimacies with me."

"Ah, but I am more interested in learning why ye refused to share such a fine meal with me when I know ye will nae sup upon anything so grand again for a long time."

He took several more steps inside her chamber and planted his feet solidly. There was something in his eyes that looked like determination. Of course it was; the man was accustomed to getting everything he desired. Norris Sutherland was every inch a Highlander, from the bonnet on his head with its three feathers pointing upward to proclaim his rank to the edge of his pleated kilt where it brushed the tops of his knees. He looked at her like he meant to have her.

So dramatic again… he can have any lass he wishes. Do nae be vain.

"Ye have no right to be cross, Laird Sutherland. Ye have been afforded the best we have."

His eyes narrowed. "I disagree, lass. Ye are the jewel in this keep."

She'd been complimented before, but a blush stung her cheeks. She rubbed at the heat, trying to rid herself of the odd reaction. "This beauty is a curse. It has brought naught but discontentment to everyone who admires it."

He moved closer, and she found herself mesmerized by his approach. She'd dreamed about him so often, it was like having her fantasy right before her. He reached out and stroked the scarlet surface of one cheek.

"'Tis men who are cursed with the nature to want to own ye like some bit of finery."

For a moment, she was captivated. There was nothing wrong with his presence in her chamber or in the way his gaze settled upon her lips. The tender skin tingled, anticipating his kiss.

Gitta's words rose from her memory and collided with the harsh ones from Father Peter.

She scooted back, her long smock fluttering and allowing the cold night air up her bare legs. "Enough,

Norris. 'Twas me serving woman Gitta who prepared the duck for ye. She hoped I'd try to lure ye into me bed so I might have yer bastard and make ye responsible for our well-being."

He crossed his arms over his chest, clearly displeased. "Ye need a new waiting woman."

"Nae. 'Tis my fault she is so desperate. I am the one who refused the match me father made. So I'll be the one thinking of a way to make sure everyone is fed." She drew in a deep breath, trying to restore her confidence. "Now go. There will be no more kissing, because I do nae prostitute meself."

"Ye did nae mind the chore of losing yer maidenhead to me. In fact, I recall yer being very eager for our union."

Her jaw dropped open, shock striking her mute for a long moment. Flashes of memory from the night they shared went through her mind like lightning.

"Ye're too bold with yer tongue," she muttered crossly.

He grinned at her. "So yer sweet cries told me, but 'tis a skill I would gladly practice upon ye."

"Enough!"

"Is it?" he demanded, his voice losing its teasing note. "Or is it time for me to toss ye into yer bed, since ye have so cleverly greeted me in a chemise thin enough to let me see the little pebbles of yer nipples?"

She crossed her arms over her chest in response. "I was seeking the warmth of me bed when ye arrived. I did nae send for ye."

"Did nae ye, lass?" He moved closer, crowding her. "Ye climbed the walls to assume the duty of leading this clan, but ye do nae break bread with me? Maybe ye're daring me to try my hand at catching ye."

Her anger froze, and it chilled every other emotion coursing so freely through her body.

"Ye are no different than any of the others." Her voice was low and hard now. "All ye see is what ye can possess because it is yer right."

She grasped her chemise and drew the garment up her body and over her head. She didn't care that the air was chilly; it suited the moment.

"Ye are me overlord, so 'tis yer right sure enough." She lay down on her bed and turned her face toward the wall. Tears pricked her eyes and slid down her cheeks. Time seemed to stand still, the space between each heartbeat long while she waited for him to touch her. She was a fool to allow him to bruise her feelings, and yet she could not seem to stop the hurt.

"I deserved that scorn in yer tone, Daphne."

As he sat down next to her, the bed shook slightly. He cupped her chin and drew her face back toward him.

"Aye, deserved it well and truly, for I'm acting like a brute," he continued.

He smoothed his fingers over her cheek, sending little ripples of delight through her. She jerked her head away, unwilling to enjoy such tenderness when he was being so arrogant.

"If ye want to make demands of me, do so, but do it quickly, for I am cold, *Laird*. Do nae waste yer breath on gentling me. I am already submissive."

It would be simple for him to take her, but disappointment tore at her. Her memories of their night together were all pleasant, yet he was shattering her illusions of who he was.

He reached into the front of his open doublet and pulled out a small round of bread. With her belly empty, she smelled it instantly, and her mouth began to water. Her belly rumbled low and loudly, shaming her with just how little they had.

"Eat, lass."

He placed the bread on the bed beside her and then stood. His gaze traveled along her length, inspecting her. He tugged the coverlet over her. Satisfaction filled his eyes for a moment; then he turned and left the chamber.

She shuddered, her body shaking as she rose and sat on her knees. When she reached for the bread, her hands trembled. Her belly rumbled, but she merely held it for a long moment, savoring the feel of it.

Father Peter was correct; she was damned.

Two

SHE SHOULD BE HAPPY.

Daphne lectured herself while dressing the next morning. Aye, she should be very pleased.

So why was she frustrated?

She realized she wasn't just frustrated. As she hurried off to church, excitement was pooling in her belly. The bell was tolling, calling the inhabitants of the tower to Mass. She lifted her chin, gathering the poise that had eluded her since Norris's arrival. If the man was still on MacLeod land, she didn't need him seeing proof that he unsettled her.

The church was full, and she made her way down to the front. Father Peter turned and eyed her sternly for being among the last to enter the sanctuary. But something pulled the priest's attention away from her. She turned to see Norris and his retainers marching down the aisle. The MacLeods made way for them, pressing tightly against one another to make the aisle wider.

"Me apologies, Father. I was slow to rising this morning."

The priest shot a hard look at Daphne, and her

face turned scarlet. She heard something that sounded suspiciously like a chuckle come from Norris across the aisle where he stood with the male members of the congregation. There was a great deal of shifting around her. Heads turned, and she felt pain stabbing into her temples. Father Peter raised his voice louder than usual when he began the service.

Her temper sizzled. It took amazing amounts of self-control to maintain her dignity and not launch herself across the distance between Norris and herself. She discovered her hands curled into talons and digging into her skirt as she tried to keep her mind on the service.

It was a lost cause. Father Peter was glaring at her at the end, and Norris's men were trying their best to get a peek at her too.

"Go in peace," Father Peter instructed them, but for the first time in her life, Daphne felt incapable of doing so.

She made the sign of the cross and hurried out of the church before the aisle became congested. A hard hand curled around her wrist before she made it all the way down the steps of the church entrance. Norris tugged her around the side of the building, and she watched his men close the way so no one might follow them. She shivered, reminded again of just how much power he had.

"Ye've done quite enough, Norris Sutherland, so take yer hand off of me."

His grip remained solid. "It is nae me fault yer priest is a suspicious man. Piety must be weighing heavily on his shoulders, for he seems to think of naught but sins of the flesh."

"Well, ye did nae help the situation by claiming to have trouble rising this morning."

His lips twitched, and he lifted her hand to place a kiss against the inside of her wrist. Ripples of delight traveled along her arm, setting off a soft throbbing deep inside her passage.

"Had I spent the nighttime hours with ye, lass, I would have risen quickly as often as ye would have entertained me." He brushed the sensitive skin of her inner wrist with his thumb and then released her. He reached up, tugged on the corner of his bonnet, and walked back to where his men stood.

"The sun is up, lads. Let's put the day to good use."

She had to crush the urge to call out. Panic was trying to send her chasing after him, but she refused to appear so weak.

Even if she felt desperate.

She shook her head, ordering herself to stop looking to the man for help. Until yesterday, she'd accepted that she was on her own, and nothing had changed.

It would have if he'd stayed in your bed last night…

She stiffened. Well, he hadn't.

Because you were less than welcoming…

Father Peter was correct. She was touched by madness, but a very different sort than the priest believed her to be suffering from. It wasn't lust; it was an infirmity of the mind, a lack of self-discipline that was allowing her thoughts to run wild.

She'd be better once Norris Sutherland was gone.

That idea made her mood turn somber, but she drew strength from knowing she'd survive. One day at a time, one task after the other. She focused her mind on the sheep and the shearing. No matter how smelly the animals were, it would be better than watching Norris ride away.

"We'll have to wait to shear the sheep," Keith announced once she'd made it into the hall. "Storm brewing. The poor things might freeze."

He was right, but she didn't like putting off the gathering of the fleece. The next time Morrell Comyn stole the animals, she doubted she'd get them back.

"Maybe until next season, since 'tis already so late."

Keith was right; the summer was fading. "Aye, ye have the right idea," she muttered at last, hating to admit it.

"I'm off to the training yard." He reached up and tugged on the corner of his bonnet.

Surprise flashed through her. Respect from any of her father's retainers had never been something she dared hope to have. Actually, she'd earned it. The feeling that filled her was warm and delightful. She realized it was pride but not in the manner she'd always thought pride would feel like. It wasn't arrogant or selfish. Instead, she was filled with a sense of accomplishment.

It made her smile, until she turned and noticed the look on Gitta's face. Triumph shone in her eyes, and hope. Daphne turned away, unwilling to destroy the other woman's happiness. Disappointment would come soon enough to them all.

꧁꧂

"I can nae believe he has nae returned." The sun set without a sign of Norris or his retainers, and Gitta was sounding frustrated.

"There is no reason for him to linger."

Gitta grunted as she pulled the laces out of Daphne's stays. She almost didn't need the garment anymore to support her breasts, because they had become so small. However, during these lean times, she needed the garment more for warmth than support. The only way to escape her wedding to Broen MacNicols the first time had been to enter a convent on Grant land. The holy order had gladly welcomed her in the hope of claiming her dowry. Living among those dedicated to serving God meant the meals were lean, even during harvest time.

"Oh, there was reason all right," Gitta groused. "I'm more than disappointed to discover he's nae man enough to see it."

Daphne sighed, drawing another grumble from her nurse. Gitta began pulling a brush through her hair. The blond strands still reached only the middle of her shoulders, so it didn't take very long to brush out. Another result of her time in a convent; she'd cut off her hair to prove she was not a servant of earthly vanity.

"Do nae start telling me what to hope for. I'm far too old to be curbing me thinking for anyone save the good Lord."

"I believe the good Lord might have an issue or two with the way ye've been counseling yer mistress toward me," Norris remarked from the doorway.

Daphne jumped. Her chemise fluttered in the night breeze, since her overgarments were all removed. Gitta dropped the brush and didn't bend to retrieve it. They both stared at Norris Sutherland.

And for good reason—the man was covered in blood.

"Sweet Christ!" Daphne exclaimed. She was across

the room in a flash, pulling on his clothing to discover where the blood seeped from.

"If that is all it takes to get ye to touch me, sweet Daphne, I'll happily tangle with a dozen stags and appear in yer bedchamber wearing their blood."

"Stag?" She looked up and gained a clear look at the smirk on his lips. "Oh, the devil take ye!" She slapped his shoulder, the leather jerkin he wore making a dull sound.

"Many would claim I'm well on the way to that." He boldly crossed into the chamber and laid his sword down next to the bed. "But the stag did not take me off to hell today, so Lucifer will have to content himself with waiting for me a wee bit longer." He raised an eyebrow at her. "I've a fair bit more sinning to do." He nodded in Gitta's direction. "Yer mistress does nae need ye any more tonight."

Gitta put her right foot behind her and bent her knee to lower herself before leaving the room on hurried steps.

Daphne's jaw dropped open, and she propped her hands onto her hips. "Ye're an arrogant one, Norris Sutherland. There will be no sinning here."

He sat down and stretched one foot out toward her. "Nae even for the man who brought a stag home to fill the pots on the morrow?"

She lost a great deal of her indignant fury. A stag was reserved for a nobleman to hunt. There were plenty about in the forest, but with no laird, there was no one who might down one.

"Ye intended to return." She slapped a hand over her mouth—but too late to mask the sound of longing in her voice.

"Aye," he confirmed. "Ye need the meat."

There was a ring of authority in his voice that was more than arrogance. She recognized it for what it was… accomplishment. He'd proven himself worthy of respect by providing for his people.

"I am grateful for the food."

"But I wonder if Father Peter will be willing to taste a bowl of stew on the morrow?"

Daphne shook her head again. "Ye never know when to leave well enough alone. Was nae me gratitude enough for ye? Was it necessary to remind me of yer hideous behavior this morning?"

His playful demeanor vanished, and he abandoned the chair. "Nay, lass. I do nae care for yer submission at all." He closed the space between them and captured the back of her head in one firm hand. "At least, nae any submission that I have nae kissed ye into."

His mouth captured hers in a kiss that was just as demanding as his nature. Excitement pierced her belly, twisting and churning like a wild storm. The taste of him kindled a need that refused to allow her to think beyond what she was feeling. She grasped his jerkin, holding him close to her as she kissed him back. For one moment, it felt like they were in the heart of a flame.

But he pulled away from her, breaking the spell. Gitta had left a candle burning, and the yellow light illuminated the glitter of victory in his eyes.

"That is more to me liking, Daphne."

She growled at him, slightly stunned by the amount of emotion he seemed able to solicit from her. "Ye need to leave me in peace. If all ye came here for was to demand me body, ye could have had me last night."

"I came for other reasons too."

He was busy working the button loops of his soiled jerkin and shrugging out of it. Daphne reached for it and eased it over his broad shoulders. His voice was low and hinted at something she couldn't quite put her finger on. Some emotion that almost struck her as caring. But the sight of his shirt shocked her.

"Some of this blood is yers…" Along his lower back was a jagged tear, but it wasn't deep.

"Well now, it was a full-grown stag, and he was nae leaving this life without a bit of a fight." He turned and winked at her before holding up his wrists so she might unbutton the cuffs of his shirt.

"Ye shouldn't look like such a delighted boy. Stags are dangerous. They can kill even a large man such as ye."

He grinned at her, unrepentant. "Well then, should I return to teasing ye like a man? I admit I enjoy hearing ye refer to me as one full well."

He took advantage of her reaching up to pull his shirt over his head to gently cup her breasts. Her chemise was thin and offered little protection from the heat of his hands. She sucked in a breath, his touch sending a jolt of sensation through her. Her nipples drew into hard nubs that looked like pebbles when she stepped back with his shirt in hand.

"Do nae ye have any shame?"

One of his fair eyebrows lifted as he pulled his belt back to allow it to unfasten. "None," he confirmed in a firm tone right before his kilt began to slide down his lean hips. He caught it and tossed it onto the table behind her. She should have been able to resist looking down his body, but failed. Her gaze slid over the sculpted perfection, helping her recall with vivid detail just how good it felt to be pressed against him. His cock stood at attention, the head swollen and ruby red.

"Are ye sure ye want to carry the burden of life alone tonight, Daphne?"

He reached out and slid his hand along her cheek. A soft sound escaped her lips, one born of pleasure. She just couldn't help it; there was something so very intense about the way she felt when he touched her. As though she had never understood how good her body might feel.

"But… tomorrow… everyone will know…"

"They already believe I spent last night in yer bed." He stepped closer. As she felt his breath against her lips once more, he gripped her hair. Her beaded nipples brushed against the harder surface of his chest, sending a bolt of pleasure down her body.

"Just because they think so, does nae mean we should…"

"Nay, lass. The way ye kissed me back is the reason we should spend the night together."

He didn't wait for a response but sealed her mouth beneath his own. The kiss was demanding, but she met him with equal strength. For a moment, he tasted her lips, taunting the delicate surfaces with teasing motions. He cupped her breast with his free hand, toying with the raised nipple before sliding his tongue across her lower lip.

She shivered, unable to contain all the sensation. The room was no longer cool; her skin warmed as he gently probed her mouth with his tongue. When she opened her mouth, he sent it deep, thrusting inside to stroke against her own. Between the folds of her sex, her clitoris began to throb, begging for attention.

But she wanted more. She needed to affect him just as strongly. Running her hands along his chest, she cupped his shoulders to hold him in place while she sent her own tongue into his mouth. His chest rumbled with a groan, and the kiss became almost savage. He released her head, smoothing his hands down her body until he cupped her bottom.

Need tore through her, and she gasped. It was a crazy twist of pleasure unleashed by his grip on her bottom.

"I haven't had a woman since we parted," he growled the admission, right before he lifted her off her feet and placed her on the table. "Ye cast a spell over me."

"I did nae," she protested, for one moment her brain resuming its ability to function. "Maybe… this is wrong… unnatural."

Her thighs parted to make way for his body, and he pressed them even farther apart. Her chemise rose up, baring her sex completely. He reached for her exposed slit, fingering it gently, and gripped the back of her head to keep their gazes locked.

"There is nothing more natural than seeking each other out when our bodies demand it so much."

He fingered her folds, sending need pulsing through her passage.

"Yer body is wet and eager, Daphne…"

She trembled, feeling like she was going to tumble off the edge of a cliff into a vortex where there was nothing to hold onto. He slid his fingers down to the opening of her passage, pushing her closer to that fall, and the walls of her sheath contracted with the need to be filled. She reached out and wrapped her hand around his cock. It was hard but smooth as silk against her palm. He jerked, sucking in a stiff breath when she slid her hand all the way to the base of it and then slowly back up.

"I am not the only one beset by need."

His eyes narrowed, hunger glittering in them. "No, ye are nae."

He kissed her again, pressing her mouth open to allow his tongue access. Her passage quivered with anticipation, and he didn't make her wait. He cupped her hips, holding her in place. The head of his cock slid easily into the slick entrance of her body. She expected less resistance, since she was no longer a virgin, but her passage protested the first thrust.

He growled and pulled free. His grip remained firm on her hips to keep her from lifting her hips to drive him deeper.

"Ye are delicate, Daphne. 'Tis a wonder ye have such a fiery spirit."

He pressed his cock forward once more, her body taking him more easily.

"Ye bled overly much the first time."

His tone was tender and his motions too slow to suit the need raging inside her. "Stop treating me like a child." She grasped him and reached around his body to hold him closer while locking her legs around his hips.

He thrust forward, going deeper this time. "I hardly think of ye as a child, Daphne."

He withdrew and thrust again. This time she lifted

her hips and broke free of his hold for just a moment. His length lodged completely inside her, stretching her passage. She pulled in a harsh breath but laughed as she blew it out.

"Minx," he accused softly.

"If ye do nae care for me demeanor, get out. No one is forcing ye to bed me."

He renewed his grip on her hips and began to work his cock in and out of her body. "It would take the hounds of hell to drag me away."

All playfulness had evaporated from his tone. It was hard and edged with determination. It had been dark the last time they spent the night together, but now she could see his face. There was a raw hunger glittering in his eyes. His lips were curled back as need took command of them both. Daphne wasn't thinking; she was responding. To every thrust of his hips and every point of connection between them. She moved to meet him with every stroke, straining toward his next thrust because she craved the hard presence of his length deep inside her. The need made no logical sense, but caught up in the moment with desire threatening to crush her in its grip, there was nothing to do but meet the demand of her own flesh.

She wasn't close enough to him. Pleasure was twisting through her belly, begging for just a bit more. She wasn't even sure what she craved, only that he could give it to her. They both moved faster, and their bodies slapped against each other as they panted. He was holding back. She could feel his body shaking, and it enraged her because she wanted to be able to best him.

But her body wouldn't obey her will. There was

no way to stop the pleasure once it began to burst. Centered beneath the hard thrust of his cock, delight shot up into her belly. She twisted and clawed at his shoulder while caught in the grasp of the climax. His hands gripped her hips, holding her in place as he growled to announce his own release.

She gasped when his seed flooded her womb. It was hot and searing, sending another ripple of enjoyment through her. Even her frantic breathing couldn't seem to provide her with enough breath. As the world spun out of control, her eyes closed.

She woke up on the tabletop, the smooth wood hard against her back. Norris was leaning over her, his elbows the only things saving her from his full weight. His skin was hot, keeping the chill of the night away from her.

"Definitely a spell," he muttered and pushed himself up.

"I'm sorry to hear ye are so susceptible to the whims of women." She tried to roll away from him, but he hooked her around her waist and pulled her back against his body. He lifted her off the table, cradling her easily on the way to her bed.

"What are ye doing, Norris?"

"Taking ye to bed."

He tossed her into the center of the bed, making the bed ropes groan and the curtains flutter. He reached for her, grasped only the shoulders of her chemise, and tugged it free. The garment fluttered onto the floor without a second glance from the man.

"Now that is me favorite position for ye, spitting and bare and ready to tangle with me."

But he didn't follow her. Norris sat down and

began unlacing his boots. He tossed one aside and then the other before standing up.

"Sweet Christ, how can ye be stiff again?"

He tossed his head back and laughed. "I swear ye are the boldest virgin I ever encountered. The most bewitching, as well."

Daphne drew herself up onto her knees. Her pride bristled beneath the casual way he lumped her into the group of women he'd known.

But what else might she expect?

"It was yer idea," she reminded him. "Nae that I'm refusing to acknowledge me share of the blame. Which is why I did nae invite ye to me chamber tonight. Ye're a knave to cry witchery."

She should have been afraid of him. One sentence uttered of spells, outside the walls of her chamber, and she'd face a trial. He was a nobleman, son of the most powerful earl in Scotland. Half of her own clan would be happy to see her done away with. But all she felt was hurt by his callousness. She reached for a pillow and sent it sailing at his head.

"Get out! If ye want to see me tried for witchcraft, ye can do it from another chamber."

He brushed the pillow aside with a fluid motion that betrayed just how adept he was at fighting. The motion was reflex from the years of training he'd endured. For just a moment, she realized how daring she was, to argue with him. There wasn't a soul who would take him to task for striking her. In fact, she could easily end in the stocks for forgetting her place.

"I was teasing ye, Daphne." He shook his head. "Ye are nae the only one who tires of the burdens of position. For the moment, I couldn't care less about who me father is or what place I have in this world. All I crave is to crawl into that bed with ye and lose meself between yer thighs. I'm nae crying witchery. I'm begging to fall beneath yer spell."

Yet his tone was full of arrogance and demand. Still, something warm rippled through her. It tempted her to smile when her better judgment warned her against letting him see too much of her emotions.

"Well… ye've already had that. So get on with ye." She wanted to snap at him, but her temper was cooling beneath his admission.

"Get on with what, lass?"

He placed a knee on the bed and then one hand. A silly little twist of excitement went through her, which sent her lips twitching up into a smile.

"Shall I get on with wrestling with ye?"

She hugged herself instantly but battled the urge to giggle. "Ye've had me."

Both of his hands were on the bed as he crawled toward her like a large predator. She couldn't resist glancing down at his cock. It still jutted out, hard and promising.

"Ye're naive, lass, for ye do nae understand the first thing about truly being had." Something that looked like a promise flashed in his eyes. "We've barely begun."

She shivered, anticipation renewing its grip on her. She shook her head, more for herself and her fickle emotions, because it should have been impossible to desire him again so soon. In fact, it was unnerving, like she was losing control of herself.

Norris grinned, the curving of his lips sensual and

beguiling. He moved closer, stalking her across the bed like a hungry beast. "Oh, aye, me sweet. I've ridden ye sure enough, but there is much more to having ye." His gaze lowered to her breasts. "And I believe I'll begin with learning what those little rosebuds taste like."

"Ye should—"

"I surely should, indeed."

He sprung at her, catching her in a solid embrace, and they both bounced on the bed. A startled giggle got past her battle to remain poised.

"Now who's encouraging mayhem?" He lifted his head and eyed her.

But she sobered quickly. "Witchery is a grave crime."

He muttered something profane then cradled her nape and rubbed it gently. "Aye, but one exaggerated these days. Believe it or not, there was a time when lads and lasses might tease one another about falling under each other's spell without a bunch of church men getting involved."

"Ye are nae just any lad." She turned over and ducked beneath his arm.

"So me word would be taken as proof?"

She scooted to the headboard and used a pillow to shield herself. Norris sat back on his haunches, considering her for a long moment.

"I suppose I can nae fault ye for nae trusting me." He shook his head. "Yet I do nae like the sound of fear in yer voice."

"I am nae afraid of ye."

He lifted one hand and curled his finger. "Then prove it."

It was a challenge, one many would tell her she was

insane to answer. But there was something inside her that refused to ignore it. Such had always been her downfall with this man.

She tossed the pillow aside and moved toward him. She hesitated only for the first moment, because as she moved closer to him, his face became an expression of wicked delight. Never once had she truly believed herself captivating.

Tonight, she did.

And she discovered she liked the feeling. Oh, it was likely vain of her or prideful or several other sinful things. *But she liked it.*

There was no longer even a hint of fear. Only fascination with the way his green eyes were focused on her. She flattened her hands on his chest, working them up his flat midsection and across the wider planes of his pectorals to his shoulders.

"Ye're enjoying mesmerizing me... admit it, Daphne."

He cupped her breasts, sending a surge of heat through her. Somehow, she'd never noticed just how sensitive they were.

"Does yer ego need polishing?" She hooked her hands over his shoulders and used the hold to help lift herself up so she might straddle his thighs. He had them braced apart, so she had to spread wide to do it, and the folds of her sex opened, allowing the head of his cock to slip between them.

"From ye? Aye." He teased her hard nipples with his thumbs. "Shall I admit how much it means to me to see ye mounting me without the glow of scheming in yer eyes?"

There was something flickering in his eyes that

made her pause, a bitterness she understood. He slid his hands down her body to cup her hips and press her down.

"Aye, I know well what yer quarrel with Broen and Faolan was. Ye do nae wish to be covered and bred for the sake of a dowry."

He'd pressed her down onto his cock, and pleasure filled her. But it was more than just the physical enjoyment of the moment; she felt like they were kindred spirits, both seeking nothing more than a companion who wanted them for themselves. She cupped his jaw, enjoying the harder, masculine feel of his skin, and kissed him. He let her lead for a moment, controlling their kiss even as she set the tempo for how fast she rose and fell on his cock.

Desire didn't flash through her; instead it built with every downward plunge. Pleasure rippled out from the friction of his member against her clitoris. As the need to move faster intensified, she lost the ability to continue the kiss, arched her back, and let her eyes close.

But Norris wasn't willing to allow her to master him. The bed rocked as he lifted her up, lodging himself firmly inside her, and pressed her back onto the surface of the bed.

"No…"

He took control of their pace the moment she felt the sheet against her back, riding her hard and deep while the bed rocked.

"Tell me yes."

There was a hard demand in his voice, just as hard as the pace he set. She gripped his biceps, pulling him closer as need began to consume her. She arched to take each thrust and gasped when each stroke threatened to send her over the edge into madness once again.

"Tell me yes!"

"Yes!" she snarled.

He growled and arched his head back. A few more strokes, and she shattered. Her climax was blinding, ripping her away into a vortex of swirling sensations. They wrapped around her, wringing her like a length of toweling. If she remembered to draw breath, she didn't recall. All she noticed was the moment when Norris ground himself deeply inside her and his seed began to erupt inside her once more. Pleasure was still washing through her, and the walls of her passage milked his cock for every last drop.

Exhaustion settled on her almost in the same moment satisfaction did. Norris rolled over, collapsing next to her, but he kept one arm around her waist. Moving her legs together took the last of her strength, and she surrendered and allowed slumber to take her away.

Tomorrow would arrive soon enough.

෴

Norris jerked awake, his mind still tired but clearing instantly. He rolled over and rose halfway off the bed before he realized it was Gahan who had startled him. His half brother locked stares with him then reached over and pinched out the candles. The scent of smoke teased his nose, and he heard the door close softly behind his captain.

The darkness suited the moment. In fact, it pleased him immensely. With no way for anyone to watch him, judge him, he was free to let his expression relax.

Daphne was sleeping.

He pulled the bedding over them both and nuzzled against her neck.

She smelled good.

He knew what clean skin smelled like, but hers went beyond the lack of grime. He placed a kiss against her temple and left a trail of them along her hairline.

This was something else…

She muttered in her sleep, shied away from him, and hugged herself. He pulled her back against him and eased her into his embrace. In the darkness, he smiled, a genuine smile of contentment.

৩০

She'd fallen again.

Daphne stared at the man sleeping in her bed but realized she was more frustrated than shamed.

Well, there was another sin to add to her list.

The sun wasn't really up yet, only the edges of the horizon turning pink. With the poorly fitting window shutters, it was enough light to wake her, since the bed curtains had never been closed.

Of course not; Norris would never allow himself to be taken by surprise simply to be warmer.

She plucked her chemise from the floor and hurried into it. Norris never moved as she dressed, but she left her shoes off when she crept from the chamber. She froze when she turned and found herself facing one of Norris's men. The burly retainer had the section of his plaid that normally rested on his shoulder raised up over his head while he slept. He was sitting on a stool with his back propped against the wall. But his hands were locked around the pommel of his sword.

Of course there was a man at the door. Maybe while they were alone it would be possible to forget who Norris was. Part of her cringed as she moved away from the retainer and down the stairs. Her chamber was three stories up in the main tower. It was also the coldest.

She sat down and put on her boots before hurrying to the kitchens to warm her hands over the hearth. The cook wasn't at the long worktable yet, which made Daphne frown. She checked the spice cabinet, but it was locked.

The cook held the keys.

She would have to hope another hour would not make much difference, even if it would increase how many eyes would know what she was about.

Daphne refused to care. She really couldn't afford to, anyway. Gitta might be of the firm opinion that a child would ease their suffering, but there was no way Daphne was going to risk her courses not arriving soon. She'd brew the necessary concoction and suffer the cramps. And that was the end of it.

Guilt tried to needle her, so she left the kitchen and walked out into the yard. The gate was just being raised, and someone ran through it. He was just a small boy with one missing front tooth. He stopped in the middle of the yard, looking at the men on the walls and scratching his head as if trying to decide how to get to them. When he noticed her, he smiled.

"Lady. Lady. Me da sent me to tell ye the Comyn are in the pens with the sheep."

Her temper flared, and the boy flinched from the sight of her. She shook her head and forced her anger behind a serene expression.

"Thank ye. Yer da should be very proud of ye. Now go inside and wait for the cook."

He tugged on the corner of his cap before scurrying away. Daphne hurried into the stable, startling the boys who slept there.

"The Comyn are stealing the sheep again. Wake the men."

She took only the time to bridle a horse and then mounted the animal.

"Lady… ye need to wait…"

Daphne rode out of the stable before she heard the rest of what the boy was trying to say. Keith would be on her heels quick enough; the man was far more at ease on the back of a horse than she was. Besides, she was on a mare, and the retainers all rode stallions.

But she'd failed to realize how close she was to the pens they'd shut the sheep in. Inexperience with riding making her ignorant of just how little time it would take her mare to travel the distance. Before there was much more than scarlet light on the ground, she was watching the sheep being herded out of the pens, and Keith had not caught up to her.

Which left her very much on her own against the Comyn.

❧

"I'm going to blister her backside."

Norris didn't give a damn about the looks he was drawing from the MacLeod retainers. There was something balled up in his gut that he didn't like at all. He understood the feeling of fury well enough, but this was something that sickened him.

He leaned low over the neck of his stallion and gave the beast its freedom. The animal surged forward, digging his hooves into the soft morning earth. Gahan was at his side as he raced up the rise and pulled his stallion to a stop at the crest. The animal snorted and danced in a circle as he obeyed.

Every muscle Norris had rebelled against stopping, screaming to charge down into the valley where the sheep had been penned, but he was not a fool or some beardless boy who had never seen a battle. The advantage was on the high ground.

"What in the name of Christ?" Gahan muttered as he surveyed the sheep milling about below them. Two of the pens were open, allowing the animals loose.

"It was a trap," Norris pronounced in a deadly tone.

Gahan took a second look at the pens and sheep then nodded.

"That fool woman ran straight into their hands," Norris added.

"But why leave the sheep?" Keith asked.

"Because Comyn does nae need to steal the animals. He can have anything he wants off yer land once he has yer mistress wed to him."

It was a ploy as old as time.

"What are ye planning to do?" Keith asked.

Norris surprised him by grinning, but a closer look showed him just how unholy the curving of his lips was.

"By God, I plan to take her back."

ॐ

"Agree to wed me this morning."

Morrell Comyn stood in front of her while his men ringed them. The morning sun was brightening the day, but all she saw was the ugliness of his expression. It was cold and calculating.

"If ye want to wed me, best ye go back to MacLeod Tower and discuss it with me overlord, Norris Sutherland."

"Sutherland's son is here?" Morrell scanned the rocky terrain behind her, losing some of his confidence for a moment, but he quickly regained his arrogance. He reached out and slapped her, to the delight of his men. "Best ye learn that I do nae tolerate scheming well. Sutherland would nae bother with ye until yer brother arrives. If the savage is still alive, that is."

Her hands were bound behind her back, and she turned with the blow, stumbling and then regaining her balance. Pain threatened to rob her of her vision, making dark spots dance before her eyes, which she blinked away. Her cheek throbbed, and she knew she'd have a bruise to mark the spot.

"Ye'll wed me, Daphne MacLeod, and I do nae mind so much just how much pain ye have to endure before agreeing." The tip of his tongue appeared and swept along his lower lip. Morrell wasn't a bad-looking man; some might even see his dark hair and square jaw as comely. Nonetheless, the lust twisting his features made him hideous in her opinion.

"And yer fortune of a dowry will be mine just as soon as ye swear before the priest that ye take me for yer husband. Since yer father is dead and yer brother is nae here, we need no contracts. Only the blessing of the Church and witnesses of a consummation."

Several of his men snickered.

"I have no dowry."

He raised his hand, and this time she only turned her head with the blow. Oh, it hurt just as badly, but she was ready for the sting and stared right back at the man in spite of the pain. Morrell smiled brighter, a gleam of appreciation lighting his dark eyes. "I do enjoy testing the strength of any beast I plan to master."

"Wedding me will gain ye naught but hungry people to provide for until me brother arrives to confirm that there is no gold."

He reached up and removed a long riding crop from his horse's saddle. The animal snorted and stepped away, obviously having felt the sting of the rod.

Morrell slapped the crop into his gauntlet-covered palm. "Swear to wed me."

"I will nae."

"I think ye will, Daphne," he taunted her. "But 'tis a shame to ruin yer fine face. I'm going to enjoy yer beauty while I labor to plant me son in yer belly. So yer bruises will have to be on other parts of yer body—some place that will nae ruin me enjoyment of yer flesh."

He continued tapping his palm with the riding crop. Daphne battled to maintain her stony expression, but the sound of that leather meeting leather sent a chill down her spine. His men were all watching, and not a single one looked disturbed by their laird's actions. More than one was leaning forward, eager to get a good view.

Morrell walked behind her and slapped the crop harder. She jerked in spite of her resolve to remain still. He chuckled softly, sickeningly.

"Yes. Yer back. Just think, me lovely Daphne. The priest will nae see any bruises along yer back. But ye'll feel them with every thrust."

He tapped her gently with the end of the riding crop, drawing it down her spine until her bound hands interfered.

"Neither will they gain ye a single bit of silver, for me clan has naught. Ye'll be saddled with a bride without a dowry."

He let out a sharp whistle.

"Unbind her, and hold her steady."

Two of his men obeyed quickly. One sliced through the strip of fabric they'd torn from the bottom of her skirt to bind her, and separated her hands. They pulled her arms out to her sides, crushing her wrists in their grips because they didn't temper their strength.

"Swear to take yer vows."

"Nae."

The crop landed on her back and sent her pitching forward as pain burned through her. While the men held her in place, she sucked in a deep breath and held it to maintain her dignity.

"Think of how much pain ye want to endure tonight, when I have ye on yer back beneath me, Daphne. I promise to ride ye half a dozen times before dawn." The crop sailed through the morning air again.

She jerked as it landed, and pain tore through her once more. It felt like it lasted longer this time, but she refused to believe it. She could endure.

She must.

"Ye'll feel every bruise while I fuck ye."

The crop sliced through the air and struck a third place, and then a fourth quickly thereafter.

"Laird!"

Daphne was suddenly free. She stumbled and turned around to see Morrell looking behind them.

"God damn ye!" he snarled, jerking back to glare at her. "Sutherland is here!"

And the man was in a rage too. She could hear Norris roaring. His men echoed the battle cry. It mixed with the pounding sound of the approaching horses. Morrell ran to his stallion and swung up onto the back of the beast. With a vicious jerk, he sent the animal charging straight at her. Too late, Daphne turned and ran, but Morrell leaned over and hooked her. Agony twisted through her back, but she refused to yield to it. She kicked and twisted, prying at the hand holding her against the side of the horse. She might well end up trampled beneath the hooves of the beast, but she preferred it to submission to Morrell Comyn.

"If 'tis a broken neck ye crave, so be it!"

Morrell Comyn cursed her and released her. She tumbled to the ground, curling into a ball to try and protect herself. As new agony raced through her body from the impact with the ground, all she heard was the thunder of the horses' hooves. Blackness didn't offer to take her away this time, maybe because the pain was too intense. But she was aware of every second that she tumbled along the ground, of all the rocks she hit and the sight of horses' hooves tearing into the earth all around her. Time seemed to slow down, giving her the chance to notice the way a hoof tore a chunk of grass from its roots and flung it up into the air.

She rolled and rolled, and finally there was nothing but silence, the thunder of the horses in the distance. When she stopped, she was lying on her back, staring up into the sky. It was a beautiful day, the sky blue with only a few clouds lingering from yesterday's storm. The ground beneath her back was moist from the rain, and the grass smelled fresh and new.

The thunder stopped, and she sighed, happy to know the sky would remain clear. But a shadow fell across her, and a moment later, Norris was beside her.

"Where did ye come from?" she wondered aloud, but then recalled the way he'd been roaring. "Ye are a fearsome man when ye want to be, Norris Sutherland."

"And ye are vexing," his words were too soft for how somber his expression was. He was smoothing his hand along her arms, touching her as if she were a babe.

"I am quite fit," she announced and sat up to prove her point. Pain stabbed into her from too many places to count. Her mouth opened, but no sound came out because her entire body was frozen in agony. She could not draw breath, couldn't do anything but endure.

"What ye are is luckier than any soul has a right to be."

He boldly flipped up her skirt and ran his hands along her legs. Then he covered her again and cupped her jaw to look into her eyes. "But ye're reeling, and that's no mistake."

"I am nae," she argued. "Me wits are in order."

He hooked her under her arms and lifted, still handling her like a child. She barely felt it when he put her on her feet, because the man was supporting most of her weight.

"I can stand."

He grumbled something, and there were other voices in agreement. She looked around to find Gahan and the rest of his retainers ringing them.

"What did that bastard want of ye?"

It took her a moment to realize Norris had asked the question, and still longer for her mind to decide on the answer.

"He… He wanted me to swear to wed him. Today. At the church."

"That accounts for why he stopped to beat her," Gahan muttered from behind her. "The priests are holding to the law when it comes to brides taking their vows."

"Well… I was doing…" Her brain felt fuzzy, but she demanded it to function. "Fine," she offered, satisfied with completing her thought.

Norris cupped her jaw, gently bringing her attention back to his face. Surprise went through her when she looked into his eyes, because she saw the unmistakable shimmer of relief there.

"Lass, when ye have yer wits back, I'm going to be pleased to tell ye just how badly ye have misjudged yer performance."

"I have?"

He nodded, and her brain refused to allow her to decide just where his thinking was wrong. In fact, a warm wave was sweeping over her body. It was hotter than warmed bath water, and it smothered her with its heat.

Norris caught her when she sagged, cradling her easily as Gahan watched. His men had turned their attention away to watch the Comyn.

"Damn fool thinks we can't best him," Gahan offered as Norris handed Daphne to him.

"Even on the high ground we could take him, but he no longer holds the prize."

Norris swung up onto his stallion and reached down for Daphne. She slept on, another kindness of fate, because the ride back to MacLeod Tower was going to be a painful one for her.

He glanced up to where Morrell Comyn was beating his shield with his sword. It was a challenge he would dearly love to take. Running the bastard through would please him mightily. But he had never risked his men's lives needlessly. Today would not be the exception.

"Leave the fool to his acting," Norris declared. "He's little better than a tone-deaf English troubadour. Certainly nae worth a drop of Sutherland or MacLeod blood. We have what they stole. Retribution can wait for a better setting. Fight hard, lads, but do nae forget to fight wisely. I'll nae see Sutherland women wailing for the benefit of a fool."

His men agreed. But Norris realized he didn't.

He wanted to run Morrell Comyn through. Rage was tempting him to do something his father had trained him since his earliest memory not to do. Use the Sutherland men to extract personal vengeance. He glanced back at Morrell and watched him lift his kilt.

Fool. The man was so drunk on his own pride, he was insane.

His day would come. There was another thing his father had taught him. No one transgressed against the Sutherlands and prospered. Satisfaction wouldn't be his today, but Norris grinned as he contemplated crushing the throat of Morrell Comyn.

The rest of the world would think it was because he'd raided one of Sutherland's vassals. Norris was going to do it because the piece of filth had struck his woman.

And he was going to enjoy it.

❧

Her dreams were powerful.

Daphne twisted and cried out when she moved, because her body ached so viciously. She wanted to wake up, but sleep held her down like a thick comforter, one that was heavy and confining. She struggled to push it aside, knowing she wanted to wake up but unable to escape her dream.

The dream swirled around her again, changing back to something pleasant. Norris was there, stalking her across her bed, and she smiled. Happiness filled her, and she giggled as he sent her that cocky grin she had never told him she enjoyed so much. She turned, and he pounced. The bed shook as they tussled like lovers. He won the day, turning her over with little resistance until she looked up into his face.

Instead of green eyes, she stared into the hard black ones of Morrell Comyn. He licked his lower lip and laughed at her. She tried to scream, but her throat was silent no matter how hard she strained to send a cry past her lips. Pain began to burn along her back, increasing as Morrell licked his lip again.

I promise to ride ye half a dozen times before dawn.

"I will nae swear!"

She broke through the hold of the dream. It took every bit of strength she had, and she tumbled right over the edge of her bed, catapulted by the strength she used to escape the clutches of the nightmare. She fell to the floor in a tangle of bedding as the door to her chamber was pushed inward. A rush of cold air came up the stairwell, but that wasn't what made her grab the bedding back, it was the sight of one of Norris's retainers peering at her. And the fact that she wasn't wearing a stitch.

"I was… having a nightmare," she muttered, not sure why the man was lingering outside her door. She looked up at the bed. Norris wasn't there, but the retainer was very real when she turned her attention back to the door. She gathered up the bedding to cover herself and stood.

He reached for the door handle, offered her a nod, and pulled it closed. She sighed with relief, but it didn't last long, because her long mirror showed her a reflection that was startling. She let the bedding go and crossed the chamber to get a closer look at herself. There was a huge black bruise along the right side of her jaw and another purple one covering her left cheek. She reached up to gently probe it, wincing as pain erupted from even that gentle contact.

That wasn't the extent of her injuries. There was something brown in her hair, and she turned her head to see a spot of dried blood on the back of her head.

She flinched when she touched it, surprised by the neat row of stitches.

"Yer back is worse."

She spun around and gasped when the movement sent pain stabbing through her.

"Do nae bite yer lip. Ye have enough broken skin."

Norris looked more formal than she'd ever seen him. His kilt was newly washed and pressed, something a more common man would never waste time on. His boots were clean, not a hint of mud on them, and they were crafted of black leather, proving again that he had coin to spare. But his doublet was made of wool, showing him to be a man of action, not useless finery. The only opulent item on him was a broach holding the feathers to the side of his bonnet. It was made of gold, with two hawks and a polished ruby the size of her thumb.

"Yer brother has arrived," he offered in explanation of his formality.

"Oh. I should dress."

He stepped closer and inspected her jaw. "I doubt ye can tolerate a dress against yer back."

"Of course I can. It is nae so terrible."

His eyes narrowed, and he folded his arms across his chest. "Is it no'? Why do nae ye have a look?"

He obviously intended to stand there while she bared herself. Of course he'd seen her body more than once, but she still hesitated.

"Unless ye're too shy."

She frowned. "Ye needn't take such a tone with me, Norris Sutherland. Ye admitted ye were a black-guard to tempt me into yer bed the first time, so do nae be insinuating I'm loose and accustomed to having men in me bedchamber. Ye just enter anytime ye please with no respect for me privacy."

She turned her head around to look at the mirror, while her temper gave her the incentive to forget about her modesty. She ordered herself to release the bedding, pausing when she uncovered bruises along her shoulders. Her mouth went dry, but she let the fabric go, and it slid lower, baring her back. She heard the sound of the riding crop and flinched as she uncovered the first point of impact. The bruise was black and brown, with red still showing in the center.

"Perhaps I like privacy as much as ye do, and like ye better in private, Daphne."

She wanted to take exception, wanted to be cross with him, but his voice was deep and husky, betraying just how much he meant what he said. He stepped up and reached around her shoulders to tug the bedding completely from her grasp.

"I find I do nae care for the way ye leash yer true nature below stairs."

His words were a deep whisper next to her ear, but she heard the heat in them.

"Ye must be as mad as they say, for no man likes a waspish female."

He chuckled and placed a kiss against her temple. "Perhaps I'm hiding behind yer chamber door because me men will nae disturb me when they believe I'm intent on bedding ye."

She turned her attention back to him, surprised by his suggestion. He was the picture of strength and authority. The idea that he felt the need to hide away from anything was almost impossible for her to grasp, and yet it seemed to touch something deep inside her. Some sense of compassion, because she realized he had as few choices as she did when it came to what life he would lead.

"Have ye and me brother already opened the whisky?"

He laughed softly. "Nae, but if ye want some for the pain, I will."

She looked back over her shoulder and sucked in a harsh breath. Every strike was clearly visible, huge black splotches marking where the riding crop had connected with her back. The mass of purple and black bruising explained the ache she felt, but she suddenly laughed.

"Now what could possibly please ye about seeing such a thing?"

Daphne ducked under his arm, his greater height making it a simple enough thing. A chemise lay over the arm of the chair, and she pulled it over her head and pushed her arms into it before facing Norris once more. The garment fluttered back down to cover her as she moved across the room.

"Ye're too delicate for such treatment, Daphne."

"No, I am nae." She lifted her chin. "I have suffered Morrell Comyn quite well."

Norris glared at her, something in his green eyes sending a tingle of warning down her back. "Perhaps yer head is nae so sound. No one would laugh over such a beating."

"Ye would," she accused softly. "And ye would laugh the next morning, enjoying the fact that ye did not swear to do anyone's bidding, no matter what pain they inflicted on ye."

For a moment, amusement flickered in his eyes. The corners of his lips twitched up, and she felt satisfaction sweep through her. But it was only a fleeting moment before his expression hardened.

"Ye would nae have lasted forever, lass. The flesh has its limits, and ye would have ended up wed to that bastard if I had nae found ye." There was a cold fury edging his voice.

"It still would nae have mattered, for he wanted only the dowry. He'd have sent me home once he realized there was no coin to be had."

Norris slowly shook his head. "Nae, lass. He'd have crushed yer throat and buried ye so he might contract himself another heiress. Annulment is messy and time-consuming. Being widowed, well, that's easy enough for a man to move past."

A chill tore through her, stealing away her confidence. She struggled to keep Norris from seeing just how much his words unsettled her. "It does nae matter what might have happened. My life is full of things that might have happened but never did."

"Ye've a stubborn nature, Daphne MacLeod," he accused her.

"No more than yer own," she countered.

A sharp bark of laughter broke through the serious expression he'd been hiding behind. "A fine point. But a man can afford to be stubborn."

"And I can nae?" she demanded.

"The world is less forgiving of women, lass. Have ye nae learned that yet?"

Now it was her turn to laugh. "Oh, I have learned a great many things about the nature of men when it comes to controlling women. Perhaps the world is less forgiving, but I am content with the fact that I am not Broen MacNicols's wife while his best friend, Faolan Chisholms, thirsts for his blood over me dowry."

"Faolan Chisholms wanted yer angelic form in his bed too," Norris countered gruffly. "It was no' just gold the pair were squabbling over."

"Well… I do nae care what I am labeled, so long as I do nae have to carry the burden of starting a feud."

"I don't give a damn who else sees the value in that, either. I recognize it full well and respect ye for no taking your comfort while men fought because of it." His eyes darkened. "Come home with me."

She wasn't sure if he was asking or demanding. There was a look in his eyes that warned her he was not in the mood to be told no.

Nevertheless, that was what she planned to do. She shook her head.

"Why nae?"

Daphne locked stares with him. "Because I am nae loose. Ye came into me bedchamber."

"A fact ye enjoyed."

"I know me weaknesses," Daphne admitted. "And knowing them makes it easier to stay away from temptation."

One of his eyebrows rose. "A temptation, am I?" He walked toward her, sending a ripple of awareness across her skin. Nature seemed to want to destroy her good intentions by making him impossible to ignore. She noticed things about him she never did with any other man. The way his skin looked healthy, his lips soft enough to kiss. Or the way he moved, every motion conveying strength and control.

He slid his hand along her hairline, careful of the bruise marring her jaw. "Well, I do admit to being tempted by ye as well, Daphne."

His lips were soft and gentle but still insistent. Even if it was a slow kiss, there was no missing the seeking insistence of it. Her belly tightened as anticipation began to stroke her flesh.

"Come to Sutherland with me."

She shivered, suddenly realizing just how Eve had fallen from grace. Norris's tone was intoxicating, clouding her thoughts so that agreeing with him seemed the most natural thing.

Aye, it was natural. Natural for him to want her to yield to his desire.

"No." She pushed away from him and heard him growl.

"Why nae?" he demanded.

"Why?" She lifted her hands in exasperation. "Because it would make me yer mistress. I never sought such a position, and I will nae become yer latest woman. Why do ye think I told ye to leave me in peace?"

"Because ye are afraid to admit how much ye enjoy being in me bed."

"And did ye nae just get finished warning me that a woman can nae be as stubborn in the pursuit of her desires as a man?"

He began shaking his head. "I meant that warning in regard to riding off without a single man at yer back." He closed the distance between them again, cornering her against the wall. "Ye need to remember that there are men out there who believe ye are an heiress, and they will nae be kind in their desires to own what ye are rumored to come with. Come home with me. I can protect ye."

She shook her head, and he cursed. "Why the devil not?"

"Because ye are a temptation I can nae seem to resist. Me brother will see to the protection of his family."

Norris contemplated her for a long minute. "Yer brother is a savage. I find I like that best about him. Morrell Comyn would do well to stay on his own land. But I confess, I hope he is fool enough to challenge yer brother."

She felt something tear inside her. Tears threatened to fall from her eyes, and she blinked to clear them away. "So, 'tis well enough, and I do thank ye for arriving yesterday."

"That's yer final word on the matter, Daphne?"

It was a formal request, one spoken in a tone she would have expected to hear in the great hall. She was facing the earl-to-be. The man who commanded one of the largest clans in the Highlands.

"Aye," she muttered.

"I'll send yer waiting woman to ye. Yer brother is waiting below to meet ye."

He offered her a slight nod and reached for the door handle to pull it open. Her throat felt like it was swelling shut, but she pressed her lips together to remain silent.

Foolish... so very foolish...

She had to watch him go. Had known it would end no other way.

He asked ye to join him…

She couldn't think on that, mustn't. It was too tempting to run after him.

Like so many others. He was the heir to the Earldom of Sutherland. He'd had a mistress since he was old enough to enjoy one and would likely always have one.

She wouldn't be one of them. But not for the reasons the rest of the world would think. They might think she was trying to preserve her virtue or at least maintain the last shreds of dignity she had. The truth was she wouldn't let Norris have her heart. He was already affecting her too much, too deeply.

So very completely.

She couldn't go with him, no matter how much her feelings needled her to change her mind. She drew in a deep breath and went to pull her stockings on. No, she'd remain firm and stay. If she didn't, she'd end up in love with Norris Sutherland.

Which simply could never be.

Three

HER BROTHER WAS A HARD-LOOKING MAN.

Daphne tried not to think of him as a savage, but she heard it being whispered by the maids near the back of the great hall when she entered. There was something in his dark eyes that made her suspect he heard them. Which wasn't possible, not with the number of people assembled to see the new laird.

Saer was dark haired like his mother. But he had their father's features. He didn't wear a doublet, just a sleeveless jerkin, and his shirt was tied up to bare his arms. Every muscle was defined. His hair was longer than his shoulders, and he had a single braid running down one side to hold it back from his face.

Daphne stopped at the entrance of the great hall, pausing for a moment to regard the son her father had so often lamented not being able to raise. Saer might hate her. He had more than one reason to. She was the child of the woman who had refused to share her castle with his mother, and she was a sister he would now shoulder the burden of either providing for or dowering.

He might send her back to the Church, but even they would not take her without a dowry. She moved forward; she wouldn't know until she faced him. Norris stood beside Saer, making it clear who had the Sutherlands' support as laird.

She stopped at the steps leading up to the platform where the high table sat and lowered herself. Daphne remained still, waiting for her brother to raise her. There were muffled whispers behind her, but she waited, making it clear she accepted Saer as her laird.

Good. That was what the MacLeods needed. Unity and an end to all the uncertainty.

"Ye are as delicate as a fairy."

Daphne straightened up instantly.

"But a fiery one by the look on yer face," Saer continued.

"Yer sister has a stubborn nature," Norris agreed. "She follows her whims no matter the consequences."

"If that were so, ye would nae be asking for me assistance," Saer boldly countered. They were a good match for each other. Both of them taller than the average man, with thick muscles attesting to just how accomplished they were at doing things for themselves. Neither man took his position for granted.

"I do nae need to ask yer permission," Norris remarked with unmistakable authority.

"But many would say I'm a savage from the isles who does nae understand anything of loyalty," Saer replied softly.

For a moment, tension filled the hall. Saer and Norris stared each other down while the MacLeods looked on.

"Even if that were so, ye'd still understand the importance of keeping blood close," Norris informed him.

Gahan had stepped up behind his laird, while another man with a dark scar running down his right cheek stood behind Saer.

Her brother turned to look at her. "I understand ye refused to swear to Comyn, and yer back is as battered as yer face because of it."

"Yes," she answered. "Fairies are creatures of the land and therefore hearty."

Saer chuckled. He shared an amused look with Norris. "I believe it is going to be greatly amusing to hear ye thank me for granting ye yer wish, because me sister is going to make ye sorry."

Norris smiled slowly and with a great deal of satisfaction. He turned his attention to her, and her knees threatened to give way. He looked like he'd won some victory, one that pleased him greatly.

"Set yer woman to packing yer things, Daphne. Ye'll be returning to Sutherland with me."

"I will nae." For a moment she forgot where she was. The sound of disapproving grunts reminded her instantly that so many were watching.

Father Peter would have her in the stocks before midday. Even that idea wasn't enough to make her lower herself. She glared at Norris, refusing to give him even a nod.

"There is nae reason for me to go with ye," she insisted.

His smile never faded; it just became more menacing. "Do ye deny sharing yer bed with me two nights past, Daphne MacLeod?"

He was adding her last name to ensure everyone heard and understood. Her cheeks burned scarlet, but she refused to lower her chin. Maybe he was the heir to the most powerful earldom in the Highlands, but she did not belong to him.

Saer added his own demand. "Answer the question, Sister. Is the man telling me the truth?"

Gahan stepped to the side, making to place himself between Saer and Norris.

"Hold," Norris told his man. "It's the God-given right of every man to fight for the honor of his sister."

"Oh, for Christ's sake," Daphne exploded. "There will be no fighting on me account." She shot Norris a scathing look. "Aye. Ye were in me bed two nights past, *me laird*."

"Then the man has the right to insist ye travel with him," Saer informed her. "Even if I have little liking for the insinuation that I can nae protect what is mine."

"As I do nae appreciate hearing ye question me motives for taking yer sister with me. A Sutherland should be born on Sutherland land," Norris remarked. "Naught was said of yer lack of ability. I'm no sniveling Englishman to offer insults through veiled pleasantries."

Norris stared at her brother for a long moment before her brother nodded. "In the short time I've known ye, that seems to be true enough. But it is still less than complimentary that ye feel the need to take me sister with ye."

"Actually, it is a compliment."

There were more than a few dry chuckles in response. Daphne lost control over her temper.

"No, it is nae. Besides, ye could send word to him if I'm"—she forced the word past her lips—"carrying."

"The decision is made." Norris spoke loudly enough for even the kitchen boys to hear him. "We leave within the hour."

Norris turned and walked away, and Saer followed him. Daphne found herself standing in the center of her own people as they watched her curiously. The men fingered their beards, contemplating her, while the women leaned close to whisper in one another's ears. Father Peter stood off to the side, his hands hidden in the wide sleeves of his church robe.

It was Gitta who cupped her shoulders and turned her around. The kind touch broke through the shock paralyzing her.

Which allowed her temper to blaze with full fury.

❧

"What is on yer mind, Laird?" Gahan asked the question the moment Norris took his leave of Saer. They were alone for a few moments while they walked through the stone hallways of the back of the keep. It was dark and musty in the passageway, the stone keeping the sun far away.

"That there is bound to be turmoil here as the new laird takes his place," Norris offered.

His half brother cut him a hard look. "She's his sister. 'Twas her father who sent the man away. If he's intent on holding a grudge, she'll have to weather it."

"She comes," Norris insisted quietly. "Make sure there is a cart for her. She'll nae be able to ride with her back black and blue." He stopped and sent

Gahan a hard look. "And I do nae want to discuss me choice again."

There were few men who wouldn't have backed off at that moment. Norris knew their reasons. Some valued their position more than their pride, while others had families to provide for. Gahan stared him straight in the eye without flinching.

"The girl has been under yer skin since Sauchieburn."

Norris started moving again. "I'm nae saying why she comes, only that she does."

"A cart will slow our pace."

"Aye, it will," Norris muttered. "But 'tis nae her choice, 'tis mine."

Gahan nodded and fell into step behind him. The passage gave way to the main yard. Norris's retainers were there, checking their horses. A two-wheeled cart was hitched to a sturdy-looking horse. It would slow them down, and many of his men were eyeing it, disgruntled.

❧

"Everything will be well." Gitta cooed like a mother trying to soothe her child. "He'll see ye have everything ye need."

Maids were bumping into one another as they tried to bundle Daphne's belongings. Gitta helped her into a sturdy wool dress that would travel well and keep her warm. Her old nurse draped a length of MacLeod plaid over her shoulder and sniffled as she secured it around her waist with a belt. The wool was pleated across her back, with a portion of it held on her right shoulder with a brooch. The arisaid would help keep her warm, and she could raise the portion draped across her back to cover her head for warmth or shelter from rain. The English scorned the garment, because it wasn't really a garment at all, simply a length of wool. But it was a traditional garment that reached back into centuries past—a Highland tradition.

"We'd best go now."

Too soon, they were on the bottom floor of the tower. Her brother stood there, his man at his back. Saer sent Gitta away with a flick of his fingers.

"The man is me overlord, and fighting with him will nae be good for any of us," Saer offered, but she could hear the discontentment in his voice. There was a hope in his dark eyes, one that sent a chill down her spine because she realized her brother wasn't very content with what Norris had demanded of him. Saer wouldn't loathe fighting him over it, if she gave him reason. But her brother was a hardened man too.

"I agree, ye have enough battles here and do nae need any with the Sutherlands. 'Tis a pitiful inheritance ye have come home to shoulder."

Saer lifted a dark eyebrow at her. "Did ye lay with him of yer own will?"

It wasn't what she'd expected to hear. Shock held her silent for a long moment.

"If not, I'll gladly run him through," her brother offered quietly, proving she'd judged him well.

"He's yer overlord. Ye'll have enough trouble trying to feed yer clan this winter."

"Ye're me blood," Saer answered. "Me only blood. Me mother taught me a thing or two about how to weather hard times. Did he rape ye?"

She shook her head.

"Demand ye submit because of his position?" Saer continued, determination flickering in his eyes.

Her cheeks heated as her memory offered up a perfect recollection of just how much Norris had demanded of her.

And ye demanded just as much in return…

She shook her head again.

"Keith told me of how yer betrothal was broken." Instead of scorn, she heard a note of appreciation in Saer's voice.

"Aye. I disgraced meself."

Her brother snorted and grinned. "The way I heard the tale, ye saved yerself from a union that was destructive to peace. Ye do look like a delicate fairy, but ye have something solid inside ye. I admire that. No boy king should be telling ye whom to give children to. 'Tis a gift a woman should have the right to decide whom she bestows it on."

"And do ye intend to choose yer bride by which woman will decide she likes ye?"

Saer smirked at her, looking just as bold as Norris so often did. "When I find the one I want, I plan to kiss her until she yields, just as Norris Sutherland seems to have done with ye. Ye look at him like a woman who knows what she likes in her bed."

"I have known no other man except him."

Her brother laughed at the stunned look on her face. "Go on, but know ye are always welcome here."

Tears pricked her eyes, but she enjoyed the feeling, because it had been too long since she had felt the closeness of family.

"Ye are nae quite the savage everyone whispers ye are."

His grin widened, and his teeth flashed. "Yes, I am. Never doubt that, Sister, for I plan never to change."

"Careful. Father Peter likes to hand out stiff penances for pride," she warned him.

"It is nae pride, Sister, 'tis who I am," Saer informed her with a wink. "Better the fine servant of the Church save his prayers for those who wrong me, because I will have no mercy on them." His gaze settled on one of her bruises. "Father Peter can begin with Morrell Comyn, for I've a score to settle with the man. While I am laird of the MacLeods, no man steals from us or touches me kin."

His teasing nature had turned cold, giving her a brief glance of the man who had survived in exile on the isles. He was ruthless, but seeing it gave her solace. The people she'd tried so hard to shepherd in the last month would not suffer under his leadership. Even if the days were hard, she believed he would be strong enough to see them through the coming year.

"There is much for ye to do, Saer. The crops will be poor, and there is no fleece. The men went off to fight at Sauchieburn instead of doing the shearing."

He continued to stare at her with solid confidence in his dark eyes. "Have faith, Sister. I'll make sure no one starves. Besides, the wool would have been stolen if it had been sheared. Now the sheep will be warm and happy through the winter. Come spring, they will be glad to be rid of their bulk. The land will yield what we need to survive. Trust that I know a thing or two about how to find enough."

Someone cleared his throat, and they looked up to see Gahan standing in the doorway. He reached up and tugged on the corner of his bonnet in respect. Saer's eyes narrowed, and he nodded in return. He shot her a firm look and raised his voice so Gahan could not mistake his words.

"But remember what I told ye. There is a home for ye here. No matter the circumstances ye discover yerself in. Ye will be welcome beneath this roof."

∽

She was shocked—but in a good way. The feeling was warm and secure, and for a few moments she lingered there, just enjoying knowing she had a place to call home.

It seemed like it had been forever since she had left for her wedding to Broen MacNicols and ended up taking refuge in a convent. It had been a full year, yet it felt much longer, for she was not the child who had left home. Was she a woman?

Norris has certainly treated ye like one...

She smiled at her thoughts and stepped out into the sunlight. The yard was full of Sutherland retainers. They wore their colors proudly and gave their allegiance to their laird without hesitation. There was a marked difference between these men and the ones who had watched Morrell beat her. It was honor, and it flowed from their laird. She had to scan the yard to find Norris, because he was doing exactly what his men were doing. There was no waiting about while his horse was readied for him. No, Norris was reaching beneath the belly of his stallion to check the strap with his hand.

But the man looked at her too confidently. He was too sure of his decision, too secure in the knowledge of his power. He was the heir to the Earldom of Sutherland. She tried not to dwell on that fact. Or on the way his men were all making ready to leave. She stared at the cart, her stomach knotting with something she refused to name, because she couldn't admit she was afraid of him.

You'd be wise to fear him…

Once they made it to Sutherland territory, she'd be at his mercy. No one there would go against the laird. Two of his retainers moved toward her, and she felt like a noose was being knotted around her throat. They tugged on the corners of their bonnets before extending their hands out toward the cart.

She shook her head, not even sure what she was refusing—the cart or the journey, only that every muscle she had was tight with resistance. The retainers looked confused. They glanced back at the cart and tried to decide what her objection was. The cart was wide and had a thick canopy stretched over its top to shield her from the weather. Inside there were plump pillows to keep her from being jostled. There was even a small basket covered with a cloth that no doubt held food and drink. But she shook her head again.

Norris wasn't as focused on preparing his stallion as he appeared to be. The moment she refused to get into the cart, he straightened and bore down on her. She felt him closing the distance between them and had to order herself to stand still, because the urge to retreat was ringing in her ears. He stopped in front of her, clearly battling his temper.

"Ye cannae mean to make me suffer the humiliation of going home with ye." Daphne insisted, disliking just how close her tone was to pleading.

He stepped past her, captured her wrist, and tugged her along behind him until they'd reentered the keep. They were in the entryway, where the stairs led to the chambers above and doorways opened to the hall and armor room. Women were working at the hearth, the muffled sounds coming from the great hall, but for the moment they were alone.

"Do ye think I'll leave ye here to sneak into the kitchen and brew yerself some concoction that will kill me seed?"

She jerked her wrist out of his grip and frowned when she realized he allowed her to escape. "That is me right, and I'd think ye'd thank me for nae trying to attach meself to ye like a leech."

He grinned at her, surprising her with how cheerful he seemed in the face of her temper. He'd been raised to expect obedience as his due. Father Peter could sentence her to time in the stocks for forgetting her place. Norris continued to grin.

"Which is exactly why ye are coming home with me, Daphne."

"I do nae understand ye a bit," she informed him, exasperated.

He reached out and grabbed a handful of her skirts before she realized his intention. With a steady strength, he pulled her against him, and she realized he was making sure he didn't hurt her by touching her back.

"But ye respond to me, lass, and that is why ye

are coming with me." There was a challenge burning in his green eyes. "Ye turned yer back on me at Sauchieburn, and it has badgered me ever since. So ye're coming home with me where we can take all the time we need to discover just what manner of connection we have."

He pressed a hard kiss onto her mouth. His lips teased hers for a long moment, sliding along the delicate surfaces and tasting them before he lifted his head.

"I did warn ye, Daphne." He cupped her hips and turned her around so she was facing the door and the cart. She could still feel him behind her, his warm breath against her neck. Her skin rippled with sensation, far more sensitive than she'd ever known it to be. So quickly, she was reduced to responding to him again.

Just like a spell…

"Run, and I'll run ye to ground. Ye may get into the cart, or I will put ye there." He kissed the side of her neck, starting a chain reaction of sensations that traveled down her body.

"Aye, I recall yer warning clearly," she offered, allowing her voice to grow sultry. "But what I'm wondering is just what game are ye playing? Have ye decided to bend me to yer will by using yer position? If so, ye are nae as different from Morrell Comyn as ye would like to believe. Ye are still a man, taking what he believes is his, and I am left feeling like a possession. Something I shall never be content as."

She had turned to face him, and he considered her from narrowed eyes. "If that were so, lass, I'd happily leave ye here to ensure ye never have a cause to pester me with demands."

"So why aren't ye?" she demanded. "What is yer game, Norris Sutherland?"

He stepped toward her, meeting her demand head-on, and caught a handful of her skirt once more to keep her in place. "Have ye never considered yerself worthy of being coveted for just who ye be, Daphne?"

Confusion swept through her. "Ye can nae claim affection for me. We've known each other for so little time…"

Yet she'd dreamed of him for what seemed like every night they had been apart. She felt so exposed in that moment, as though he might reach forward and clamp a manacle around her heart. Then she'd be his possession by her own will.

"Such is nonsense," she announced and pushed him away. As she felt the steady beat of his heart beneath her hand, a little ripple of awareness traveled along her arm. It unleashed a curl of anticipation in her belly, and she failed to hold back the memory of just how intimate it had been to be held against him in the dark hours of the night.

It had been bliss.

He cupped her chin and raised it so their eyes met. There was something burning in those green orbs that promised her that he was willing to challenge her rejections. He leaned down until his warm breath was teasing her lips, tormenting her with the idea of another kiss.

"As I said, lass, I'm taking ye home to see what it is about ye I can nae ignore. If ye want to view that as a demand, well then, I admit to enjoying yer responses to me demands."

Her jaw dropped open, but at the same time, a flare of heat flashed through her. Part of it was arousal, but the other part was enjoyment. A savage, primitive sort of enjoyment from some part of her she hadn't really realized she had. Deep inside, she was excited by the idea that he couldn't ignore her.

"Ye're a blackguard, Norris Sutherland."

He chuckled. "Aye, and ye are more than me match, fairy."

"Oh, now 'tis a fairy I am and nae a witch casting spells over ye?"

He grinned mockingly. "The fae folk are far more mystical and enchanting than a mere witch. Yer brother was right. Ye're a fire fairy."

"Then best ye mind yer fingers, else ye'll end up blistered, *me laird*."

This time he released her when she shoved against him. She stumbled back a step because she'd been pulling away from him so much.

"That's me promise to ye, Norris Sutherland."

She listened to him laughing all the way to the cart. His men turned to see what amused their laird, and she heard several muffled chuckles too. But the man had admitted he couldn't ignore her, and nothing else seemed to matter.

❧

Oh, damn the man and his pride.

Damn her for her lack of willpower…

They were a fitting pair; that much was for certain.

As expected, the cart slowed their pace. For the most part, they traveled by road to accommodate the cart she rode in. It was almost as if he enjoyed having her be seen with him. Those working in the fields stopped to look at them, many tugging on the corners of their bonnets as the son of the great Earl of Sutherland passed. He was more well-known than the king, and since James IV was a boy of only fifteen, Norris was more respected. Of course, there was no way for those passing to know who was in the cart, but they would guess it was a woman.

They'd whisper it was a bride.

She sighed. Well, she'd refused to become a bride once already. She still wasn't sorry; she lamented only the need for her behavior.

Liar. Broen MacNicols never made ye feel like Norris does…

There was a truth in that that colored her cheeks, but what shamed her was the fact that she was so relieved. She might have lived her life never knowing what true passion felt like. Maybe she was mad, for it would make things much easier if there was not such a pull between her and Norris. It wasn't normal. Or at least she suspected many would tell her to resist the attraction.

Her possessions were tied to several horses that followed the cart. Throughout the day they passed fields being harvested. Once they passed beyond MacLeod land, the fields were fuller. She discovered herself looking at the undamaged crops enviously while at the same time battling guilt for having left her people behind to suffer the winter. But her brother looked able to see to the MacLeods, which left her

with nothing to contemplate but her own fate. She saw
Norris only a few times throughout the day. He took
command of his men very personally. The expression
on his face was focused and intent. As he moved into
different positions throughout the day, he surveyed the
lines of retainers and the progress of her cart. There
was nothing to do but think, and her mind wanted to
dwell on Norris. Which wasn't the brightest idea. She
sighed and tried to contemplate something else, but her
thoughts returned to where she was bound.

By his command.

That part rubbed her temper. It also seemed rather
fitting. Father Peter would certainly think so, as well
as delight in telling her how her own behavior was to
blame for where she had landed.

But just where was she? The man's mistress? No,
she wasn't that. His lover? She doubted their nights
together entitled her to such a title. His vassal? Yes,
but the custom of claiming the laird's daughter on the
night of her marriage didn't really apply. Their entire
relationship was a contradiction of everything she had
been raised to expect from life. Of course, she'd been
the one to step off the path of righteous behavior first,
but it was very possible Norris had never set a single
foot on it himself.

The man was such a blackguard. Yet, she had
difficulty labeling him such. He was tender toward
her, controlling his strength when there was no one
to tell him otherwise. He'd saved her from a loveless
marriage too, but taken her virginity as his price. He
could have helped her deceive Broen MacNicols, but
he hadn't, and she realized it was because he might

be a marauder, but he was not a liar. It couldn't have been because he couldn't resist her. To believe such a thing would be arrogant of her, but that left her pondering why he'd offered to help her avoid her wedding at all. Perhaps that was the saving grace of going to Sutherland with him. She just might learn the answer. Even if it cost her her heart along the way.

❧

As the afternoon began to wane, some of the men took up their bows to shoot rabbits. They enjoyed keeping count and tied the downed ones to the backs of their saddles. They were farther north, which accounted for the chill once the sun began to set. The retainers buttoned their doublets and sleeves for the first time when they stopped for the night. Daphne crawled out of the cart, determined to stretch out her legs.

Fires were lit, and the rabbits were set to roasting. The scent of smoke tickled her nose. The men joked with one another as they tended to the horses. Norris had stopped them near the bank of a river, nestled next to a rise. She could hear it roaring. The men led their horses down to it to drink before returning and rubbing the animals down. There was ample grass for the animals to graze on, and they began slowly wandering as far as their bridle ropes would allow.

Daphne walked into the trees, seeking privacy. Once she reemerged, she realized she hadn't been as unnoticed as she'd believed. Two younger men were halfway into the trees with their backs to her. They heard her steps and waited to make sure she was returning before looking back at her.

The cart had two wheels. While in motion, it was level. But when the horse had been unhitched, it tilted toward the ground. A pair of men were busy tying the long poles that had secured it to the horse to large rocks. Once they finished, the cart was level again, giving her a very pleasant place to sleep. They pulled the edges of the cover in tighter, to shield against rain, and pulled down two lengths that had been over the top to act as doors. Luxury, indeed.

But before she entered the cart, there was a cry and a flap of wings, and a peregrine falcon landed on one of the canopy poles. It considered her for a long moment from its large, dark eyes then fluffed its feathers and settled down. It was brown with white feathers along its belly and inside its wings. Tied to its ankle was a small leather pouch.

"That is Bacchus. He seems to like ye, which is rare." Norris informed her as he approached. Already wearing a leather gauntlet, he extended his hand. Between his fingers he held a piece of raw meat. With a soft click, he summoned the falcon. Bacchus jumped onto his arm and took the offered meat with a soft cry.

The peregrine was another blunt reminder of just how much the Sutherlands had. The only purpose the raptor had was to ensure swift communication between Norris and his father.

She shouldn't be envious, and yet she was.

Which was childish. It was like wishing she were born a princess without ever knowing one or listening to the demands such a royal daughter had to endure. No one's life was free of responsibility. Norris might not want for food or a warm fire, but he was accompanied everywhere he went and had no doubt been raised on strict lectures about what he was expected to achieve because of who his parents were. Even Bacchus did not come freely. A raptor gave its loyalty only to the master who trained it. Norris must tend to the bird, else it would not have come to him.

Yet he seeks ye out…

It was a humbling thought and one that warmed her heart. She climbed back into the cart to avoid looking at Norris while thinking about him. The task proved more difficult than she'd imagined. Her back protested. Pain tore through her when she tried to lean over to duck beneath the cover. She had to hold her breath, only to lose it in a long hiss as she crawled into the makeshift tent. She collapsed onto the pillows, grateful for the flaps to shield her pride. Sweat had popped out on her forehead from the agony.

"That is why I did nae allow ye to ride," Norris muttered softly from beside her feet. She lifted her head and glared at him when he peeked inside. "The pounding would have been torment for ye."

"I'd have endured."

The scent of roasted rabbit tickled her nose, and her belly rumbled. He offered her a stick with a steaming portion of meat on it.

"There is ale in the basket, to help with the pain."

The flap dropped back into place the moment she'd taken the meat.

"Norris…"

He nudged the flap back, just enough to look in at her. His expression shamed her, for it was clear he expected her to argue with him.

"Thank ye."

For a moment, his stony expression softened. He looked as though he even appreciated her gratitude, but she didn't have long to consider just what she saw in his green eyes. He gave a short nod and dropped the flap again.

The light faded quickly, and the men did not keep the fires going. Soon it was pitch black inside the cart, with only a dull glow from the moon. But with her belly full, it was easy to slip into sleep. She pulled her arisaid up and over her head, shook out the folds that had been secured to her waist all day, and used it as a blanket. The pillows helped keep her back warm, but as the night grew colder, she shivered.

The wind was blowing down from the north, heralding the approach of winter. Her teeth began to chatter, and she gripped a pillow tighter against her chest. She pulled her knees up, curling around it to try and get warm, but her body shivered more violently.

"Here now, lass... What ails ye?"

She was half-asleep when Norris swept the flap aside.

"I'm well enough." But she couldn't stop her teeth from chattering.

"Ye're thin and injured," he pronounced in a soft voice. "I should have realized the night air would cut into ye."

"I'll endure... well enough."

"Aye, we will."

She lifted her head at the use of the word "we." The cart rocked when he climbed in and set his sword along the side. There was suddenly not enough space, but she could feel his body heat.

"Come here, Daphne. We'll argue later about why ye do nae want me near."

He gathered her close, touching her gently until he was pressed along her back. The man radiated heat. It felt like she was soaking it up, her body eager for more.

"Why…"

He smoothed his hand over her lips, silencing her. "We'll nae sleep long, and ye need yer strength to continue to make me dance once we've made it to Dunrobin."

"I am nae making ye dance."

She wanted to stay awake, but her body was warm, and she yawned. Sleep was suddenly very easy to fall into. His scent filled her senses, granting her a contentment she felt only when he slept next to her. She flattened her hands against the arm he had draped over her waist and lost the battle to stay awake.

❧

"Aye, ye are making me dance to yer tune," Norris muttered once slumber had settled over her. He drew in a deep breath, savoring the scent of her skin. Sleep eluded him. Thoughts of Daphne kept him awake.

He should be frustrated. Instead he was amused by his emotions. They were insistent and impossible to shake. The only thing he feared was that Daphne didn't harbor any feelings for him. He wouldn't be the first man she'd refused. Neither would it be the first time she'd left him.

His arm tightened around her waist momentarily before he realized he was responding. He had no idea how much further his feelings might go, but he would find out soon enough. Even if Daphne spit in his eye the entire way.

❦

Norris left at dawn. At least that's what the man called it. Daphne rubbed her eyes, and with nothing but a faint pink glow on the horizon, stumbled from the cart to relieve herself. The Sutherland retainers were all massaging their horses' legs to get the animals ready to ride.

Her back ached, but she still stopped and looked longingly at one of the horses burdened with her clothing.

Maybe she could ride…

The choice was taken from her as Gahan swept her right off her feet. She sputtered, but he carried her the last few paces to the cart and deposited her inside it while his men held the flaps open. The man had the audacity to tug on the corner of his bonnet before flashing her a smirk.

"I can ride well enough," she informed him. But the cart jerked and began moving forward. He swung up onto the back of his stallion and dug his heels into its side to send it galloping up to the front of the line where Norris was.

She settled for hitting a pillow, but the soft impact offered her little satisfaction. The cart rumbled over the ruts in the road, making her scoot back into the corner to brace herself. The sun rose, and she enjoyed the warmth on her skin. By midafternoon, she'd taken shelter beneath the canopy to avoid getting sunburned, but the chill returned the moment the sun began to set.

Tonight the men did not hunt. They pushed on, lashing the cart to two horses when the road became steeper. The animals snorted with the effort but dug their hooves into the rocky ground that took her cart farther north.

She heard the village and pulled a corner of the canopy aside at the front of the cart to see it. The bells in the church began to ring, several of them, confirming just how well-off the Sutherlands were. The church was a sweeping structure, built in the shape of a huge cross, and rose several stories into the air.

But Dunrobin Castle dwarfed it. It was a true castle, not like MacLeod Tower. This had three large keeps, protected by a curtain wall. She could hear the sea behind it. Every ten feet along the curtain wall, the dark shapes of cannons reflected the light from the torches. In the darkness, it looked black with only the orange fire dancing along its stone surface.

In spite of the lateness of the hour, people came out of their homes to line the road. Children tumbled out of their beds, wearing nothing but their shirts, to wave as the retainers went by. The women pointed at the cart, turning their heads to watch it pass. The village was large, and people ran down the cobblestone-paved roads to see their laird's son returning.

Norris was a prince here.

He raised a hand and waved, even tugging on the corner of his bonnet when he made eye contact with an elder of the clan. His people cheered, while in the distance she heard the large gate that secured the curtain wall begin grinding its way up.

The sound of the horses' hooves clattering over the

stones echoed loudly as they made their way beneath
the gate. Even the inner yard was paved with cobble-
stones. It didn't stink, telling her the Sutherlands did
indeed have wealth, for they had enough servants to
see to the removal of animal waste.

"It's good to be home, lads!" Norris declared.

His men cheered as they dismounted.

"And fine it is to have me son home!" a new voice
offered, one cracked by age. Everyone turned to look
at the top of the stairs that led into the center keep.

"Thank ye for the welcome, Father." Norris
inclined his head toward the gray-haired man standing
there. He was leaning on a cane, but there was still a
sharpness to his eyes.

Every man in the yard offered the laird a tug on
his bonnet before they set about taking their horses
through an arched opening to the right of the keep.
The animals pranced happily, clearly recognizing
their home.

She was the only one not at home. Daphne hesitated at the edge of the cart, unsure of what to do. It
would be foolish to stay inside the cart as if it offered
some sort of protection, but she was also loath to step
boldly forward as if she were arriving as some sort of
honored guest. She wasn't sure what she was.

"Here, mistress."

One of the retainers had handed off his horse to a
boy and was now offering her his hand. Another one
did the same, giving her no more time for lingering.
They lifted her up the moment she placed her hands
in theirs, neither one of them content with just her
hand. They slid their hands to her wrist for a more

secure hold and used their greater strength to whisk her out of the cart.

Men watched from the top of the wall, some of them pointing at her the moment her dress made it clear she was a woman. There was enough light from the torches to show off her MacLeod arisaid. As well as the bruises on her face.

"May I present Daphne MacLeod, Father."

The retainers helping her relinquished their hold the moment they'd guided her near Norris. "Lytge Sutherland."

She lowered herself, not truly thinking about it, but the motion had been instilled in her since childhood. The earl peered at her, studying her face for a long time before grunting.

"MacLeods are welcome here." He turned, the frailty of his body evident in his faltering steps. But he waved away the men who tried to offer him assistance.

Norris captured her hand and led her up the steps to the doorway of the keep. It was a huge, arched entrance, with ten full steps to climb before reaching the landing.

"I need to speak with me father," Norris muttered softly. "This is Asgree, head of house at Dunrobin. She'll see to ye."

He lifted her hand to his lips, bestowing a kiss on the back of it while the head of house looked on. A line of maids stood neatly behind the woman, and they smothered their giggles. Norris winked at her then tugged on the corner of his bonnet and followed his father. For just a moment she watched the firelight dance off the hilt of his sword, where it was secured across his back the same as any of his men. The longer folds of his kilt swayed as he moved rapidly to catch up with his father.

"I should think a bath would suit ye well."

Daphne turned her attention back to Asgree, grateful for the darkness, because it hid the color staining her cheeks. She chided herself for getting caught staring at Norris like a besotted fool—or an enchanted mistress. The older woman hid her thoughts behind a pleasant expression, but her eyes were full of knowledge.

"Yes, thank ye."

Daphne still found it hard to walk through the massive doorway, because it felt like a surrender of sorts.

Like admitting she was Norris's mistress.

She shuffled her feet and earned a sidelong look from Asgree. The maids were still standing in a line, their heads all covered by linen caps that looked ironed. They wore matching household livery, to keep strangers from easily infiltrating the earl's staff.

"Are ye stiff from the journey?" Asgree asked.

Daphne shook her head and cringed when she heard the gate being lowered back into place. There was nowhere to go but in, so she stepped over the threshold. Candles illuminated the inside of the keep. There were stairs to the right and an entrance to the great hall on the left. The scent of bread lingered from supper, making her mouth water. Her belly rumbled long and loud.

"There will be stew from supper and fruit, fresh from the harvest," Asgree extended her hand toward a smaller doorway near the base of the stairs. "I think we should wash yer hair first, so it might dry while ye're breaking yer fast."

"Thank ye." Daphne lowered herself out of habit, earning a curious look from the head of house.

"Ye are me laird's guest. But I see ye have pretty manners. Such a thing is a skill many forget to value."

But it was clear from her tone she thought Daphne was there to warm his bed and nothing more. Clearly, she wasn't the first woman Norris had brought home. Or was she? There was no way to know except to ask him.

And what will ye do if he tells ye there have been no others?

What indeed. It was tempting to smile, because the idea pleased her. Asgree led her through the doorway and down a section of steps to a hallway. The candles were lit in the sconces, their yellow flames dancing as the women walked by and disturbed the air. The scent of beeswax spoke of the means of the Sutherlands once again, because, even here, there were no tallow candles, only the best beeswax.

Asgree snapped her fingers, and two of the maids grabbed up their skirts so they might hurry ahead. The girls pulled open the doors that led to the bath-house. Daphne could smell the water, but it wasn't dank. There was a slight scent of lye and rosemary but no mold.

"The men have their own bathhouse near the stables. We will nae be disturbed." Asgree snapped her fingers again, and the maids began to prepare a large tub. It had been stored against the wall so water would not pool in its bottom. They placed it on the floor and pushed it toward a large hearth. Another girl was adding wood to the hearth and pushing it into the ash. She picked up a bellows and blew air into the coals until they flashed with a bright yellow flame. The wood popped as it caught, and soon the room was brighter.

The last two girls began to take off her clothing. They reached for the lacing that ran down the back of her overdress, but Daphne stepped away from them.

"I do nae require service."

They peered at her like she'd gone mad. To their way of thinking, she had. Norris was the heir, and whomever he brought home as his guest would be served.

"Ye can nae unlace that dress yerself." Asgree spoke evenly as she walked in a circle around her. "The laces are down the back. Ye must have had a waiting woman help ye into it."

"Gitta was me nurse. We helped each other, really."

"And here we shall make sure she would have naught to critique us for," Asgree insisted. She sent the girls back toward Daphne with a flick of her fingers.

Daphne forced herself to stand still. It was ridiculous to worry so much about having other women in the room with her while she was bare. In fact, it was dangerous, for there might be rumors that she was misshapen or had marks from the devil. Inhabitants of a castle always gossiped. There would be plenty to keep the maids talking once her back was bared. There really was nothing to worry about, because Norris's men knew how she had come by the bruises. The castle folk might talk, but it would not be malicious gossip. Still, she cringed when the maid lifted her chemise and let out a startled cry. Asgree had walked over to the tub to oversee its filling, but she hurried back.

"Sweet Mary."

"It truly is nae so terrible," Daphne offered, crossing her arms over her breasts.

"No wonder the laird had ye brought by cart. These are deep." Asgree snapped her fingers once again. "Tell the cook to brew up something for the ache."

One of the maids lowered herself before moving off toward the doorway. Another girl brought a stool forward for Daphne to sit on while her boots were removed.

In short order, she was easing herself down into the half-full tub of water. Asgree oversaw the entire bath, proving she was a dedicated mistress of Dunrobin. The older woman wasn't satisfied with leaving any detail to her maids. She frowned when Daphne's hair was loosened and its short length revealed.

"Were ye ill with the fever?" she asked. "I do wonder why ye are so thin. Ye are nae healthy."

"Nae." Daphne chewed on her lower lip, but the head of house had stopped in front of her and aimed an expectant look at her. As head of house, Asgree did not suffer having her questions ignored. "I went to a convent to avoid the match me father had made. Since I was nae content, I spent every hour at chores to keep me mind off me dilemma, and the food was very humble."

Asgree's eyebrows lifted until they practically disappeared beneath the edge of her linen cap.

One of the maids spoke up. "Ye were betrothed to Broen MacNicols."

"Alice, mind yer tongue," Asgree warned the girl. The maid lowered herself immediately. "I've

no tolerance for gossip. Go and make sure the cook
knows our guest is hungry. Flanna, go with her, and
the pair of ye make sure the star chamber is ready. One
of ye tell the cook our guest will eat in her chamber.
Tomorrow will be soon enough for ye to suffer
having a dress tightened against those bruises," Asgree
declared, "as well as let the rest of those chattering
hens get a look at ye in the hall."

The two maids left, and another brought forward
a clean chemise. As much as Daphne hadn't enjoyed
being stripped, she was very happy to have clean skin
and clothing. Asgree knew her art well, and her staff
was trained to perfection. Before long, a thick dressing
robe was keeping her warm, and a pair of carpet slip-
pers shielded her feet from the chilly stone floors.

❧

"She's the MacLeod lass with the fortune," Alice
declared once they'd cleared the hallway.

"Ye do nae know much more about her than I do,"
Flanna accused.

"It is true," Alice insisted in a whisper. "Why else
would the laird have her beaten if there was no fortune?"

"He does nae need to beat her to make her wed
him," Flanna argued while peeking at the doorway
of the star chamber to make sure Asgree or one of
her assistants didn't notice them. There would be hell
to pay if they were caught gossiping. The room was
empty, and they began to pull the sheeting off the
furniture to make it ready.

"Yes, he does. Did nae ye hear? Do nae ye know
why her hair is short?" Alice smiled with glee. "Me

cousin heard it from her husband's niece. Daphne MacLeod refused to wed Broen MacNicols. She went into the convent on Grant land and cut her hair."

Flanna covered her gaping mouth with one hand. "Surely the Church would nae let her get away if she had a fortune for a dowry."

Alice shrugged. "No doubt it was the battle of Sauchieburn that allowed her to escape, but she's learned the power of nae bending to any man's rule over her. She must have refused the laird when he sought her out now that his own bride is gone to Laird MacNicols. A fine trade if ye ask me, but she is overly proud and thinks herself above having a husband to master her."

"Just like the priest says…"

"Aye," Alice agreed. "She's acting unnatural now that she's been allowed to think herself able to make her own choices."

"No doubt the laird helped her lose her virtue so he might claim her fine dowry too, but his father had gone and made the match with the York bastard," Flanna continued. "Now that he's free to wed again, it makes sense he'd go looking for that fortune."

The two maids finished in the chamber then made their way to the kitchens to tell their friends of their discoveries. Everyone at Dunrobin was curious about the female Norris had brought home.

❧

"The laird's wife, Norris's mother, had a passion for painting," Asgree explained.

"It's lovely," Daphne murmured as she slowly

turned about to survey the paintings on the walls of the chamber. It was easy to understand why it was called the star chamber, for there were paintings of the night sky all over the walls. The detail was impressive, the different constellations clearly portrayed during different seasons.

"We've other chambers decorated with her visions."

Daphne held out her hands to warm them over the fire. "Ye do nae have to waste wood this early in the season for me."

"This is Sutherland. It is already freezing at night because of how far north we are."

"Oh." She turned to discover Asgree extending her hand toward a chair. The chamber itself was twice the size of the one she used at MacLeod Tower. There was a table and four chairs off to one side. A tablecloth was spread out already, making Daphne bite her lip over the amount of effort the staff was going to for her comfort. It was certainly a stark contrast to life at the convent. Of course life at MacLeod Tower had been stark too.

She felt guilty as she sat down, the faces of those she'd left behind needling her. But the determination in her brother's eyes helped ease her worry. Saer was not a man easily defeated. She smiled as she contemplated what her brother would think of her pity. He'd spit on it.

"This is young Alice. Ye can trust any food she brings ye. Her family has served Dunrobin for three generations." Alice lowered herself then held a silver serving tray while Asgree lifted each dish and inspected it before setting it in front of Daphne. There was a soup terrine, bread, fruit, and even cheese.

"Do nae take anything from a maid ye do nae know."

The scent of warm stew had distracted her, but Asgree's warning startled her. "Why? I am of little importance."

"Ye are the personal guest of the Earl of Sutherland's heir. Many would consider ye a target worth hitting to strike at him or his father. Those seeking vengeance often lack honor."

Personal guest... *Mistress* was the word going through all their heads.

"We have no arrangement." Daphne squelched the urge to lower her gaze to the tabletop. Instead, she stared straight into Asgree's eyes. "But I have known him. Yer laird brought me here to prove I am nae carrying his child. He claims the Sutherlands keep their blood close."

There was no point in denying it, and yet she took a certain satisfaction in telling the head of house herself.

"Ye spoke the truth about living in a convent for the last year," Asgree muttered as she lifted the lid off the bowl, releasing a white puff of steam. "Ye have learned to speak plainly, no matter what others might decide to judge ye for. 'Tis a trait a woman learns only when she's on her own."

Daphne's mouth watered, and she lost the battle not to stare at the food. It was a thick stew with chunks of meat and root vegetables. There was barely any broth, and she stared, soaking up the sight of it. It had been a very long time since she'd seen such a bountiful meal.

She was shaking when she reached for the spoon, and it clattered back to the tabletop. She grabbed it again.

"No one will enter without knocking."

With the spoon against her lips, Daphne looked up at Asgree. The head of house lowered herself, and the six maids with her did the same. They turned in a swirl of burgundy wool skirts and left the chamber.

She heard the sound of the spoon scraping against the sides of the bowl as she tried to get every last bit of stew. Before she sat back, she broke off a piece of bread and used it to soak up what residue remained. There was nothing but a slight gloss left on the bottom of the bowl when she relaxed against the back of the chair.

She straightened up instantly when she made contact with the hard back of the chair, pain ruining her enjoyment of the meal. Well, it really wasn't enough discomfort to destroy the contentment of having a full belly—overfull, really. She looked at the cheese and knew her stomach would not accommodate even a small nibble. So she placed a small square of linen left for her to wipe her lips on over the cheese and fruit. Maybe later.

She shook her head at her gluttony. At least it was one sin she wouldn't mind being able to commit for a change.

Ye did nae mind partaking of lust with Norris either…

Personal guest. Well, she was that, sure enough, and she had enjoyed having Norris in her bed.

As yer lover…

Now there was a word she had never thought to have personal experience of. As long as she could recall, her future had been planned. It had never been something she fretted over, either. Many girls never met their intended grooms until the wedding; she'd been fortunate to know Broen MacNicols. He was even a friend. They might have been content with each other if fate hadn't decided otherwise. Many would condemn her for not taking her place—but at the cost of peace? Even the meager food and cold in the convent hadn't made her regret her choice.

That didn't mean she didn't enjoy the lingering taste of the stew on her lips. Or having a fire to warm the floor she walked across. Dunrobin was the finest place she had ever stayed in.

She walked across the chamber, marveling at the size of it. There was enough space between the table and the bed for her to dance. The bed itself was huge, with large posts that held iron rods for the bed curtains made of thick velvet, and she smoothed her fingers along one panel in awe. She might have expected to find such a lavish fabric hanging around the laird's bed, or Norris's—but not here, in a guest room.

Someone had turned down the bedding, exposing the sheets. They were creamy and smelled of heather. With her belly full for the first time in too long, she crawled under the covers and fell asleep before she had time to further enjoy the luxury encasing her.

Four

"WHAT DO YE WANT?"

Gahan didn't take offense at his laird's tone. In fact, his half brother smiled smugly on his way through the chamber door. He reached up to tug on the corner of his bonnet but raised his middle finger instead.

Norris chuckled. "Well now, me brother. I'd have guessed ye were in the mood for fucking, but I never noticed ye taking a fancy to me."

Gahan grimaced. "Ye're in a fine mood. Why? I'd have thought ye'd be quite pleased to have the little MacLeod lass where ye want her."

Norris's cock twitched. "She's close to where I want her."

Gahan shrugged. "So go and claim her. What is stopping ye?"

"Those bruises darkening her back, for one."

"So let her do the riding," Gahan suggested wickedly. "The pair of ye can nae stop nipping at each other. It would be a service to the rest of us if ye'd take that passion off to bed where it belongs."

"It's a damn irritating skill ye have, Gahan. No one

needles me quite the way ye do." Norris sat back down and looked over the supper the staff had brought up. He settled for grabbing a mug of ale and extended his arm in invitation to his brother. Gahan was more than his captain; when their father left this life, he'd become a lesser noble. It was his birthright and Sutherland tradition.

"Or makes ye face yer feelings," Gahan offered as he sat down. "She's under yer skin."

"I admit it… to ye," Norris muttered. "And to meself, as far as needing to discover what it is I feel for her."

"Many would brand ye a fool for talking that way, unless ye mention the fortune of a dowry she has." Gahan picked up a slice of apple and bit it in half.

"I do nae give a rat's arse about her dowry." Norris held up his hand when Gahan opened his mouth. "Which makes me a double fool in the eyes of the rest of the world, or at least the majority of them. But the only one I'm interested in is Broen MacNicols. His opinion I'd very much like to know."

Gahan tossed the other half of the apple slice into his mouth and chewed on it for a moment; then he nodded. "Because the man is in love with his new bride, Clarrisa?"

"Call me a fool, but I'll tell ye something, Brother. There was a look in his eyes when he was ready to challenge the king and Lord Home for that woman. It was nae fueled by anything she came with. It was pure need for the woman herself."

"Aye, I recall that well enough. He'd have died for her, which was rather astounding considering the man had just escaped Sauchieburn with his life and should have been more enamored with staying among the living," Gahan added.

"Daphne's dowry meant nothing to him, for he could have had both, Clarrisa for his mistress and Daphne for wife, but it never seemed to cross his mind." Norris flattened his hand on the table. "The only reason I can think of for such a thing is Broen did nae want to bruise Clarrisa's feelings. That is the thing that has me attention."

Gahan raised an eyebrow. "Are ye saying ye have affection for Daphne MacLeod?"

Norris frowned. "I'm admitting she's the only woman I've ever turned down another willing lass for. It was nae something I decided to do, and I thought it would pass, but it persists. I'd think meself mad if I had nae seen that look in Broen's eyes. There is something to it, and I want know what it is."

"Well now, ye may get the answer ye seek…" Gahan stabbed a piece of meat with a small dirk. "If the lass does nae carve out yer heart for demanding she come home with ye like some sort of prized mare." He chewed and swallowed before smirking at him.

"Aye, well, she's here."

And that was all that seemed to matter to him. It made no sense, but it pleased him. It wasn't even a sort of satisfaction he was familiar with. This was something deeper, more intense. It frustrated him as much as he enjoyed it. His emotions were churning like the sea during a storm, completely unpredictable. There seemed nothing to do but ride it out. So that was what he'd do. And, by God, Daphne would be there to share the ride.

ﮙ

Summer was truly waning in Sutherland. Daphne woke to a chill that left no doubt about how close winter was creeping. It was tempting to stay in bed. The thick comforter was soft and warm, so only her nose was cold, but she lowered her chin, and the bedding eased even that discomfort. She sighed and giggled—a happy little sound she couldn't recall making in a long time. So she did it again.

"I'm glad ye approve."

She gasped, tightening her grip on the comforter, then realized what a foolish response it was. Norris had seen all of her, and more than once.

He stood near the bed, looking every inch the son of the earl. His kilt was once again bearing marks from an iron, and his shirt even had a collar on it with tiny box pleats. His jerkin was leather but dyed black, proving he didn't worry about expense when it came to selecting his clothing.

But it wasn't his clothing that drew her gaze to linger on him. It was the way he stood, his body poised and full of strength. It was almost like he battled to contain it, but his control was firmly in place today. The collar of his doublet was open, as were the first few buttons of his shirt, allowing her to see a deep V of his bare chest. Oh yes, he was a savage in the clothing of a civilized man.

She knew what he looked like when he'd been pushed past his limits…

"I admit I enjoy watching ye inspect me, Daphne." His eyes narrowed, making him look like a large feline. "Almost as much as I enjoy inspecting ye."

"Well... I am nae dressed yet."

He flashed his teeth at her. "My favorite way to see ye—bare. Every pink part unveiled."

Her nipples tingled. The chemise she'd worn to bed suddenly felt thin and delicate. A teasing flicker of heat awoke between her thighs, making her groan with frustration.

"Enough, Norris. Why are ye here so early to torment me? Ye did nae come to tumble me, for ye are fully dressed." She sat up, feeling too vulnerable lying down.

"Tumbling can be done without disrobing, lass. Have ye never seen what a man wears beneath his kilt?" He tugged on the edge of his plaid suggestively.

"Christ, Norris! Ye're a braggart this morning," she groused as she climbed out of bed. Her back was stiff, but it had improved. "I was nae aware that being yer personal guest meant I'd have to suffer yer needling when I first open me eyes."

"Who titled ye me personal guest?"

The teasing tone had evaporated, and she looked over her shoulder to see him frowning at her.

"Asgree." His eyebrows lowered, but she shook her head. "It is a kinder word than mistress. What else do ye expect yer people to think of me as? Yer leman... yer slut?"

"Mine," he stated in a hard tone. "*Mine* works very well to my way of thinking."

"I see." She shrugged into the dressing robe, but left it open. For some reason she felt the need to challenge him or at least push him until the controlled look left his green eyes. She closed the distance between them, watching the way his gaze was trained on her.

"And yet… I do nae see at all." She stopped in front of him. Her heart accelerated as she caught the first hints of his scent. "Ye have frustrated me with all yer demands, Norris."

He leaned down, closing the gap between their lips. "And satisfied them too."

She slipped her fingers beneath the edge of his kilt and teased the bare skin of his thighs. His jaw tightened, the muscles cording. "Which makes me yer slut." She delivered her comment with a slicing tone and then pushed him away from her. "Something I do nae agree with. Ye should have left me at home."

He moved only a single step and caught himself. "So ye could starve?"

"So I might uphold me place and shoulder me duty," she replied. "Perhaps MacLeod Tower is nae as grand, but it is where I was born. Ye are nae the only one who was raised to perform your duty to your clan. I am a MacLeod."

Something flashed in his eyes that looked very much like a promise. She shivered, the response instantaneous. It sent her back a pace, and then another when Norris followed her.

"Ye have starved for the welfare of yer clan, Daphne. Half yer clan is blind to the sacrifice ye made for their benefit. Maybe I'm doing me duty as yer overlord to bring ye here before ye waste away to naught."

She hugged the robe close. "'Tis nae so terrible. I endured well enough." She turned and moved away from him. When she realized she had given him her back, she whirled back around to face him. Such a stupid impulse, and yet when Norris was about, she seemed to make such blunders often. "Ye might have sent a few wagons of grain, if that was yer concern."

"I already did that at sunrise."

Her eyes widened. "Ye did?" She chewed on her lip and tried to swallow the shrewishness she'd been unleashing on him. "I suppose I owe ye an apology."

He moved closer, stalking her across the large chamber. "No, ye do nae. I could have told ye of the grain in the great hall, but I came here to make sure I could catch ye alone. So spit at me, lass. I'm behaving like a knave. Ye seem to bring out the worst in me."

She slowly shook her head, feeling a strange tightening in her belly. It was anticipation, but this time, she wasn't shocked by it. She was expecting it.

She was enjoying it...

"Aye, ye are behaving poorly." Her voice had turned husky, betraying her emotions. "Which is why ye should nae get what ye seek."

He paused and straightened up as formally as any lad waiting his turn for communion. "Should I attempt to court ye with all pomp and formality? Beg for yer hand so I might kiss the back of it as a true gallant?" He extended his hand, palm facing up in invitation.

A sharp bark of laughter escaped her. "I'd have to insist on checking ye for fever if ye did."

He captured her wrist and slid close enough to press her hand against his chest where the jerkin was open. "I'll happily stand still while ye touch every last inch of me."

In a flash, she was breathless again. The passion in her belly twisted, sending a jolt of yearning through her. It was sharp and insistent, and refused to be ignored. Norris lifted her hand and pressed a hot kiss against the delicate skin of her inner wrist. A small sound escaped her lips. It might have been mistaken for distress, but he growled softly in response.

"Come and touch me, Daphne. As ye did the first night we tasted each other."

"But 'tis morning… there is Mass…"

He pressed her hand back against his heart. The steady beating drove her own heart to move faster.

"Do ye think lovers taste passion's delight only under the cover of darkness?" He chuckled ominously. He grasped her hips, lifting her off her feet and depositing her on the top of the table she'd supped on.

"Ye truly are a knave." Her tone lacked any true reprimand.

He parted the top of her dressing gown and boldly cupped her breasts, with nothing but her chemise between their skin. Her nipples drew tight, rising up into hard nubs beneath his thumbs.

"I believe it's the way ye like me best." He leaned forward and placed a kiss against the side of her neck. "I know I like ye best when I am making ye breathless."

She wanted to argue with him, knew she was honor bound to. But when she leaned back, he cupped her nape and brought her close again. He pressed closer, parting her knees with his body. At the same time, he pressed a kiss against her lips, sealing her protest beneath his mouth.

It stole her breath and her wits. The desire to argue vanished, burned away by the need flaring up between them. It didn't build slowly. No, her body knew he might feed her longing, and it was impatient to experience all the delights he could deliver. She slid her hands up his chest, seeking the bare skin where his doublet was open.

He moved her legs apart, spreading her wide enough to allow his hips to nestle between her thighs. But she didn't want to be taken so easily. She reached down, far enough to reach beneath the edge of his kilt, and brought her hand up to cup his cock.

"Holy Christ!" he cursed. "I'll never behave decently again."

"Ye never have with me," she muttered and stroked the length of his member. His teeth were bared, each breath hissing as he leaned his head back, and the muscles along the side of his jaw began to twitch.

"Maybe I should have taken ye in hand before now."

The skin covering his cock was smooth and soft, but the organ was swollen stiff.

"I've never been so happy about being reined in."

She pulled her hand all the way to the crown, teasing the slit at its top before pressing her hand back down to the base. He trembled, the reaction betraying how much her touch affected him.

"I doubt ye have ever been reined in, Norris."

He lowered his chin and offered her a smile that was full of arrogant pride. "Ye know me better than most, lass, for ye are correct."

He flipped open her dressing robe, proving he wasn't as helpless beneath her touch as he might have appeared. He leaned forward and boldly licked one nipple. She gasped and would have scooted back, but he hooked an arm around her waist to keep her in place.

"But ye do have a way of making me feel like taking control."

He captured her nipple between his lips, sucking the puckered tip completely. She'd never realized a man's mouth might feel so hot or that it might give her so much pleasure. She arched, offering her breast to him, and he happily increased the suction. Delight spread through her, traveling from her nipple to her passage where she ached. The air brushed the open folds of her sex, making her aware of them and just how sensitive they were.

"And I admit the idea of making ye weep with pleasure is something I covet." There was some sort of promise in his tone. She opened her eyes and straightened up to see his expression, but he lowered himself to one knee before she got a good look.

"What... what are ye doing?"

He tossed up the edge of her chemise, completely baring her sex.

"Giving ye something to shock the priest with, and living up to me boasting about positions holy men have likely never heard of."

She still didn't understand, but Norris didn't grant her time to debate the matter. As he held her steady with one hand on each of her hips, he leaned forward and boldly licked her slit.

"Ye cannae!"

"Oh, but I just did, lass."

And he wasn't finished. He returned to lap the exposed center of her sex with a long swipe of his tongue. Pleasure ripped through her, threatening to tear her in half. Her clitoris throbbed so hard she almost climaxed before he'd finished. She'd failed to draw breath and had to drag in air once he'd lifted his mouth, but it went rushing out again when he treated her clitoris to the same treatment he'd given her nipple. He sucked it. Drawing the little button into his mouth while worrying it with the tip of his tongue.

She twisted and strained, caught in a storm of need and impending pleasure. Norris held her steady as he continued his assault on her body. He would release her for a brief moment while teasing the rest of her slit with his tongue, then return to her clitoris to suck again. Her passage ached, demanding to be filled, but that need didn't stop the tightening under his mouth or the explosion of pleasure that erupted beneath his lips. It twisted through her, raising gooseflesh along her limbs. When it was over, she was nothing but a mass of limp, quivering muscles. Norris chuckled softly, delivering a few final laps before rising and gathering her close.

"That's known as being 'Frenched.'" He rubbed her back gently, soothing her strained muscles. "More than one lady of court enjoys it before her wedding, because she can still fly a bloodied sheet."

"That is… insane…" Her heart was still thumping hard, making anything but panting difficult.

"Ye sounded as though ye enjoyed it well enough."

She swatted his shoulder. "I meant the part about flying the sheet, ye rogue."

He offered her a wolfish grin. "Just because a woman has been Frenched, or Frenched a man, does nae mean she is nae a maiden. Ye do nae lose that until ye fuck."

The head of his cock teased the opening of her passage, slipping easily between the slick folds of her sex. She sighed, and her body burst with renewed need. She lifted her hips for his next thrust, holding onto his shoulders while he drove his entire length into her.

"Which I've always found to be a good companion to Frenching." He groaned softly, and his cock stretched her passage as he lingered deep inside her for a long moment. "But I confess I enjoyed pushing ye to the edge of madness while ye could do naught but wait for me to grant ye release."

There was a hard note of savageness in his tone. She could see it in his eyes, as well. Part of her wanted to rebel, and she drew her fingernails down the sides of his throat in a slow scratching.

He shuddered and lost the control to remain still. The table began to shake with the strength he used to work his body against hers. He pressed her back until she was lying across the surface of the dark wood, her breasts bouncing with every thrust.

"Perfect," he growled, primitive satisfaction glowing in his eyes. His attention moved from the mounds of her breasts to the point where his flesh entered hers. He looked every inch a savage, but the sight of his delight unleashed something deep inside her. It rose up, brushing every learned behavior aside in favor of pure reaction. She lifted her hips, meeting his thrusts and moaning as pleasure filled her. She felt wild, and strained to move faster.

"That's it, lass, do nae be content with what I give ye. Demand more from me."

"I shall!"

She sat up, clamping his hips between her thighs, no longer content to lay spread for his taking. She gripped his shoulders and arched to take his thrusts. Her heart was racing, but she was absorbed in the moment, in the wildness. It consumed her and gave her the greatest sense of freedom she'd ever known. There was only what she wanted and the man who could give it to her.

"Yes," he snarled against her neck, pounding into her body in thrusts so continuous that she couldn't decide where they ended or started. It was a constant, flowing motion, one that fed the need tearing her apart.

"Yes!" Norris shouted again as his body went rigid and his seed began to flood her. That last, hot spurt was the final sensation she needed to unleash another jolting climax. It shredded her, swamping her with wave after wave of blinding rapture. This time it was deeper, and she couldn't contain it all inside her. She moaned, lowly and loudly, as the walls of her passage tried to milk the last drops of seed from him.

She'd have collapsed onto the tabletop if he hadn't supported her. His breathing was harsh, and he held her with only one arm while the other was pressed against the table for support.

"Ye enchant me, Daphne." He pressed a kiss against her neck. A soft, tender one before he nuzzled her hair. "And then ye destroy me."

It was an admission, one that touched something inside her, something she was uncertain of. For a moment, she felt closer to him than to any other

person she'd known in her life, more understood by
him than any other.

The doors suddenly opened, letting in a gust of
morning air. She jerked, stiffened, and sent her head
into his chin. He didn't move away; instead he held
her still so he shielded her.

"Yer mistress will be ready for ye in a moment."
There was a firm note of command in his voice.
"Henceforth, ye shall knock before entering. Be gone."

The maids looked at the floor and scurried from the
chamber. Horror flooded her, rendering her speechless.

"Do nae look so stricken, Daphne."

Her temper flared up. "Do nae tell me how to
feel." She shoved him back, snarling softly when he
stood fast and refused to let her recover her dignity by
closing her thighs. He still gripped her hips, and she
drew in a harsh breath when his cock stiffened again.

"I much prefer experiencing how I make ye feel,
Daphne. Be very sure of that."

He cupped her nape again, holding her steady for
a hard kiss. There was no mercy in it, and he allowed
her no escape. In that moment she felt claimed.
What bothered her the most was how much she
liked the sensation. He lifted his lips away from hers
and granted her a moment to look into his eyes. The
green orbs were alight with flames so intense they
threatened to send enough heat into her to make
her malleable.

He stepped away, and his kilt fell down to hide his
erection.

"And be sure that I do nae care so much what
anyone else says. This matter is between us."

He was already on his way to the door by the time she scrambled off the table.

"What do ye mean? What matter?"

He turned and offered her an arrogant look. "The matter of ye meeting me demands, lass, as me personal guest."

"Why ye... ye..."

"Blackguard?" he offered.

She searched her mind, trying to recall the foulest language she had ever overheard.

"Presumptuous, arrogant, rutting savage!"

He laughed at her, tossing his head back so his pale hair went flying. When he looked back at her, his eyes were full of devilish intent.

"No' too bad, me cock-sucking bitch."

"I have nae sucked yer—" She slapped a hand over her mouth when she realized just what she was saying. "Well, I have nae."

"But I'm stiff again just thinking about ye trying yer hand at mastering me."

"I would never—"

Norris wasn't waiting for her to finish. He tugged on the corner of his bonnet and opened the chamber door. The maids were clustered in front of it, clearly listening at the crack. They squealed when he yanked both sides wide open, and tumbled out of his way in a swish of burgundy wool.

She would never suck his cock.

Why not?

Her cheeks burned, and she struggled not to race after him and argue the point. The blunt reality of what might happen if she did kept her still. She turned her back on the open doorway and struggled to keep her mind from latching onto his suggestion. Oh, it had been a suggestion sure enough.

One ye would nae mind trying.

She was wicked to the core, because the idea of reducing him to the same quivering state she'd experienced appealed to her—more like beckoned. Like being drawn to the only candle on a winter night, her very nature made her seek it out, even if she knew every inch of the room she was in. She'd still long for light.

Long for Norris...

Just as he'd sought her out. She drew a deep breath, slightly frightened by just how strong their reactions were. It wasn't normal, possibly wasn't sane.

God help them both.

❧

Norris looked up, not because he heard anything, but because he sensed someone. Asgree lowered herself and waited for him to beckon her into the laird's chamber. His father had long since retired, leaving Norris the stacks of letters and books that never seemed to be finished. He waved Asgree forward, happy to have something else to occupy his mind.

"The lass is too thin," his head of house informed him.

Norris didn't have to respect Asgree, but he'd learned to. The woman was wise and had the most amazing way of discovering information. She gathered it from a large network of extended family relations who worked all around her. The damnable part about it was the woman was almost always correct.

"Why are ye telling me that?"

Asgree's eyes narrowed in reprimand for just a moment. "Because ye told many she was here in case she was carrying. Ye could have left her on her own land if a bastard was yer worry. That is nae yer reason, for she is hardly the first lass ye've dallied with."

He was suddenly seven years old and caught with his finger in the sugar drawer. Asgree's lips rose into a small, knowing smile.

"Now that ye've reduced me to a lad willing to beg yer pardon for filching sweets before supper, tell me why ye came to me. Ye never do anything without a reason, woman."

The table in front of him was stacked high with letters and rolled documents that needed his attention. His private secretary was scratching away with a quill at a letter. But he was far more interested in why Asgree had interrupted him.

"Ye are far too good at putting me in me place, even now that I'm grown."

Pride appeared on her face for a moment before she focused on the matter at hand. "She's too thin to carry or bleed. The lass told me she was at a convent for the last year."

"Aye, she was."

"There is the reason she is nae bleeding regularly. The body must be nourished in order for a woman's courses to be consistent. I'd say she is nae with child, nor likely to be until she gains some weight."

There was a note of warning in Asgree's eyes that Norris had seen before. He was accustomed to seeing it when she was defending his father or himself.

"Ye like her," he stated in a firm tone.

"I respect her."

Norris pulled in a deep breath. The head of house was known well for her high standards. Many a maid had struggled to earn just such words from Asgree.

"It would have been a simple thing for her to wed the man her father contracted with no care for the suffering that resulted. There are nae many lasses with that sort of strength. It would nae please me to see her suffer." Asgree nodded firmly.

She lowered herself, but there was a glint in her eyes that sent him a warning, even as she offered him a courtesy meant to be submissive. There was no mistaking her threat, but he discovered himself grinning after the door closed behind her. Daphne had made a conquest.

"The insanity is spreading, it seems," Gahan muttered from one of the side arches. His half brother enjoyed shadows as much as Norris did but was able to seek them more often, since he was not the heir.

"So it seems. Perhaps ye'll admit I am nae as mad as ye thought last night, since Asgree has a good opinion of me guest."

Gahan looked at the secretary, whose hand had gone still. The man was looking at the parchment, but it was clear he was listening.

"Take yer leave," Norris instructed.

The secretary was startled, though he fought to control his expression. For a moment, it looked as if he was going to make an argument in favor of remaining. A too familiar sting of suspicion teased Norris's nape. He'd learned to watch his back since he was young.

Gahan had, as well. Dunrobin was one of the finest fortifications when it came to protection from attack, but inside its walls there was an entirely different sort of danger to avoid. The secretary lowered himself before disappearing through the doorway.

Gahan abandoned his hiding spot. "I'm thinking it fitting to fetch me sister up."

"Isla?" Norris grinned. "I thought ye worried I'd toss her skirts, since she's only yer half sister."

"I'll bust yer jaw if ye do. Ye need a new set of eyes on that little sweet ye've brought here. Better to be sure who her maidservant is loyal to," Gahan offered. "When it gets out that ye've brought her here to see if she's carrying, I wouldn't doubt someone would be willing to poison her to remove her hold over ye."

Norris stiffened. "I already warned Asgree about that possibility."

"Still, me sister is nae even loyal to Asgree, for me sister does nae need a position at Dunrobin to keep a roof over her head, and do nae forget that Asgree is loyal to our father before either of us," Gahan argued. "And the young king is nae too pleased with young Daphne. Father does like to consider what will bring the most gain out of any situation."

His father was the one person he'd failed to consider as a threat. Norris cursed, realizing the error he'd made. He had a close relationship with his father, which was rare, but that didn't mean his sire wouldn't consider it a duty to the clan to make sure Daphne MacLeod didn't present them with a Sutherland-blooded babe.

"I'd rather nae think our father would do such a thing." But he could not leave it to chance. "Go and fetch Isla and bring that younger brother of yers too. She'll need someone to watch her back."

Gahan tugged on the corner of his bonnet, proving he was taking the matter seriously. Norris stood up and went to find his father.

❧

"The laird's son would see ye at the high table."

Daphne jumped, startled by how easily Gahan had appeared close to her. She hadn't heard a sound. The book she'd been reading went flying across the room and skidded to a stop on the stone floor. She blushed, embarrassed to be caught wasting the daylight in the library. But what a library it was. An entire floor of the keep was used to shelve books. The shelves went higher than she might reach without the aid of a ladder. She'd never seen so many books in a single place and had quite simply been draw in.

"I'll escort ye there."

"Oh… yes."

Her blush deepened as she realized Gahan was still waiting. He was such an opposite to Norris, with his black hair and dark eyes, but he had similar features. It reminded her of Saer and the fact that most men fancied more than one woman.

Ye have no reason to be jealous.

And yet, she felt unease tugging on her confidence. She followed Gahan down the stairs to the bottom floor of the keep. She'd set off that morning with some notion of exploring but had stopped at the library, only a single story beneath the bedchamber she'd slept in.

And dallied in…

Her blush never faded. She ended up appearing in the great hall with her cheeks bright. Dinner would be served soon, and many of the long tables were full of the Sutherland retainers. They were all burly men, proudly wearing the colors of their clan. Younger boys sat halfway down the hall, many of them sporting bruises on their faces from training. Instead of swords, they wore wooden blades across their backs.

Beyond them sat the elders, men who had served the clan and had reached the age where rest was their reward. Scars bore testament to the times they had bled in defense of the castle. Next came the older women or ones heavy with child, who were not expected to help serve the tables. These were only the inhabitants of the castle and the men charged with its defense. Outside the curtain wall, there were homes aplenty where more Sutherland families were having their supper. If there was a threat, the villagers would crowd into the yard to hide behind the curtain wall.

At the end of the aisle was the high table. It sat on a raised platform with huge chairs for those afforded the honor of supping at the earl's table. A large banner with the Sutherland crest was draped from the balcony directly behind the center chair. It glittered with threads containing gold and silver as well as rich, deep colors that were expensive. Lytge Sutherland sat there, watching her. Norris was seated to his right. The hall became as silent as a tomb as she approached.

She stopped at the stairs that led up to the high table and lowered herself.

"Straighten up, lass, I want to get a look at ye." The earl's voice crackled with age, but his eyes still looked keen and sharp. "Ye are the beauty the rumors claim ye are." He waved at her. "Turn about."

There was nothing to do but obey him, though her temper didn't care for it. When she turned, every man in the hall was watching her. She felt their gazes slide along her curves and battled to finish circling all the way around to face the earl once more. Leaving was more to her taste.

"Ye do nae care for me instructions, do ye, Daphne MacLeod?"

The hall was so silent she could hear the wind blowing through the open windows.

"Nae."

Soft grunts of disapproval met her reply. Behind her, the Sutherland retainers grumbled. But the earl chuckled, his voice crackling as he slapped the table.

"Well... ye are nae a liar. A trait I like." He pointed at her. "Even if ye are half-starved. Still, the tale of how that came to pass is one I find interesting. Why did ye disrespect yer father and the match he made for ye?"

"Because it was going to cause bloodshed, but he did nae know that when he sent me off to wed." Her father had been many things, but he had never been cruel. The match with Broen had been designed with alliances in mind.

"Ye do nae think a fortune for yer dowry is worth fighting over?" he demanded.

"Nae."

The earl was silent for a long moment. "Little wonder ye're half-starved with an attitude such as that. Perhaps the convent was the place for ye." He looked at Norris for a moment. "Then again, I hear ye have a taste for men."

"Father," Norris interrupted softly. She could see the muscle on the side of his jaw was corded, and his hand was tightened into a fist, but that single word was his only argument.

The earl smiled at his son. "If ye did nae want me to hear of it, ye should nae have allowed the king's men to catch ye with her blood on yer sheets."

"'Twas me choice," Norris informed his sire firmly.

"And mine," Daphne added.

"No it was nae," Norris argued. "I lured ye into me bed."

"Only because I was nae accustomed…"

"Exactly," Norris interrupted her. "Now stop arguing with me."

The earl suddenly slapped the table again and laughed. Daphne realized where Norris had learned to be so arrogant, because the earl laughed long and hard without a care for the fact that everyone was watching him. Lytge was laird of all he surveyed. Yes, Scotland had a king, but the boy was very far away. So far north, the Sutherlands were absolute rulers, and even with gray hair, Lytge didn't lack confidence. He resided over the hall like a king. Norris might be his heir, but he was still bound to obey his father. She'd be a fool to forget that the earl's power was absolute. With a single sentence, Lytge could have her shipped back to MacLeod land.

Wasn't that what she wanted? If so, why did the thought of it send a spike of pain through her heart?

"Ye're a spitfire, all right," the earl said at last.

"I'm tempted to pray ye are with child, for I have no stomach for weaklings. That York-blooded bride was a good match, for her blood was blue, but yers is full of spirit." He nodded but suddenly lifted one of his aged hands and pointed at her. "Providing ye have the dowry the rumors also speak of."

"I know nothing of it."

There were whispers behind her now, and she watched the earl frown. "Then yer child will be bastard born."

∽

The bedchamber she'd been given was a fine one. Among its many luxuries was a full-length mirror like the one her mother had left her. Daphne approached it slowly, wondering just what she wanted to see. Her temper was hot. The scene in the great hall still stung her pride. She smoothed her hands over her belly, flattening the front of her dress. There was no proof she was with child, and yet there was no sure sign she was not.

She looked at her face for the first time in a long time. There had simply been so much to do when she returned home that vanity hadn't been afforded much of her attention. Her cheekbones were harshly defined. Her chemise had a rounded neck, and her collarbones were just as noticeable. Where she noticed the difference was in her breasts. They no longer swelled up when her stays were laced into place.

Norris had seemed to like them well enough...

Yet his father had described her as half-starved.

"Ye'll gain the weight back easily enough."

She twisted around at the sound of his voice,

sending her skirts swirling up to let the chilly after-noon air at her thighs.

"But nae if ye skip yer meals," Norris continued. He walked farther into the chamber like he owned it.

He did. Or at least, one day he would.

"Am I to be afforded no privacy? Nae even a knock upon the door before ye enter?" Her hurt feelings were betrayed by the tone of her voice, further irritating her.

One of his fair eyebrows rose. "From me? Nae. Ye are me personal guest."

"I have nae agreed to be yer mistress." She propped her hands onto her hips. "Or do ye demand it of me because ye are me overlord?"

He closed the space between them, sending her heart beating faster. His green eyes were full of promise as he reached out and stroked her cheek. "I demand it because we are drawn to each other."

"Me cheeks are red because of the humiliation yer father just forced me to endure. But I do nae expect ye to understand, for ye sat there while he declared me sins to one and all."

"Our sins, Daphne. Do nae forget that," he warned her. "Or the fact that I made sure everyone knew I considered yer arrival in me bed my doing."

She bit her lower lip for a moment, shamed that she had overlooked that fact. Norris was using his rank to protect her good name, for there were many who believed in the old customs of allowing the nobles whatever girl they fancied. But she knew she had wanted him just as much.

"I came up here to be done with threats."

"And to worry that ye are with child," Norris accused her. "Me silence does nae mean I agree with me father."

"It does nae matter what it means." Her voice turned soft as she struggled to mask her hurt feelings.

Norris shook his head. "It matters a great deal to me that me father does nae see me eager to take his place."

His words cut through her hurt, filling her with remorse. "I did nae think upon it in that manner."

"Most do nae, but I do." He nodded. "His days will be done too soon, and I will nae raise me voice above his while there are others listening. Ye may label me a knave, but ye'll nae have reason to call me a disrespectful son or a greedy bastard who cares for his father's title more than his own blood."

Tears pricked her eyes. She tried to turn away and ended up facing the mirror. Norris stepped right up and wrapped his arms around her, watching her in the polished surface of the glass.

"I came up here to soothe ye, for I could see the hurt in yer eyes. Me father must think of the entire clan, nae just me feelings. He was reminding me that with whom I dally matters. For that, I apologize to ye, lass."

She quivered, enjoying the idea of what he promised immensely. How long had it been since anyone had soothed her feelings? Not since the night she'd yielded her purity to him.

"Ye did nae need to."

He pressed a soft kiss against her hairline, just at her temple. A ripple of contentment traveled down her body, and she struggled to hold her emotions in check.

She lost the battle, and the tears ran down her cheeks. He kissed one wet trail before moving his head to her opposite cheek to kiss the other.

"Aye, I did because I can nae seem to find the discipline to stay away from ye, when I know it would shield ye," he whispered. "Do ye think ye are the only one feeling the noose of duty and expectation about yer throat?" He kissed her neck, right where her shoulder began. "Or that ye alone struggle to maintain yer composure while those around ye are telling ye what yer life should be?"

His words were muffled against her skin, but she felt him tremble against her back. She'd never thought of his battling to be an obedient son. She smoothed her hand along his arm, drawing in a deep breath when he tightened his embrace.

He released her instantly. "I forgot about yer back, lass. Forgive me."

"Ye did nae hurt me," she assured him.

He moved back a pace, his expression tightening and hiding the tender emotions she'd shared with him so briefly. For a moment, she witnessed something she'd never seen in his eyes. It was the unmistakable sight of vulnerability—but only briefly. The man she knew so well returned, standing firmly in the face of what he felt was his duty. She admired him for it, more so because she knew just how it felt to cast her own feelings aside in favor of doing the best thing for her clan.

"I was foolish nae to understand why ye held yer silence. Ye are a fine son, Norris."

Something that looked like gratitude flickered in his eyes. It was only a quick look at his deepest feelings before he masked them once again.

"I've someone to introduce to ye." He let out a sharp whistle.

The doors opened in response. Gahan stood there, along with a female with the same dark hair. She lowered herself before entering the chamber.

"This is Isla, Gahan's half sister," Norris informed her. "She's to be yer woman."

"I do nae need—"

"Ye do," Norris cut her off with a tone that was as solid as steel. "Ye'll go nowhere without her, eat or drink anything she has nae brought to ye. The young pup waiting at the door is Cam, her brother. He's going to help make sure no harm comes to ye."

"Yer mistress has nae had dinner." Norris sent them from the chamber with a flick of his fingers. Gahan went too, pulling the doors closed behind him.

Norris cupped her chin. "Do nae challenge me on this, Daphne. Asgree is loyal to me father, and I would nae have a reason to be angry with him."

He pressed a kiss against her lips, parting them for a moment of bliss. Delight filled her and glowed inside her as he teased the delicate surfaces.

He was gone a second later, the longer pleats of his kilt swaying as he walked toward the doors and whistled. Gahan opened them in time for Norris never to break his stride. She was left marveling at the side of Norris she had just met. She had enjoyed the introduction quite well. But it chilled her too. She turned back to her reflection, looking at the fading bruises along her jaw.

Asgree is loyal to me father…

Of course she was. Daphne should have considered that sooner. If the earl didn't think she was fit for his son, it would be a simple matter to have his head of house deliver something to ensure she began to bleed.

Ye had the same idea…

A chill raced down her back as she acknowledged the hard truth. It had been her plan to drink a bitter brew to ensure she did not ripen with child. How strange to discover herself grateful to Norris for providing Isla to protect her.

Ye do nae make sense… Decide what ye want.

She wished she knew, but what had seemed so logical a week ago at MacLeod Tower was somehow twisting into a terrible deed. It was the tender way Norris had just apologized to her. She—the disgraced daughter of a defeated clan laird. A penniless one at that. He had everything she did not, and yet she realized he did not have everything. He was still bound by duty and honor.

No… He chooses those things…

That thought made her smile. He was an honorable man, and such a virtue had nothing to do with station.

It had to do with the man.

❧

"I am nae certain the laird would wish ye to go to the kitchen," Isla warned.

Daphne reached for the linen cap dangling from the younger girl's hand and placed it on her head herself.

"I can nae simply eat and sleep." Daphne turned to make sure her hair was all tucked beneath the cap. "There must be chores aplenty."

"Oh, there are," Isla assured her. "The earl keeps over a hundred servants on his pay."

"A hundred?" The cost must be outrageous.

Isla nodded. "The earl does love to entertain. Me mother used to say it was a jest with his old friend Laird Mackenzie, whose land is below Sutherland, that his table fare was grander and would draw more visitors than Mackenzie might."

Daphne left the chamber, and Isla followed her.

"Was it very different where ye were raised? To have a fortune for dowry, yer father must have enjoyed a fine table."

"Aye, he did," Daphne admitted. "But that was before Sauchieburn and the raids that followed. Nae much was left, and what was had to be shared with the villagers who lost all."

Many of those villagers staffed MacLeod Tower in exchange for their meals and shelter. Their homes had been burned, and with so many of her father's retainers dead, there were not enough men to rebuild them.

"No one has ever breached Dunrobin."

"I doubt they ever shall, unless they can learn to fly," Daphne muttered. The walls were too high, and the sea was at their back.

Daphne and Isla descended to the ground floor and began making their way back toward the great hall. The few people they passed looked at Daphne curiously.

The kitchens were massive. There were several long buildings, each with their own specialty. The butchery was at the farthest edge. An angler was bringing in his catch of the day, the fish no doubt intended for the next day's pies. The scent of bread was heavy and rich. Daphne smiled, enjoying the way it was almost overwhelming, because it had been too long since she'd smelled the scent of plenty.

"I can nae grind another," someone groused from the stillroom. Dunrobin was large enough to have a separate stillroom where the precious spices and sugar were worked with. In many castles, such ingredients were so costly, only the lady of the house was allowed to handle them.

"May I help?" Daphne asked.

A middle-aged maid looked up from the table she was working at. Her expression brightened as she recognized Daphne.

"Ye're heaven-sent, miss." She waved Daphne forward eagerly. "The earl has himself a taste for marzipan. I've been at it most of the day, yet there is more to do, and I can nae ask just any simple-headed miss in here to help me. But ye are a laird's daughter. Ye've worked sugar, no doubt."

The woman had already judged her fit for the task, but Daphne nodded anyway. "I recall well the amount of work it takes to make a marzipan centerpiece."

The woman smiled gratefully and happily watched Daphne pick up one of the mortars and a pestle. Inside were thinly sliced almonds that would need to be pounded into flour. A bowl already held two batches, but that would not make a tart large enough for the size of the laird's table at Dunrobin. Isla began to work on the sugar as she hummed. The amount of sugar was worth a small fortune, and when added to the almonds, the cost was unimaginable.

The tart began to come together as the three of them worked on it. Once the ingredients were pounded and mixed with rosewater for a paste, the first servant began to form it into the tart, and Isla worked on tiny petals to form roses for the top.

"There's still the nutmeg to be ground, and the cloves and cinnamon for the pies."

Daphne picked up one of the nutmegs, taking a moment to marvel at it.

"Are ye mad?"

All three women jumped, startled by the head cook. He was a plump man, who clearly enjoyed tasting his work.

"Ye're a simpleminded fool to let this harlot near the spices," he scolded the servant. "She might already have stuffed some of those nutmegs down her bodice!"

"I am no thief," Daphne insisted. "Ye have no reason to accuse me of such."

The cook wasn't accustomed to being challenged. His eyes bulged, and his cheeks turned ruby as he sputtered, trying to speak through his anger. "No one challenges me in me own kitchens! I am the head cook here, by order of his lairdship!"

He reached out and slapped her, the sound popping loudly throughout the stillroom. Daphne hadn't even raised her hand to cover the stinging spot before Cam grabbed the cook and yanked him backward. Pandemonium erupted in the kitchen beyond the door of the stillroom. Maids screamed as plates and other things went crashing to the floor. Retainers from the great hall rushed in to investigate the cause of the commotion.

The cook stood his ground. "No one touches the laird's food without me say so. Do ye think I allow just anyone near his supper? It's me duty to make sure no one poisons him!" He reached out and delivered a slap to the woman Daphne had helped. "Ye should know better. That sugar costs more than gold and is meant for the laird himself. I judged ye more careful than to let a stranger near it. It will be both of us ended up hung if something befalls the laird through our carelessness."

The woman's eyes bulged as she rubbed her cheek. "I... I... I did nae think..."

"What is all of this?" the Earl of Sutherland demanded. His retainers cleared the space around him, making sure no one ventured too close.

The pudgy cook opened his mouth and bellowed, "Her!" He pointed at Daphne. "She was in the stillroom with her hands on the nutmeg and cinnamon! No doubt she has a few down her bodice to remedy her lack of dowry. She snuck in there, never asked me permission. Sure as the blessed Mother was virgin, she's a scheming harlot. She did nae ask me permission... me laird..."

The rest of the kitchen staff cast her disapproving looks. Daphne could see them condemning her, and the retainers were no different. They shook their heads, disgust clear on their faces.

Daphne stepped forward. "I am no thief, and the fact that I came down to do an honest day's work does nae make me a schemer."

"Then what were ye doing in the stillroom with the sugar? It's more expensive than gold. I am in charge of the kitchens. If it was honest work ye were seeking, why did ye nae ask me for a task?" the cook demanded. He puffed up his chest and pointed at her. "She needs to be stripped."

"Hold." Norris's voice shook some of the pans

hanging on the walls. "Touch her again, and I will have ye lashed."

His hair was wet and his doublet open, indicating he'd come straight from the training yard. Gahan was at his back, his shirt collar dark with sweat.

"Well now…" the cook sputtered and drew his hand back toward his chest. "It's me duty to account for the spices."

"Enough!" Norris barked and shot his father a hard look. It was clear to one and all he was not pleased with his father's silence.

"Aye, enough," Lytge agreed. "The lass is nae some English noblewoman, raised to think herself above doing her share. Unless someone is willing to speak against her? A witness?"

"Mildred was in the stillroom. It was her duty," the cook insisted.

"I was there as well," Isla offered.

"But ye will only back yer mistress," the cook accused her, "for ye have no place here at Dunrobin."

Cam stepped forward to defend his sister. "Mind yer accusations, man."

"For Christ's sake!" the earl roared. "Have the lot of ye gone mad? I need a cook who can keep order in these kitchens."

"I was keeping order." The cook was quick to defend himself. "The spices ye trust me with are handled only by the most trusted. She"—he pointed at Daphne—"did nae have my permission to be in the stillroom. Such actions are suspicious. I'm right to be so cautious with my duty. It is an easy task to slip a nutmeg down a dress. I do nae allow just any lass into the stillroom, ye understand, me laird. Why, a couple of nutmegs are worth a fortune, and though there are plenty of rumors about her dowry, no one seems to know if she has one or not. Why wouldn't I be suspicious to find her in the stillroom without permission?"

It was a valid point, one that drew dark looks from those watching. Daphne had to admit she would have questioned the matter if their roles were reversed, for nutmeg was rare and terribly expensive when it could be purchased. Yet the facts failed to keep her temper from rising.

"Shall I strip here, in order to appease ye? I have naught to hide and will prove it." Her temper was boiling, else she never would have suggested such a thing. Shock appeared on Norris's face, and his father's, right before the earl choked with amusement. He bent over and slapped his thighs.

"Och now, well, little lass. I wager there are a few men hoping I'll take ye up on that offer, and if me son is half the man I believe him to be, he'll toss ye over his shoulder and take ye off to a chamber to ensure me the deed is done, since ye have so boldly offered."

The old man's brogue grew thicker with his amusement. Norris shook his head, fury dancing in his green eyes. Then he cursed in Gaelic and did exactly as his father suggested.

Daphne shrieked as she went over his shoulder, her skirts threatening to flip all the way over her head. Norris clamped an arm around her thighs and strode out of the kitchen to the sound of muffled laughter.

She was furious.

No ye aren't; ye're relieved to be free of the kitchen...

She wasn't.

Ye're being stubborn…

Fine. She was, and she wasn't going to change her mind.

❧

"Ye've got a nerve," Daphne groused.

Norris grinned like a moonlight raider as he stood between her and the doorway.

"Do ye never tire of making a public display of me?" She discovered herself looking away because of the flare of excitement that went through her. She shouldn't enjoy it.

Really… she shouldn't.

"Nae when it comes to making sure everyone knows ye're under me protection." He aimed an unwavering look at her, one she was beginning to recognize and might even have called possessive—if she were foolish enough to think he cared so deeply about her, that is.

Yet ye do hope… That's why it excites ye…

She cast a look about and realized he hadn't taken her to the chamber she'd slept in. This one was twice the size and furnished with a bed worthy of the laird of the castle. The bed was hung with scarlet and purple velvet. She almost gaped like a simpleton and unconsciously chewed on her lower lip as she stared at the thing. It was huge, with heavy wooden posts carved with vines and leaves. Beneath it was a true Persian carpet. Or at least she thought it was, having only heard descriptions from her relations at court. Five swords hung on the wall, each one gleaming from recent polish.

"It's as comfortable as it looks, but I would nae want

ye to say I was telling ye what to think, lass. Ye're very welcome to test it for yerself." When she looked back at him, he was smirking. "But of course, ye did offer to shed yer clothing to prove yer innocence first."

Her jaw did drop open. "Ye are a marauder."

He shook his head. "Nae. I'm conducting meself as a true laird of the castle. Making me judgments based on fact, nae me personal feelings."

He shrugged out of his doublet and tossed it onto a large, ornately carved chair with a padded seat. "But I will be happy to play the blackguard with ye—too happy."

A curl of heat unfurled inside her belly. It was intoxicating, dulling her wisdom and allowing bold-ness to rise up.

"Oh no, ye shall nae." She propped her hands onto her hips and stood her ground against the slow advance he'd begun. "Since ye are determined to behave so very correctly, I would nae dream of distracting ye from such a noble purpose."

He pushed out his lower lip, looking ridiculous and utterly adorable at the same time. "Ye would nae?" he asked, sounding pitifully disappointed.

"Nae," she assured him firmly.

He grunted and crossed his arms over his chest. "Where's the fun in that?"

"Well…" Daphne reached up and tugged the linen cap off her head. She dropped it onto the table near the fireplace. "I do believe this was more of a duty…"

His eyebrows lowered as he tried to understand her meaning. Daphne removed the few pins holding her shoulder-length hair up so the blond strands cascaded down.

"So ye should sit down, me laird."

His eyebrows shot up with disdain, bringing a smile to her lips. Daphne enjoyed the surge of daring that filled her and pointed at the chair.

"Sit down, Norris Sutherland, or I shan't remove a single garment."

He plopped into the chair like an eager little boy. There was a slant to his lips that was pure man, but his eyes glowed with anticipation too. A tingle raced along her arms and down her body, an awareness of just what her actions would lead to. She'd never felt so confident of her own sexuality or her ability to dictate the pace of their union.

"Do ye need help with yer laces?" he suggested hopefully.

Her cheeks heated, her memory recalling just how easily he'd overwhelmed her the first time. She'd boldly teased him too, and tonight, she wanted to unleash more of that devilish side of her nature.

She shook her head, gently fingering the edge of her bodice where it hooked. With a tiny pop, the first hook gave way, and then she was working her fingers down to the waistline.

Norris sat back, abandoning all hints of boyhood. Now he was very much an adult male, contemplating doing things only men did with women.

"I'll have the tailor make ye up more of those," he murmured suggestively.

"Ye are nae telling me what to do." She had the bodice open, and the dress sagged, the weight of the skirt pulling it down her body. She rolled her shoulders back, and it easily slithered down her frame to the floor.

"Ye enjoy satisfying me demands."

She shrugged, toying with the end of the lace that tightened her long stays down the front. "Ye might well find being on the receiving end… enjoyable too."

His expression became one of impending challenge. He reached up and stroked his face. "I can nae wait to test yer theory."

And neither could she. With a tug, she opened the bow the lace had been secured with. His gaze settled on the swell of her breasts. Hunger flickered in his eyes. It was fascinating the way he stared at her. She hadn't realized how long she'd been in the stillroom, for the sun was setting and the light fading.

Twilight was the time when fairies were strongest…

With a single finger, she pulled the lace through the first few eyelets. Her breasts were still small and didn't sag once their support was removed. The stays came off easily, and soon they were abandoned on the table with her cap.

Only the flicker of the fire lit the chamber. The dancing tongues of orange and scarlet cast a primitive light over her chemise. Norris's face had been a tapestry of tension and need. One hand curled around the arm of the chair as though he fought the urge to rise.

"Come here, lass, and I'll help ye with those boots."

His voice was low and tempting and edged with a promise that made her tremble. It was the sure knowledge that he was aroused. She recognized the timbre of his tone. Beneath his kilt, his cock would already be stiff, and her passage was growing moist in response.

All of the reasons why they shouldn't give into desire's pull were missing as she sauntered toward him.

He was mesmerized by her. His green eyes narrowed as his gaze slipped over the curve of her hips, and he patted the spot between his thighs. She wanted to be bold, wanted to let the desire to toy with him consume her.

He didn't reach for the tie on her ankle boot first. Instead, he cupped her calf, gently rubbing it until he reached where her garters held her stocking secure at her knee. Without looking away from her, he worked the small buckle of the garter and released it.

"Courtesans learn to captivate a man by disrobing." He slid his hand down to her boot and began to work the lace free of the antler-horn buttons along the inside of her ankle. "But I admit I'm the sort of man who enjoys getting his hands involved more than just watching."

He lifted her foot out of the boot and let it fall to the floor. He massaged her foot, working his hands up along her calf until he reached the top of her stocking. He lingered there for a moment, teasing her bare skin. And then he boldly stroked the top of her thigh. When he drew his hand back, he curled his fingers into a talon, sending a ripple of sensation straight into her core. He felt it and chuckled softly as he tugged her stocking free.

"It seems ye like having me hands on ye as well, lass."

He released her foot, and she touched it down onto the floor. The stone was cool and felt good against her skin. Her heart was racing, warming her and making the chemise feel like too much.

"So demanding again," she admonished while offering her second boot to him. "Be careful. If ye believe ye know everything, what new experiences will there be for ye to have? What will there be to tantalize ye?"

He dropped her boot next to its companion. "I'm naught but yer humble student."

She laughed at him while he unbuckled her garter and rolled her stocking down her leg. It fluttered to the floor, but he didn't release her ankle. He held it prisoner while stroking her calf. This time he smoothed his hand along the inside of her thigh, awakening a thousand different points of sensitivity she'd never realized she had. The desire to lean her head back and let her eyes close so she might sink into the sensation was strong.

"I can see several advantages to sitting down," Norris muttered.

He stretched up his hand, teasing the curls on her mons and then stroking her slit. She jumped, her eyes half-closed, and he steadied her with his hold on her ankle.

"Keep yer eyes on mine, lass."

It was a honey-coated demand, and one she wanted to obey. He wasn't the only one who wanted to know if the other was as moved. His green eyes were full of passion as he teased her folds, stroking them and parting them to circle the opening to her passage.

"No quite wet enough, but I recall well how to remedy that."

Anticipation ripped through her, tightening her nipples. Her clit throbbed for the touch of his tongue again. Nevertheless, her pride rebelled.

"Ye are doing me bidding tonight."

He thrust the tip of one finger into her passage, unleashing a need that was staggering with its intensity. "Is that a fact?"

"It is," she countered and lowered her leg. Her clit ached with frustration, but she was too absorbed with the idea of reducing him to the same state he'd had her in that morning.

She sank to her knees, remaining between his open thighs, and flipped up the folds of his kilt. He sucked in a harsh breath. Just as she'd thought, his cock was rigid, the length of it standing straight up now that there was nothing to press it down.

"And I am going to enjoy matching ye, me fine laird."

The skin encasing his member was soft and smooth. It was hot too. She clasped it, taking a moment to listen to the sounds he made as she stroked his length. Her confidence swelled in response, giving her the daring to lean forward and lick the head.

"Holy fucking Christ!" he swore.

"Norris Sutherland! Christ was pure."

Norris's eyes glittered with a savage need. He reached out and cupped the back of her head, gripping it just tight enough to send a prickle of sensation across her scalp.

"If ye had been between his thighs with yer little rosy nipples peeking at him, he'd have enjoyed ye as much as I plan to." His eyes narrowed in challenge. "Unless ye've lost yer nerve."

"Only gained more of it." She stroked his length with her fingers. "Ye'll nae count me as another conquest, Norris. I am going to be the woman ye remember as being able to best ye."

Sure, she was boasting, but she didn't care. She leaned forward and licked the crown of his cock. His grip tightened, confirming she was doing the job right.

So she continued, teasing the slit and the spot beneath the head with her tongue.

"Ye've a natural instinct, sure enough." His voice was raspy, and he'd leaned back in the chair, offering his cock to her. But he wasn't shaking as he did right before he climaxed. For a moment she faltered, until her memory offered up a few comments she'd heard when the maids on MacLeod land hadn't thought she was close enough to hear them.

"Likely sucks him off…"

She smiled as understanding dawned. Opening her mouth, she took the entire head inside and heard him growl. The sound was all she needed as encouragement. Rising up so she could take more of his length inside her mouth, she mimicked the motion of thrusting. Moving her head up and down, taking as much of his member as she could while sucking her lips around it. Both of his hands gripped her head while he thrust upwards into her mouth. She felt him shaking, his cock hardening even further before it suddenly erupted, filling her mouth with his seed.

"Ye're a creature of enchantment for certain," he snarled, pulling her head away from his sex. For a moment, she soaked up the satisfaction shimmering in his eyes, letting the sight fill her with confidence. It was like nothing she'd ever felt before. The woman inside her was pleased, and there was no shame involved.

"Ye enjoyed that, did nae ye?"

"Why shouldn't I? Ye nearly crowed with victory this morning after… ummm…" she stumbled over the word.

"Frenching ye? I surely did."

She understood his tone now. It was arrogant, yes, and she enjoyed the feeling as it swelled up inside her chest. She stroked his member, breaking eye contact with him because his length had not lost its stiffness. It was still swollen and ruby red.

"Men are nae limited to one offering a night, Daphne." He captured her wrists and drew her off her knees. "I wonder, though, if I am nae making a mistake in showing ye just how good it feels to meet yer lover on an even footing."

"Ye mean instead of lying meekly on me back while me husband labors to plant his seed inside me?" She wrinkled her nose and shrugged. "I suppose that would be one way to ensure ye'd send me back to MacLeod land."

He stood up, catching her close and wrapping his arms around her. Something appeared in his eyes that looked almost like insecurity, but she couldn't believe it. She lost sight of it when he kissed her. His mouth moved across hers in a sultry motion she was insatiable for. It felt like days since their last kiss, and she reached for him, slipping her hands over his chest and around his neck as she kissed him back.

"I'm tempted to lay ye on yer back in me bed and labor over ye as long as it takes to make sure ye are so satisfied being with me, ye will never even jest about leaving."

His words offered her something she'd never thought to have from him—affection, or at least the desire to have her near.

"But I'm more interested in discovering just how far yer streak of boldness goes."

He sat back down, moving his kilt out of the way to expose his erect member once more.

"What do ye mean?" she asked.

"Since ye claimed I was at yer service tonight, sweet fairy, does that mean ye intend to mount me and ride me until ye are satisfied?"

Her eyebrows rose, earning her a chuckle. He wrapped his hand around his cock. "I promise to give ye a spirited ride if ye are bold enough to ride me without a saddle."

On top of him. She considered the chair, with its wide seat, and realized it would allow her to do exactly what he'd suggested. No doubt it was wicked, but she was already climbing up onto the padded surface of the chair before she finished thinking. He cupped her hips, guiding her over his cock and pulling her closer to his body so she could take his entire length. As she felt the head of his cock parting the folds of her sex, he nuzzled her neck. She was so wet his flesh slid easily into her passage, stretching her as she lowered her body down until he was completely encased inside her.

"Now show me what fire ye have inside ye, Daphne."

The seat of the chair was wide enough for her to brace both of her knees on the padded surface on either side of his hips. She rose up and let her body weight press her back down. A gasp escaped her lips when the entire length of his cock rubbed along her clitoris. Pleasure went ripping through her, setting off a need to move faster. She gripped his shoulders and answered the demand.

"Aye, ye've got it."

His voice was dark and savage. She wanted to snarl a response as he helped increase their pace with his grip on her hips. But he suddenly released her, grabbed the chemise, and tore it up and over her head.

"Better!" he grunted as he cupped her breasts, teasing her hard nipples with his thumbs. "I want to see everything ye hide from the rest of the world." His eyes snapped with demand. "And listen to the sounds ye make when I'm deep inside ye."

He was lifting his hips every time she plunged down, making their bodies connect harder with each thrust.

"That's it, lass, keep pace with me, or I'll give ye a touch of the whip."

"Ye'll like me pace, Norris Sutherland, and be satisfied by what I give ye," she snapped at him.

"Will I?"

His tone was full of arrogance again, so she rose off him, stopping when only the tip of his cock was still inside her.

"Aye, else ye shall have naught."

He released one hip, and a second later, delivered a light slap to her bottom. It startled her, and she plunged back down while he snickered gleefully.

"Some lasses like a little spanking. Ye might just be one of them."

"I am nae!" she insisted, but he smacked her opposite cheek, sending her up and down in a quick motion. Her clitoris threatened to burst with climax. She didn't want to tumble over the edge into rapture; she wanted to make sure she took him with her. But the sting from his slap jolted through her lower body, triggering an intense burst of pleasure.

"Ye do like it," he cooed softly. "I can feel yer passage tightening."

He delivered another blow, and her body responded instantly. This time he rubbed the spot, but there was no slowing down the reaction. She was becoming desperate, grinding herself against him. The need to climax overwhelmed her. She was poised on the edge, needing just a touch more friction to send her tumbling into the vortex.

He smacked her twice more and lifted his hips to impale her on her downward plunges. She cried out as rapture tore her away. But she didn't go alone. Norris clasped her hips, his cock buried to the hilt, and his seed erupted into her womb. Their cries mingled, bouncing between the stone walls until there was no way to tell one from the other, which was perfect.

Daphne ended up slumped against his chest, and Norris seemed to have no more strength than she. The chair held them as he smoothed his hands along her back in gentle strokes and she listened to the sound of his heart slowing down. Perfect.

✑

Norris wanted to sink down into sleep like Daphne, but there was one thing he wanted to do even more. His body had been well and truly satisfied, but it was nothing compared to the feeling he got when he settled Daphne in his bed. He enjoyed it on a level he'd never felt before. Or at least he hadn't unless it was with this woman.

Although she looked fragile in his bed, he grinned because she'd shown him her spirit and proved her strength. He pulled the bedding over her and walked over to the table to pour himself a drink. He had left one side of the curtains half-open so he could enjoy the sight of Daphne's face resting on his pillow. She sighed and snuggled against the plump pillow and pulled the comforter close. He was feeling too protective by far, though he didn't bother to check the feelings that were running through him. In fact, he allowed them free rein.

He was everything his father wanted him to be, the leader his clan needed. But for the moment, he was damned pleased to be sharing the night with a woman who wanted nothing from him but what the commonest man might give her.

The night was suddenly a welcome place. He crawled into bed and gathered Daphne close. She was warm and soft, and he buried his nose in her hair. Her heart beat softly against his side as slumber beckoned. He saw no reason to resist.

Five

DAPHNE ROSE WITH THE DAWN, HER MIND TOO ACTIVE to allow her to sleep. Norris was sprawled on his back, only his lower body covered by the bedding. His chest was completely in her view, and the morning light illuminated the red in his chest hair. She found her chemise and hurried into it to fend off the chill of early autumn. Her stockings were on the floor, each laying on either side of the chair, and she blushed as she recalled how much she'd enjoyed the piece of furniture. Once she'd tied her boots, she realized her dress was neatly draped over the table.

Gahan certainly took his duty seriously, it seemed, for she doubted there was anyone else who would dare enter Norris's private chamber while he was entertaining. Of course, it couldn't have been the first time. That knowledge stung, tearing through her fragile happiness.

Foolish…

For sure she was acting the fool to be so tender-hearted, but she seemed to have no control over her emotions. She liked knowing she'd woken up in

Norris's bed, and part of her enjoyed knowing the information would be all over the castle before the morning meal was finished. Father Peter would have a great deal to say to her.

Nonetheless, Daphne left with a smile on her lips because she was going to enjoy the days until she had to face the consequences of her actions. She had no doubt that day would come. Norris Sutherland would wed only a bride who came with a dowry, and she had none. However, she did have courage, and there was no way the cook was going to run her above stairs to do naught but wait to warm Norris's bed.

There were retainers in the hallway. They stared at her, one reaching for the corner of his bonnet in respect and stopping midway because his companion failed to offer her any deference. She swept by them and went down the stairs until she reached the bottom floor. Norris's chamber was in a different tower than the one she'd used. This one was farther back in the castle for more protection. Along the walls were large paintings of the Sutherland earls and countesses.

The hallway opened into a large armory. There were full suits of armor and at least two hundred breastplates alone. It was an amazing display of wealth. Pikes, axes, and swords were arranged in racks, their deadly tips shiny with oil to keep the metal from rusting. No one was set to guard the room, because it was deep in the personal tower. As she walked through it and opened the doors, she heard the sounds of the great hall.

Plenty of people noticed her now. The conversation died momentarily before rising once more. Eyes narrowed, and many people pointed. She watched some of the maids shaking their heads; no doubt they'd had to endure the cook's ill temper. To be employed as the head cook at a castle such as Dunrobin was a high position. One sought by many. The cook wouldn't be happy with her for angering his noble employer. Well, she wasn't very pleased with his accusations, either.

Daphne held her head high. If she'd wanted to cower and take shelter under Norris's wing, she would have waited for him to wake. That had never been her way.

She walked through the hall, heading toward the hearth where porridge was being ladled into bowls for the morning meal. The retainers were being served, but the animosity coming from the maids warned her not to expect the same. Something else she was not unaccustomed to. It mattered little. But she did admit to having compassion for them; likely the cook had been unpleasable for the rest of the evening. The Mother Superior at the convent had been a laird's daughter, and as such, she often took her frustrations out on the novices within her care. Daphne had been lower than the newest novice and the last to finish any time there was additional work.

Daphne reached for a wooden bowl and waited her turn in front of the woman serving the porridge. She hesitated before dropping a ladle full of thick oat-and-barley cereal into Daphne's bowl. There were small bits of fruit in it too, and the heat warmed her hands.

She'd learned to appreciate the simple things while at the convent, a skill that had served her well once she'd returned to MacLeod land. It hadn't been so long ago, and yet it seemed ages. Maybe she should be the one accusing Norris of bewitching her, for the man seemed to have overwhelmed her senses completely. Now, even time felt affected.

She walked toward the benches, and the women sitting there made it clear she wasn't welcome to sit among them. Several scooted over to fill up more space between them and their friends to ensure Daphne understood their message. Well, if that was the way they wanted to be, she'd have to begin wearing her MacLeod arisaid again. If she was going to be treated like an outsider, she would look the part.

Scorn brings naught but bitterness...

She sat down in the far corner of the hall. Shame colored her cheeks, for the words rising from her memory had been spoken by an older nun who had not chosen the life of dedication to the Church but had been born a third daughter and been promised to Christ on the day of her birth. Sister Naomi had been content, though, and a true friend. Fate had dictated that the girl grow old never knowing the delights Daphne had shared with Norris, never feeling fine bedding against her skin or tasting a marzipan tart, even if her hands ached from preparing it.

Daphne scolded herself for being so irritable. True, Norris would most likely send her back to MacLeod land, but Saer had promised her a place. A home. Tears burned her eyes, making her even more frustrated with her fickle emotions. It should please her to know she had someplace to go.

"I hear she had naught... penniless..."

"But to steal?"

"I hear the laird already beat her once. Her back was black and blue."

"And still he brought her here? I'd mind me tongue if I were ye. She has him under her spell…"

Daphne cringed. Telling herself to ignore the whispers wasn't working very well. The muscles along her neck tightened as she tried to keep her gaze on her breakfast instead of glaring at the women discussing her. Every castle had gossip. That knowledge didn't give her any comfort when she looked up and caught the harsh stares of several women. Her appetite vanished, but her pride refused to let her show them she was frightened by their judgment. She would endure well enough.

The tension was thick enough to cut. Her belly was knotted from it, but she forced herself to lift her spoon and swallow the porridge. The single bite felt like a small rock going down her throat, and she had to drag in a deep breath before digging into her bowl for a second spoonful.

"Ye lack the basic instincts of a child when it comes to safeguarding yerself." Norris was furious, though his voice was low. He scooped her up off the bench from behind, and the bowl of porridge went rolling across the table.

"Put me down—"

She might as well have saved her breath, for Norris wasn't listening to her. He carried her out of the hall, and it erupted into hurried conversation.

"Damn ye, Norris! Ye shall nae simply haul me about like some goose ye have decided to make yer pet!"

"Ye are me pet," he snarled as he deposited her on her feet and captured her wrist.

She gasped, so outraged, words failed her. Norris took advantage of her shock, tugging her up a flight of stairs and another and a third with a pace that kept her struggling to keep up. She followed because she'd not have the beast tossing her over his shoulder again. He grabbed a door handle and swung open a heavy oak door, pulling her through.

"We require privacy," he growled, and she turned her head to stare at the retainers following them. Isla and Cam were also there, along with Asgree and two more maids. Her face flamed scarlet before the door shut to allow her some dignity.

"I warned ye nae to eat anything Isla did nae bring to ye. The damned cook has every reason to want to see ye suffer now."

"I was served from the same pot as others," she said, defending herself.

Norris was wearing only his kilt, shirt, and boots. His blond hair was messy, the strands obviously not brushed.

"It would take only a moment for a maid to slip something into her ladle below the table."

Her temper sizzled so hot she thought it might consume her. But the fury dancing in his eyes made her throw up her hands, and she desperately tried to maintain her hold on rational thinking.

"Why does it matter so much to ye, Norris? Yer father does nae want me here. Neither do yer people. Why can ye nae understand that I would nae willingly birth a child that must be branded a bastard?"

"I never said our child would be illegitimate, only

that I would nae allow ye to risk yer life to be rid of it." He shook his head. "Do ye think that because I am a man I do nae know women die from drinking those concoctions? That I have nae heard of the suffering they endure before death takes them away from the pain? Do ye think I value ye so little, that taking ye to me bed means I expect ye to risk such a thing because yer body is only a plaything for me amusement?"

He'd closed the distance between them and cupped the sides of her face. In his eyes, she witnessed a torment that tore through her anger. She'd frightened him in a personal way she would never have dared to believe she held the power to do. And it shamed her. Shamed her because hurting him hurt her.

She placed her hands on his chest, needing to soothe him, but he stiffened. His expression became guarded.

"Ye'll stay here so I do nae have to worry what ye are up to."

"Here?"

He stepped back and extended his hand. "Me mother's solar."

"But…"

He made a slashing motion with his hand. "Ye'll stay here, Daphne MacLeod, because I have decided it will be so."

He was striding toward the door before she could think of what to say, his kilt pleats swaying with his quick pace. There was anger in every motion he made. His knuckles turned white when he grasped the door handle and pulled it open. Men had to scramble out of his way, because he didn't pause as he strode past.

She should have been furious with him. Her pride should have rebelled. Instead, she was ashamed for causing him worry.

Damn her for a fool.

⌘

"What is yer fancy piece doing in the lady's solar?" Lytge Sutherland sat behind his desk while Norris stood before it.

"Being kept safe from meddling," Norris replied.

His father raised an eyebrow at his tone, but Norris didn't offer any apology.

"The way I hear it, the girl meddled with me cook and upset the man plenty. I like his cooking and do nae need him nursing a bruised ego."

"Nae for a woman ye consider unworthy of me, ye mean."

His father frowned and pointed at him. "Everything ye have came from yer ancestors making good decisions. No man in this line has taken a wife that came with naught."

"She's a MacLeod, sister to the new laird."

"A laird that has yet to secure the allegiance of his clan," Lytge shot back. "A clan that is already ours."

"Let her be, Father."

His father sat back in his chair. "Ye sound like ye are warning me, lad. Why?"

"Because she is important to me," Norris answered. "Very important. It would grieve me to argue with ye, but I will over Daphne. Let her be."

The older man peered at him through narrowed eyes. Norris reached up, tugging on his bonnet to offer his father the respect due to him before turning to leave. It wasn't in his nature to disagree with his sire, but Daphne unleashed things inside him beyond his control. It unsettled him, because a laird had to be as solid as stone when it came to his sense of judgment, not in jeopardy of being manipulated. Some men would see Daphne's effect on him as a prelude to being a woman's puppet.

"I wonder if the lass values ye so highly."

Norris turned around to meet his father's pointed gaze. "Well, does she? Ye keep having to carry her to yer chamber. If the lass does nae return yer regard, what use is she?"

Norris slowly grinned, earning him a grunt from his father as the older man shook his head.

"Ye are bruising the feelings of yer clan members for her when there are plenty of yer own kinswomen to dally with," the earl continued.

"The cook was being presumptuous to accuse Daphne of thievery."

His father nodded but also appeared unmoved. "Yet that attitude keeps our food free of poison. No small feat in times like these. His father was head cook before him, and his grandfather before that. There is none more loyal. The man also keeps the kitchens running smoothly and on a budget—something to remember since ye sent yer royal-blooded bride away and have left Dunrobin without a mistress to see to the books."

"Daphne has been educated and is practiced in the skills of running a large house."

His father slapped the table. "She has no dowry, something ye can demand from a bride." He pointed at a small stack of letters sitting to his right. "There are offers for ye, me son. Ones that include lasses eager to warm yer bed and fill the coffers while they do it."

"I run our land well enough to ensure there is a steady stream of income," Norris remarked, refusing to look at the stack of letters. The knowledge that they were there made him want to cast them into the hearth. "Do nae negotiate another bride for me."

"It is nae like ye to be so disrespectful," his father grumbled.

"We're in private, Father, and I mean no disrespect, but I am nae interested in wedding a stranger."

"Then perhaps ye should go to court," Lytge suggested. "With a new young king on the throne, there is bound to be a good crop of young heiresses there."

"No doubt."

However, he wasn't interested. Norris tugged on his cap to show respect and left his father's study. He paused in the hallway, considering the stairs that led up to the lady's solar. The day was only beginning, and the sounds of training came up from the yard. He hadn't been bragging about managing the estate well. They profited each season, but it took diligence.

His father's question needled him. It was true he continued to chase Daphne. His cock twitched in response, but for once he ignored it. Would she choose him? Come to him if there was another option? Part of him needed to know. Too damn much so.

⁓

"Ye should nae have gone below stairs alone, mistress," Isla scolded softly. The girl was busy pulling the covers off the furniture in the solar. "The laird is terribly worried something will befall ye. He had Gahan select several men to be under Cam's direction to make sure no one trifles with ye."

"Except for himself, that is."

Isla surprised her by aiming a knowing stare at her. The girl looked more knowledgeable than Daphne might have expected.

"Are ye sure ye want to look that gift horse in the mouth?" Isla muttered. "Ye sounded right pleased last night."

Oh, she had been… and so had Norris…

Her cheeks burned crimson as she contemplated the fact that Isla had heard her.

Isla returned to pulling sheets off furniture. "Men can be fickle, especially ones with position and title. They do nae have to look far for a willing partner to tumble. Nor would ye with yer fair looks."

Daphne stood up and began helping. The work helped dispel her dark humor, and soon she was happily anticipating the next discovery. The solar was richly appointed. There were chairs with padded seats and tables. A full harp was under one sheet, along with mandolins and even a set of virginals. The mandolins were potbellied style with intricate borders painted around their flat faces. The virginals had gleaming white and black keys, and each rested on four ornately carved legs. There were boxes of music and even a music stand to complete it all.

Next came several lace-making pillows. They both gasped when they opened the boxes of silk floss to be used in making the finery. There were bobbins in wood and silver, and even four glass ones. What stunned Daphne was the gold and silver thread stored openly on the bookcase near the window where the light would be best for making lace.

"I heard the late countess was a grand maker of lace and other finery," Isla said softly. "These were her things, but she had no daughters to teach her skill to."

There was a trace of longing in Isla's voice. When Daphne turned to look at the girl, she was gently stroking one of the glass bobbins. As the earl's bastard daughter, the countess might have dictated Isla's education. But since the mistress of Dunrobin hadn't taken any interest in her husband's bastard daughter, Isla had not been educated as a lady. Such was often the fate of well-blooded bastards.

"I will show ye, if ye like."

Isla looked up, startled. She was shaking her head in a moment. "Oh… I could nae. Ye're me mistress, and such fine things are nae for me fingers."

"No, I am nae so different than ye, and I prefer we were friends, for ye are right. I should enjoy the time that I have Norris's attention. Fate will no doubt intercede soon enough." Daphne picked up one of the pillows and began to push pins into it. "For the moment, let us enjoy being able to pass the day like princesses."

❧

Daphne rubbed her neck, but it was still stiff. By late afternoon, her hands ached from working the bobbins, but delicate lace was growing inch by inch. The pillow was the easiest to use, for you simply turned it round and round, moving the pins. It was detailed work, requiring focus to make sure every thin thread was moved at the correct time.

Isla was beaming. She fingered the lace she'd made, her face shining with triumph. "I never thought to make something so fine."

"Ye have a natural talent and a keen mind," Daphne offered, standing up. Her back was tight, but the ache was nothing compared to the way she'd felt after the beating Morrell Comyn had inflicted upon her.

She strolled around the solar, pausing at the windows. Although the sun was setting, the men still trained in the yard, and the sound of their wooden swords drifted up through the open windows. The evening air was chilly, and Isla began to close the glass windows, doing it gently to ensure she didn't crack one of the costly panes.

The sound of horses rose above the clacking of the wooden weapons, and Daphne looked down to see Norris riding into the inner yard. He truly was a master of the stallion he rode, though the animal still tossed its head. Norris reached up to rub its sweaty neck and then cast a look up at her. Their gazes connected, and she felt her belly twist. So quickly, so immediately.

Pure response.

So far above him she couldn't be sure, but she thought she saw his lips twitch up into a smile. He reached up and tugged on the corner of his bonnet, making her want to lower herself like some lady spying her gallant suitor arriving. Maybe she should greet him as such and await his courtship.

Ye mean his seduction...

"Supper will be on the table later, and the earl does enjoy having his son and guests at the high table. There are always clàrsach players."

How long had it been since she'd heard the Celtic harp, known as the clàrsach, played? Too long. However, that wasn't what made her interested in attending supper. It was her gallant suitor.

"I believe I'd like to bathe."

Isla grinned, flashing her teeth in her excitement. She rubbed her hands together and opened the door to the stairs. The sight of the retainers standing there made Daphne hesitate, but anticipation was brewing inside her.

"The mistress is to bathe."

They reached for the corner of their bonnets and moved out of the way. It was unnerving the way they followed her, insisting on going into the bathhouse to inspect it before allowing her enter. Asgree appeared, slightly flushed from hurrying, and shooed them away. They went only as far as the doorway and turned their backs.

"Ye'll have to become accustomed to such things so long as ye are important to the earl's son," the head of house muttered. She snapped her fingers, and two maids began the process of filling a tub.

"Disrobe yer mistress."

Isla was only too happy to assume the duty. The two maids working with the tub shot her envious looks as she carefully began to unlace and help Daphne from her dress. Asgree watched the process with an experienced eye, merely having to point, and her staff understood her. The woman was an accomplished head of house. Isla removed Daphne's clothing and handed each piece to another maid, who would in turn drape it over a rack.

But when her underdrawers were removed, Asgree snapped her fingers, and the maid brought them to her.

Daphne blushed scarlet. "I'm nae bleeding."

Asgree didn't take her word for it. "I doubted ye would be," she remarked after handing the intimate garment back to the maid. "Ye are too thin. I've seen it before. Many a lass suffers such near the end of winter when there has been little on the table for too many months, and their clothing is sagging. A year in a convent would no doubt account for how thin ye are."

Daphne sat down in the tub, trying to relax as Isla began to wash her. The girl wouldn't let her take the cake of soap from her hand, and Asgree brought over a rare sea sponge to use on her skin.

"Ye have much to learn about being waited on," Asgree teased her gently.

"A wasted effort, since I do nae plan to have need of such knowledge once I return to MacLeod land." For a moment, tears stung her eyes, because she doubted she would ever wed. What man would want her? The disobedient daughter of a defeated laird and one who had defied the king, as well.

"Fate likes to make up her own mind," Asgree instructed her gently. "None of us know for sure what tomorrow will bring."

For a moment, a tiny flicker of hope warmed her. A vision of her belly large with a babe sprung up in spite of her warnings not to allow herself to daydream. She did desire children.

Norris's children.

Once again the thought was simply there, in defiance of her better judgment. The vision continued, with Norris reaching out to rub her swollen belly with a cocky grin on his lips. But tenderness in his eyes.

"Well, I do find meself agreeing with ye, Asgree. Tomorrow is something we know naught about." Daphne stood up to let the cold air distract her from the daydream. It hit her wet skin, sending gooseflesh spreading across her limbs and puckering her nipples.

Asgree snapped her fingers, but Isla had already brought toweling forward. The head of house went to a small wardrobe and used one of the keys hanging on the ring at her waist to open it. The keys were the symbol of her position at Dunrobin and responsibility, for if the account books didn't balance, Asgree would be the one called on to answer for any shortages. There were locked cabinets and chests that held items of value, such as the wardrobe she opened now. Inside were robes, some of them made of expensive fabrics, but any cloth cost a fair amount of coin, even wool. There were no doubt plenty of sheep on Sutherland land, but shearing took time. So did carding and spinning and weaving. Those who produced cloth had to eat.

"This will keep ye warm until we decide what ye shall wear to supper." Asgree selected a gold-colored robe, and Isla helped hold it up so Daphne might slip her arms easily into the sleeves. It was lined in something so soft, she looked down and gasped when she realized it was silk.

"When the mistress was alive, she enjoyed fine

things," Asgree said with a touch of nostalgia in her voice. "I believe ye shall find something among her things to wear. Velvet never goes out of fashion."

Asgree didn't give her time to argue. She pointed toward the door, and Isla encouraged her to come along. The robe fell to her ankles, keeping her warm as she climbed the stairs to the lady's solar once more. This time Asgree pointed to the next floor, and once they reached it, the head of house fitted one of her keys into the door to open it.

"The mistress insisted on private chambers once she'd conceived." There was a note of sadness in Asgree's voice. "Such likely accounted for the fact that she had only one child, for she never returned to the master's chambers for more than a few hours."

It was the way for many marriages, and yet it sounded sad. Lying beside Norris through the night had been satisfying on a level Daphne had never known before. The maids lit the candles, which were all placed in the candelabras as if the mistress might return at any moment. When they pulled off the sheets covering the furniture, there were no puffs of dust. Every inch of the chamber was spotless and as silent as a tomb.

"There are dresses aplenty in here," Isla murmured, as excited as a child on May Morning. "Me mother told me stories of the velvet and silks, all trimmed with lace made by the mistress."

There came the jingle of keys as Asgree unlocked the wardrobes in the chamber. They were set around the circular room, one wardrobe between the windows so one might turn all the way around and always be staring at one of them. They were arranged by season, as well. The lighter colors were obviously the summer clothing, so Daphne turned to find the darker-toned fabrics. Asgree was there, gently searching through the hanging garments.

Isla withdrew a delicate chemise and carried it to Daphne. "There is lace all around the neckline. It must have taken a week to make it."

The two maids didn't hesitate to remove the robe, leaving Daphne blushing as she was stripped bare. Isla lifted the chemise, and Daphne hurried into it, desperate to have something to protect her modesty.

"That convent tried to teach ye to be ashamed of yer body," Asgree observed drily. "It is nae a natural thing to be so timid when there are only women here."

It was gentle scolding, but a reprimand nonetheless. Nothing bred gossip faster than the unknown. If it was said she let no one see her body, there would be those who whispered it was because she was marked by the devil.

"Modesty was indeed stressed," Daphne replied, forcing herself to uncross her arms and allow the darker hue of her nipples to show through the thin fabric. "I suppose I picked up a few habits I did nae have afore."

Asgree nodded, and there was a rustle as she withdrew an undergown of russet silk. "I believe this one will fit well enough. When the mistress arrived, she was very thin from serving the queen at Court. They have strange notions of what is attractive in Edinburgh. Highlanders like women the way the good Lord intended them to be. Curvy."

One of the maids giggled and took the undergown from Asgree. It crinkled as they lifted it up and helped her into it. Once on, the skirt fell in generous pleats all the way to the floor.

"Still, there are a few things I agreed with the mistress on." Asgree lifted something from inside the wardrobe, and it unfolded. "I hear the French are the creators of lace stockings. The Church preaches against them, while men pray to see them."

Daphne giggled this time, the other girls joining her. Asgree grinned mischievously as she brought the stockings forward. One of the maids brought a chair close, and she sat down. Asgree refused to let anyone else handle the delicate creations. She gathered them up gently and worked her thumbs down the inside of them. Daphne pointed her toes and pressed her foot into one. Asgree drew the stocking up her leg and secured it with a ribbon garter just behind her knee. The second one went on just as easily, and a maid brought a pair of heeled shoes for her. Daphne stepped into them, unable to stop herself from moving toward the full-length mirror to see her reflection. She lifted up the undergown to admire her legs. The candlelight cast a warm yellow glow over her, clearly illuminating the black lace against her skin.

Asgree admired Daphne. "I believe I understand why the priests preach against them… and I'd wager a month's pay that Norris would willingly fall onto his knees if he thought ye'd wear those."

Daphne laughed in a tone both husky and full of anticipation.

Ye enjoyed the last time the man was on his knees full well…

Indeed she had.

"She does nae need the long stays," Asgree told one of the maids. "And it is nae yet cold enough to wear them for the warmth."

The girls looked at Daphne's breasts, trying to learn the skill their mentor had. To be chosen to serve the mistress of the house was one of the best duties, for it came with the nicest surroundings. The girls lifted a dress and carried it like a babe, making sure not even the hem touched the floor. It was a rich shade of blue, and once it was close enough to touch, Daphne realized it was made of velvet.

"I can nae wear that. It is fit for a queen."

"Or the Countess of Sutherland," Asgree informed her in a tone full of authority.

"Which I am nae, either," Daphne whispered. For just a moment, doubt punctured her enjoyment. What if Norris would not welcome her at the high table? No invitation had been issued. She'd look the fool sitting at one of the common tables in his mother's finery.

"'Twas the laird who placed ye in the lady's solar when he might as easily have taken ye to the chamber I put ye in the night ye arrived. He gives ye personal attendants when he has never done so before." Asgree propped her hand onto her hip and aimed a hard look at Daphne. "Norris has ever been a bold one. Timid lasses never catch his eye."

So subtle, yet sharp as could be. Asgree knew her art well, for she spoke her mind without ever over-stepping her position. Daphne lifted her arms for the gown. It settled into place, and the maids began to lace up the back. The chamber was silent, allowing her to hear the laces pulling through the eyelets. Once again, the head of house proved her ability, for the dress fit her well. Norris's mother had been slightly shorter than she, but the dress still touched the floor.

The bells began to ring, announcing to all that the cook was ready to serve supper. The maids hurried to comb her hair and pin a caul over the back of it. Asgree brushed Daphne's cheeks with colored powder and used a tiny brush to paint her lips.

"Ye need naught else," she announced at last, "except the boldness to show the young master ye can stand steady no matter the situation."

"Thank ye," Daphne murmured.

Surprise flickered in the old woman's eyes, and her lips curved into a satisfied smile.

"Get on with ye now. Ye have no need of this old woman any longer tonight. The dark hours belong to lovers, be they wed or no'."

The maids gasped softly, but Daphne felt Asgree's words blow air across the embers that had been smoldering inside her all day. Passion burned again within her, and she turned to go find the man she dreamed of sharing it with.

Fire fairy… perhaps.

Well, the man had best be ready to deal with what he had insisted on bringing home.

❧

The hall was filling up. The sun had set, and everyone was ready to take some time to relax after the day's demands. Her undergown rustled, announcing her arrival. Heads turned in her direction before she had even made it to the doorway. The conversation died then rose again in hushed whispers. Daphne held her chin steady, ordering herself to not pluck at the skirt of the gown. She kept her toes on the floor when she moved, using slow, flowing steps as her mother had once taught her some ten years ago.

A lady did not hurry on her way down the aisle.

She made sure everyone had time to admire her and the costly garments her family had provided her with.

A lady was meant to be noticed.

A lady studied dance, music, literature, and language to ensure when she was noticed, it was for her poise and sharp wits.

Nonetheless, she wanted to hurry to Norris's side. At least she did until their eyes met. She felt the connection all the way to her toes. His green eyes were full of surprise, which burned away to reveal astonishment. His expression became a mask of enjoyment, stealing her breath. What really stunned her were his actions.

Norris Sutherland, heir to the Earldom of Sutherland, stood.

It was the height of compliments, the pinnacle of gestures that only his betters might have demanded of him, and that list was very short. It included the king and other earls, but even her father had been this man's vassal. The hall went silent, and then it was filled with the scraping of benches being pushed back as every Sutherland retainer followed their laird's son.

She walked past them all, catching the tugging on the edges of bonnets out of the corners of her eyes because she never looked away from Norris. She did stop at the base leading up to the high table. She lowered herself, waiting for the earl to raise her.

"Join us, since it seems me son can nae remain in his chair while ye are nae beside him."

The earl was frowning, but there was a hint of amusement in his voice. Daphne didn't have time to dwell on what that meant, because Norris descended two of the stairs and offered her his hand. She could feel everyone's attention on them, making the moment seem important somehow. Like the first time Broen MacNicols had welcomed her to his home as his intended bride. What had gone before didn't matter. When she placed her hand into Norris's, there was a soft sound of approval from behind her.

She didn't look over her shoulder. What drew her attention was the look in his green eyes. There was an intensity there that melted every doubt she had. There was no reason to ponder what tomorrow might bring, because she trusted in the man grasping her hand so securely.

❧

Supper began with the wailing of pipes. The great hall was ringed by a balcony where musicians might stand out of sight. The clàrsach players followed, filling the hall with sweet melodies while maids carried platters of food to the head table. Each serving plate was covered with a silver dome to keep the food hot. Once the dome was removed, steam rose from the dishes, proving the Earl of Sutherland lived as finely as a king. Personal attendants laid silver plates in front of those dining at the head table, the serviceware having been guarded to ensure the earl was not poisoned.

Isla stepped up and took the goblet brought for Daphne. Both the earl and Norris had men assigned to their goblets, and those men would not let the drinking vessels out of their sight. It was a necessary precaution in a world riddled with power-hungry rivals. Now that she had publicly stepped up to sit beside Norris, she too would have to behave cautiously or risk having someone poison her in order to empty Norris's bed.

There were meat pies and fresh, sweet bread. Cheese arrived with late harvest fruits. Norris delighted in filling her plate while his people watched.

"Enough," she whispered. "The hounds will end up believing they have transformed into knights when they see the scraps tonight."

He raised one eyebrow suggestively. "Are ye saying ye are finished, lass?"

"Aye," she answered before recognizing she had played right into his trap. A wolfish grin appeared on his lips, and he pushed his chair back so fast the man holding his cup had to jump aside or be hit.

"I bid ye good night, Father."

"Do ye now?" the earl drawled slowly. "Before we've sampled the marzipan tart yer companion assisted in making? Nae, ye must stay and enjoy the sweet."

Norris dropped back into his chair, looking pitiful. He cast a frustrated look toward her. "Ye had to help make that tart."

She grinned softly and fluttered her eyelashes. "How could I fail to tempt ye with me skills?"

He reached beneath the table and squeezed her

thigh. There was a promise of retribution flickering in his eyes as the tart was brought down the aisle. It seemed to take a small eternity for the cook to unveil it and slice it into servings.

"Well now, ye do know a thing or two about preparing one of me favorite dishes," Lytge muttered after licking his lips. "Perhaps ye might join me in me study to explain yer methods."

Norris growled at his sire. The earl pretended surprise, but there was a familiar flicker of wickedness in his eyes that she had often witnessed in Norris's.

"Off with the pair of ye, then."

This time, the man holding Norris's goblet moved out of the way fast enough. Norris was on his feet and dragged her chair back to the delight of the retainers at the lower tables. They raised their mugs, slapping the tabletops and making their wooden dishes bounce.

Norris offered them all a nod before clasping her wrist and nearly running down the aisle. Her silk skirts flew up, flashing her lace stockings as she lost the battle not to giggle.

"Ye marauder," she accused when at last she stumbled into his chamber.

"If that were the case, I would have tossed ye over me shoulder."

"As if yer people have nae seen that afore," she answered, walking in a small circle as she caught her breath. To be honest, the rapid rate of her heart wasn't due solely to the brisk pace Norris had set. Anticipation was flooding her with excitement now that the chamber door was closed and they were alone. She froze when she realized she and Norris had begun

to circle each other. Surprise appeared on his face, and
he offered her a bow.

"Ye bring out the savage in me. But I admit tonight
I wanted me people to see ye following me." It was
an admission and one a man like Norris didn't make
easily. He was on guard, waiting to see what she'd
make of his words.

"They saw me dressed for ye too."

He tossed his bonnet onto the table. "Aye, lass, and
it meant a great deal to me."

She could see that. It confused and astounded her
but, most of all, it drew her toward him. She reached
for the top button of his doublet, working it free. The
scent of his skin teased her. He shrugged out of the
garment when she finished and dropped it over a chair.
A soft rap came from the door, and it began to open.

"Be gone," he bellowed, drawing a giggle from her.

The door jerked shut as he raised an eyebrow, and
she opened the collar of his shirt.

"Amused by my being caught half-dressed, are ye?"
He cupped her cheek, rubbing the delicate surface for
a moment, and then he circled around her and tugged
on the ends of the laces that held her overgown closed.

"Let us see how ye like having the tables turned
on ye."

She was going to enjoy it full well...

The silk underslip crinkled as it was released and fell
toward the floor. Norris grasped her waist and lifted
her free of it.

"Sweet Mother of Christ. Where did ye get those?
And where are yer stays?"

She stretched out one leg to ensure he gained a

good view of the lace stocking. "Asgree suggested I wear them, and I do nae need stays."

He cupped her breasts through the thin fabric of her chemise, teasing her nipples with his thumbs. She worked the buttons of his cuffs loose, impatient to be pressed against him.

"I don't want to talk." The words simply escaped, her emotions unwilling to be controlled. Her yearnings wanted freedom, and she was in complete agreement.

"Neither do I."

He backed up and pulled the end of his belt loose. Another jerk, and he'd released the buckle that held the strap of leather tightly to his waist. His kilt fell, but he caught it before it hit the floor. He tossed it on the chair, then sat down and unlaced his boots. She leaned over and pulled one off.

"Now there is a service I can become accustomed to."

The front of her chemise was gaping open to afford him a clear look down her body. Beneath the tail of his shirt, his cock hardened and stood.

He grunted and pulled his other boot off himself then stood up. "I want ye in me bed tonight, lass."

He pinched out the candles, encasing them in darkness before he swept her off her feet. She didn't gasp but made a sound of pleasure instead. Cradled against his chest, she listened to the sound of his bare feet crossing the stone floor to the carpet by his bed.

As he sat her down and pulled her chemise loose, the ropes holding the mattress groaned softly. With no light, she never saw it flutter to the floor, but she felt her lover join her. His lips pressed against hers in a kiss she felt she'd been waiting months for. She reached for him, pulling him against her, and they twisted and stroked each other. Time ceased, and she was willingly trapped in the moment. Clinging to her companion, she held him with her thighs when he pressed himself inside her. They moved together in perfect harmony, straining toward each other as the need to be together consumed them. When release came, it was pure rapture, burning away everything and leaving them content in each other's embrace.

❧

Daphne awoke to a hand smoothing along her back. She rubbed her eyes and blinked when sunlight burned them.

Norris was staring at the bruises on her back. "How bad is the pain now?"

She rolled away from him and earned a frown.

"I hardly notice them." However, as she moved too quickly after waking, a small twinge of pain twisted through her. He didn't miss it.

"Really, it is fine, just a bit stiff in the morning." She looked at the window and realized the sun was up. "Why are ye still here?"

He chuckled, stood up, and walked across the chamber to a wardrobe. "Maybe I wanted to enjoy a few more moments of being with someone who enjoys me company simply for meself and nae the things to be gained from befriending me."

He shrugged into a shirt and sat down to put on his boots. "Or maybe I woke up early and resisted falling back asleep for fear ye'd slip out of me bed again."

"Ye do nae fear anything."

He stood up and leaned against the angled table that held his kilt. To have a piece of furniture devoted to only one item of clothing was a luxury indeed. The length of his plaid was already folded into even pleats with the belt held in a wide groove behind the fabric. He grasped the ends and buckled his kilt in place.

"At this moment, I am nae so sure, lass." He stared at her for a long moment before crossing the floor and cupping her chin. "I'm scared ye'll repent during Mass and feel the need to sleep somewhere else tonight, and I do nae think I even care who hears me say it."

He kissed her, smothering any reply she might have made, but honestly, she was stunned by his admission. Norris Sutherland was not afraid of anything. There was a flap and flutter, and Norris chuckled softly as Bacchus flew through the window. The peregrine perched on the curtain rail and screeched at Norris.

"I knew ye raised him," Daphne offered.

"From the moment he was fledged." Norris reached into a leather pouch that hung from a rack on the wall and pulled a strip of meat from it. The falcon watched him, lowering its head as it caught the scent of the meat. Norris tossed the scrap into the air, and with another cry, Bacchus caught it before it fell. The raptor returned to the curtain rod and began to feast.

"Are ye frightened of him?" Norris asked.

Daphne shook her head, fascinated with the bird and being able to watch him so closely. "Where is he trained to fly to?"

"Dunrobin," Norris answered. "We have others trained to fly to many of our vassal's lands. They have birds trained to fly here, but Bacchus is mine."

Of course he was. Now that she was looking closer, she could see marks on the rod from the falcon's talons.

"I hope ye'll be here tonight, lass, it would please me greatly."

She simpered like a child being given a piece of sugar candy. Her heart was suddenly full of happiness, and her logic was nowhere to be found. She nodded, not trusting her voice, and he grinned.

Someone rapped on the door, and his expression hardened. "Duty calls. No matter what ye decide, do nae be foolish. Stay with Cam and Isla. Me life is full of threats no matter how loyal I believe me staff to be."

"I shall," she promised, earning a pleased look from him. For a moment it looked like he might say something, but the door began to open.

He grunted and sent the bed curtain closed to hide her. His men muttered morning greetings before the door shut again behind them. Bacchus cried out. There was a flutter, and she knew the bird had left.

She'd worn the lace stockings to bed, but her chemise was hanging over the back of a chair, indicating someone had crept into the chamber after she and Norris had fallen asleep.

After they'd made love, that was... She bit her lip and shrugged into the garment, not in the mood to be caught bare skinned by Isla.

As if she does nae know what ye've been about...

Her inner voice was trying to needle her. Daphne struggled against it but couldn't completely dismiss the feeling of foreboding that crept past the happiness warming her. Perhaps it was the bright light of day, but she couldn't ignore the fact that each night with Norris might well be her last. Oh, she knew it was foolish to worry about such things, for every love affair ended.

She simply wondered if she'd survive having her heart broken.

❧

The bells rang out, loud and clear. But not too fast, so Daphne didn't worry that it might be an emergency.

"Looks like Laird Fraser's come to see the earl," Isla informed Daphne after leaning out of the open windows of the solar. She made a low sound and turned to look at Daphne, worrying her lower lip. "He's got his sister along. Sandra is ripe for marriage, and they've been dangling her in front of the master for the past year. She's quite fetching."

Daphne tried not to care. But failed. Today there were other women in the solar with them. Asgree had arrived with two new attendants for her and refused to take no for an answer. Daphne couldn't deny the spike of apprehension that pierced her heart. She had no right to be jealous, but it went surging through her as hot as a fire poker.

"Ye should go and meet her."

"Why?" Daphne asked Isla and bit back the rest of her comment when she realized the other women were nodding.

"Go and show her the laird is taken."

"Ye should nae say such things. He does nae belong to me," Daphne muttered.

Such... bold things. There was no understanding between them beyond tonight, and a man might change his mind as easily as he changed his shirt. Thinking such things might make her discontent with her lot. She'd be the only one to suffer if she began to long for more from Norris. It would be her heartache to bear. Isla lowered herself, but her expression was far from repentant. Exactly like her thoughts, Daphne grumbled to herself. But she was worrying her lip, and Isla stared at the telltale motion.

"Oh, fie. Ye are correct." Daphne gave in.

A timid lass has never caught his eye...

Asgree's words rose from her memory like a warning. There was something more, a need to protect the right to join Norris in his chamber. Sleeping alone seemed too much to tolerate. What sent her out of the solar and down the stairs was the fact that she knew Sandra Fraser was there to see Norris. It was more than Isla's words. It was something Daphne felt rising up from deep inside her. Some instinct was warning her to be on guard or risk losing what she treasured.

When she entered the hall and witnessed Bari Fraser presenting Sandra to the earl, her feelings proved correct. She gave Lytge only the briefest courtesy then turned her full attention to Norris. Sandra took her time as she lowered herself before him. She looked up into his face, ensuring he had an unobstructed view of her cleavage. Sandra held up her hand, and Daphne's vision turned red.

Norris had no choice but to lift it and kiss the back of it. Daphne still resented seeing his lips touch the other woman's skin. Norris must have felt her gaze on him, for he looked past Sandra, locking stares with Daphne.

"Allow me to introduce Daphne MacLeod." His voice was strong and edged with authority. Sandra wasn't pleased, but masked her irritation well.

"Good… good…" Lytge mumbled. "The lasses can share some spiced cider while we talk business at the high table."

Asgree had obviously anticipated such a request, and her staff was already setting out dishes on one of the tables. Daphne would rather have returned to the solar, but she sat down, mindful of her behavior. Sandra whipped her attention back to her brother, but the earl had already turned and was on his way to the high table. Norris followed his father, and Bari shrugged. Sandra propped her hand onto her hip for a brief moment. A sharp look from her brother saw her straightening her posture. Bari Fraser went after his hosts, and Sandra turned to look at Daphne.

It seemed neither of them was pleased with the company they'd be keeping.

Daphne would have to thank Isla later, for the girl knew what she had been talking about. Sandra Fraser had her eye on Norris. No doubt about it.

❧

Sandra Fraser was prettier up close.

She had red hair, the darker shade of it. Her eyes were blue and her complexion blissfully free of freckles so often found on redheads. She glided on graceful steps, her dress perfectly fitted to her. The stiffened corset beneath the bodice pushed her young breasts up into a tempting display. When she sat down next to Daphne, she did it with a smile on her rosy lips, but it was directed at the retainers at the next table. When they turned back to their game of dice, she sighed and looked at Daphne.

"Ye are as comely as the rumors claim." Sandra spoke softly.

"Some believe so," Daphne replied. She was on guard. Tension squeezed her as she watched the other girl contemplate her.

Sandra lowered her chin and raised a mocking eyebrow. "Let's not be coy when there are no men about to impress. Ye're a beauty, and ye've used it to snare yerself Norris Sutherland. At least for a lover. For that much, I congratulate ye. He's never taken a woman to his personal bedchamber. The star chamber is where he prefers to tryst."

"How do you know all of this?" Daphne asked incredulously.

Norris's warning rose from her memory.

Me life is full of threats no matter how loyal I believe me staff to be.

Sandra laughed softly, mockingly, before offering a bright smile. "He is a very important man, so what he does and with whom he does it interests me. We can still be friends, ye know."

"Is that so?" Daphne couldn't help but ask. There was an arrogance in the woman she was in awe of, simply because it was so ridiculous. Sandra was full of pride and seemed to have supreme confidence in her ability to do whatever she pleased.

Sandra leaned closer. "Tell me what makes Norris

hard, and I'll make sure ye have someplace to go once he turns ye out in order to wed me."

A hot flash of denial went through her. It was stunning, and like everything else she felt in relation to Norris, it threatened to overwhelm her better judgment. She wanted to lunge at Sandra and smack her mocking face.

Sandra snickered. "Now do nae be too hasty," she cooed. "Nae many women would offer ye anything."

"Ye assume I want something from ye," Daphne snapped.

Sandra's expression turned harsh. "Every woman seeks something. Life is nae kind. I'm here to snare Norris for me husband. With or without yer help." She shrugged. "If ye decide to play nicely and tell me what the man likes in his bed, I will make sure ye do nae end up dumped in the road like the strumpet ye are."

"How generous of ye," Daphne snipped.

Sandra fluttered her eyelashes. "Oh, it is. Do nae be a fool. I know the truth of ye, and soon, me brother is going to make sure Norris knows it also."

"And what truth is that?" Daphne demanded.

Sandra slowly smiled, seeming to enjoy making Daphne wait for her reply.

"Ye have no dowry," she delivered in a mocking tone. "None. Naught to yer name at all."

"Norris knows that well enough." However, she couldn't dismiss the fact that he might not believe it. A horrible sense of foreboding hit her, threatening to strangle her confidence and the happiness she'd enjoyed for the last few days.

"Ye really are nae very intelligent," Sandra decided. "I may be pretty like ye, but I am also very clever. No wonder ye are naught but the man's conquest. Or, should I say current conquest, because a man such as Norris will never be satisfied with one woman. Ye're such a little fool to believe he'll care one bit about ye once he's spied another woman he fancies."

"I believe I've heard enough of this." Daphne made to stand, but Sandra surprised her by clamping her hand on Daphne's wrist to keep her at the table.

"I will be the next woman. Better ye accept that fact now. More than his woman, I shall be his wife and mistress of Dunrobin once that old man does us the favor of dying," Sandra hissed low and with a tone full of venom. "I always pay me debts, but I also never fail to collect me vengeance. Tell me what he likes, or ye'll regret it."

Isla suddenly stepped forward, her eyes narrowed as she looked at the way Sandra was digging her fingers into Daphne's arm. Sandra shot the girl a hard look.

"Yer mistress does nae need ye. Be gone."

Isla lowered herself, but it was clear from the stiffness of her motion she lacked any sincerity. Cam stepped up behind his sister, tugging on the corner of his bonnet while his eyes remained narrowed.

"Tell them to be gone," Sandra demanded.

Daphne shook her head. "They are nae fools. If ye are as clever as ye claim, better learn to respect the fact that just because someone serves ye, it does nae ensure they will like ye."

Sandra rolled her eyes. "Why should I care? As mistress of Dunrobin, I'll be the one deciding who serves here"—she turned her head and sent a hard look at Isla—"and who does not."

Daphne stood up. Sandra didn't want to let her go and ended up hanging onto her arm. Her eyes were rounded in shock, proving that her brother allowed her free rein.

"Good day to ye, Mistress Fraser."

Sandra released Daphne and gave her skirts a vicious shake before lifting her chin arrogantly.

"Best ye consider me offer. Every hour ye make me wait for what I desire, ye shall have less from me when ye need it."

She brushed by Daphne, her carriage as regal as a queen's. Norris looked up, and Sandra instantly changed. Her body lost its haughty stance, becoming sultry as she lowered herself. Norris's lips lifted into a grin that was far too appreciative. A chill twisted through Daphne, and she turned to hide it from him. As if he'd notice while looking at Sandra.

Ye're jealous…

She was. There was no denying it or the fact that there was nothing she might do about it. Norris was the earl's heir. He'd do what he wanted. What frightened her the most was the certain knowledge he'd do what he considered his duty. Sandra was the daughter of a laird and had a dowry. When it came to marriage, the Earl of Sutherland would look at the bride who came with the most for his eldest son.

Sandra might just gain her wish and became mistress of Dunrobin.

❧

"There will be no supper at the high table tonight. The earl has retired." It was Asgree who appeared just before sunset to inform Daphne of the news. Two maids followed her, freshly pressed linens stacked in their arms.

"I hope the earl is well."

The head of house scoffed softly. "I believe his stomach is soured by the endless prattle of his guests. I confess I've used the task of informing ye of supper's change in order to escape the demands of young Mistress Fraser. Half the maids in the bathhouse have suddenly gone ill. When she set herself to inspecting the kitchens, the cook took to sharpening his knives."

Daphne felt her eyes widen, and she raised a hand to stifle a small sound of amusement that tried to escape her lips. Asgree didn't miss her lapse in discipline.

"Go on, laugh. Lord knows I want to. That lass is presumption wrapped in a siren's form."

"Still. I shouldn't be judgmental. I am hardly without me own sins," Daphne offered.

Asgree moved forward to inspect the lace Daphne and Isla had been making. "Ye have polished skills, something some lasses like to talk about more than prove."

The compliment warmed her. The older woman shifted her attention to Daphne's face, studying her for a long moment. "His lairdship asked me where ye would like to take yer supper. Which chamber?"

And it seemed Norris would not be the only one at Dunrobin wondering what her choice would be. It really wasn't a decision. She'd stepped onto the path she was set on the night before.

"I would return to the laird's chamber."

Asgree's eyes brightened, and she nodded. She turned and pointed the maids toward the doorway. Then she paused, waiting until they left.

"A fine choice," she offered and left the solar on silent feet. It had been a long time since anyone with any authority had approved of her, and Daphne discovered herself stunned. She stood still, allowing herself to savor the moment, for she admired the head of house. Asgree was no fool and knew one when she saw one.

Isla was brimming with excitement too, worrying her lower lip once again as she waited for Daphne to decide it was time to leave the solar.

"Well then, I suppose I shall bathe and make sure those working in the bathhouse are properly thanked for their service."

It was a small thing, one that fate might decide to take away from her at any moment, but for today, Norris had set her above the other women in the house. Daphne planned to make sure she did not abuse the position.

Sandra would not be so kind.

Daphne shook her head, pushing her thoughts aside. The sun was setting, and she would not waste the night, for it was hers to share with Norris. With her lover.

❦

Sandra Fraser was waiting on him.

Norris didn't know which was worse, sitting at the high table while her brother droned on endlessly about the merits of the Frasers or the certain knowledge that the moment he followed his father's example and left the high table Sandra would waylay him.

The woman held no appeal. She might be a beauty, blessed with a body most men would have no trouble desiring, but all he could see was the calculating look in her eyes.

Sandra Fraser was a cunning bitch, and she'd set her sights on him. It wasn't the first time he'd been the target of such. Maybe sometime, many years ago, when he'd been young enough to be impressed with his own power, he'd have enjoyed it. Becoming a man had tempered his ego, and it was a fact he was very pleased with. Too many viewed him as a man who had everything, when the truth was, no one had it all. He had privilege and position but no freedom to wed the woman he wanted. A common man had no land of his own but could follow his heart.

At the moment, Norris envied every retainer wearing his father's colors. Sandra Fraser wouldn't be waiting on them. No, she was a coldhearted jade. She was waiting on him but casting sly looks at some of his men. Not only would she rule his house like a shrew, he'd have to put a watch on her else wonder if her children were his.

Asgree appeared at the kitchen door and made her way toward the high table. Norris discovered himself watching her, his anticipation rising as she made a steady progress toward him. She stopped and lowered herself before climbing up the side steps to come behind him and Laird Fraser. He lifted his hand, and Bari made a low sound of frustration but closed his mouth anyway.

"Mistress MacLeod has decided to accept yer invitation. She awaits ye."

He didn't think three words had ever filled him with such joy. Daphne was waiting for him. He stood up, gaining a grunt from Bari.

"Can nae yer mistress wait until we've finished?" he whined. "I hear she's new. Is she that talented on her back?"

Norris cast a hard look at his guest. For once, he abandoned diplomacy completely, allowing the other man to see his true emotions. Bari Fraser swallowed roughly. "Mistress MacLeod is a woman I respect," Norris informed him quietly. "While ye are near me, ye'll do the same or keep yer opinion to yerself."

Bari wasn't accustomed to being told to mind his words. It was clear that the man ruled with absolute power on Fraser land. It was also clear Bari put his own desires above the other members of his household. He'd never suggested inviting Sandra to the head table to see if she and Norris found each other pleasing. No, Bari Fraser was more concerned in finding out what sort of alliance he'd gain when Sandra was handed over to Norris to occupy his bed.

Aye, he knew well that was the way of most noble marriages, but he wanted something else, and it was waiting for him but a few stories above his head. Norris headed out of the great hall through the side entrance. He had no desire to listen to Sandra do her best to impress him or to hurt the girl's feelings on the off chance she wasn't as cold as he'd judged her to be.

Asgree was there, beyond the doorway.

"Shall I send supper up?"

"Aye, and then give yer staff their leave."

Asgree lowered herself and left. Norris looked up and muffled a curse. Sandra had taken the opportunity to close in on him. She sank down into a graceful courtesy, her velvet dress pooling like water. The color suited her perfectly, and every hair on her head was artfully arranged. Nevertheless, he felt not even a twinge of attraction.

"Forgive me, mistress, but I'm set to retire for the night."

Her eyes narrowed for a moment, and her gaze slipped down his length. "It is nae very fair of ye to tease me so, Norris."

He had to reach out and stop her before she pressed herself against him. "I've teased ye not at all."

She pouted and shrugged in the face of his harsh tone. "For certain ye are accustomed to being so harsh with the women who fall under yer spell, but I was hoping ye might consider being just a wee bit tender with me."

She fluttered her eyelashes and aimed a pleading look at him. She reached right out and stroked his neck. The touch disgusted him because of just how practiced it was. He could see her judging his response, no hint of reaction in her own eyes. He might have been a stallion for all she cared. Her mind was on the matter of making him her conquest. So very different from the way Daphne's eyes filled with hunger when she touched him.

"Good night, Mistress Fraser. I suggest ye find someone else to offer ye tenderness."

Her eyes widened, and her expression became hard.

"I do nae care if ye keep yer mistress. Me brother has made it clear he would like a match between us. I hear the MacLeod girl is barren, that she has nae bled in a very long time. Ye need heirs. Besides, she has not even a silver penny to her name. Let us come to an agreement. I'll give ye yer heirs, and neither of us shall be jealous of where we find our pleasures. I can be discreet, I assure ye, Norris."

"Of that, I have no doubt."

Sandra lifted her chin stubbornly. "As if ye are as pure as Saint Peter. Daphne MacLeod is a sack of bones." She boldly stroked the swells of her breast above the edge of her bodice. "Do ye nae long to have a pair of tits ye can rest yer head on when yer cock is spent?"

"Enough!" he barked at her. "I suppose there are men aplenty in this world who will take a liking to yer bold tongue, but I am nae one of them."

He left her behind, glad to be finished with her. What chilled his blood as he climbed the stairs was the fact that he might well find himself battling his father when it came to contracting a bride. What twisted his gut was the worry that Daphne wouldn't be content as his mistress.

For the first time in his life he was tempted to use his position for his own purposes. The temptation was intoxicating with the relief it offered. Relief from worrying when Daphne would leave Dunrobin. There were plenty of men who wouldn't have bothered battling the urge. But his father had raised him to consider his position a duty, not a privilege. He'd shouldered that duty more than once, performing as expected rather than as he wished. However, tonight he wondered if he'd ever be able to let Daphne go.

⤌⤍

"What did Sandra say to ye?" Norris appeared only a few moments after Isla had taken her leave. Daphne had just pinched out several of the candles, leaving the chamber in semidarkness. It suited Norris, though. Or perhaps it suited her mood, for it made the moment seem intimate and hidden away from the sharper edges of reality.

So much easier for her to slip into her fantasy world where she need only please herself…

"It doesn't matter." She reached for the pitcher of wine Isla had left and poured some of it into a goblet. She held it out for Norris. He took it but didn't lift it to his lips. Instead he set it back on the table.

"It matters if ye are intent on distracting me from learning the answer to me question. Isla says Sandra refused to let ye leave. Why?"

"It was a matter of little importance. Be careful ye do nae encourage me to make demands of ye whenever something displeases me. Better that I retain enough of me wits to know the difference between sense and foolishness."

Daphne moved closer to the fire, letting the heat fill the long dressing robe Isla had produced for her to wear once her dress was unlaced and hung in the wardrobe. She laughed softly, gaining a raised eyebrow from Norris.

"I was noticing how easily I have become accustomed to being undressed in yer presence." The words felt wicked on her tongue, but she laughed again. "Father Peter is sure to have something horrible to say about it."

"A situation easily remedied by yer remaining here, where Father Peter can nae demand yer attention."

It was mad the way his words made hope flare up inside her. She hadn't realized just how frightened she was until he put her mind at ease.

Norris cursed softly behind her. "So that's what the bitch said to ye."

Daphne jerked her attention around toward him. "I said naught."

He'd unbuttoned his doublet and tossed it over the back of a chair. His collar was open, making him look rakish, but he shook his head. "What I saw in yer eyes, 'tis the truth that I did nae recognize it."

Confusion held her in its grip as he closed the distance between them. He cupped her chin and stared into her eyes.

"Never once, even when I pulled ye out of Morrell Comyn's clutches, have I seen fear in yer eyes. Until tonight." He held her chin when she would have turned away. "That bitch threatened ye."

It wasn't a question, and she couldn't hide her emotions. She never had been able to mask her true feelings with him. "It does nae matter. I've made me choices and understand ye are nae bound to me."

He slid his hand up her face, and tenderness filled his green eyes. "I am surely bound to ye, Daphne, and God forgive me, but I am happy to see ye fear to be parted from me, for I do nae think I can bear having ye leave me. I swear I will never wed Sandra Fraser."

He sealed her mouth with his, the kiss slow and deep. She reached for him, desperate to feel him pressed against her. Nothing else mattered. Nothing at all.

∽

Something woke Daphne. She opened her eyes and stared at the canopy stretched out above Norris's bed. His arm was draped over her chest, one large hand cupping her breast. The air was still cold, the fire reduced to ashes long ago. Only the barest amount of light teased the horizon. She should go back to sleep, but her belly ached. It was dull but persistent, and when she shifted her legs, she realized her thighs were wet.

She sat up, staring in horror at the soiled sheet. It was a terrible waste of such fine cloth. Even in the dark, she could see the stain. Norris jerked, jumping to his feet in a motion that betrayed just how powerful his body was.

"What is it?" He turned his head, clearly listening for the bells, but only the morning birds could be heard.

"I'm sorry... I didn't mean to wake ye."

He sat down and rolled his shoulders. "Ye may wake me early anytime, lass. I am sure we shall find something to do with the time."

"Nae." She pushed against him when he tried to pull her close. He settled for pressing a kiss against her neck and growling softly against her hair.

"We can nae, Norris."

He caught her hand and carried it to his member. The flesh was hard and hot in spite of the coolness of the morning air.

"We surely can…"

"I'm bleeding, and I've ruined yer fine sheets." She stood up, going to the garderobe to fetch a linen. Tears pricked her eyes, but she forbade herself to cry. It was a prayer answered. The very thing she had desired. She should be happy. Yet she sniffled.

"Here now, Daphne… do nae be so distraught."

Norris scooped her up and carried her back to bed. He tossed the soiled sheet aside, spreading the top one over the mattress.

"I'll ruin that one too," she warned.

"I do nae care."

He pulled the bedding back over them and wrapped his body around hers. "I am nae giving up even a moment of me time with ye. Me duties may own me during the daylight hours, but the sun has nae risen, so I am free to be yer disciple."

He was warm and welcoming, folding her against him. With the dawn yet to break, it was simple to be tempted back into slumber where she didn't have to worry. For the moment, Norris was hers. Perhaps the last moment. But hers nonetheless.

❧

Sandra Fraser was furious.

And she always extracted vengeance on those who crossed her. Oh, it would be a bit harder this time, because Norris was the heir to an earldom, but she enjoyed a good challenge. He would pay for the way he'd brushed her aside. She tapped her lower lip with one slim finger and grinned. It really wasn't much of a challenge after all. His bitch whore was the way to get to him. After she dealt a blow to Daphne MacLeod, the man would learn to fear her wrath for sure.

Casting a look about, she made sure no one was following her. She made her way toward the chamber her brother had been given for the night. His men allowed her through the door once they recognized her, but her brother frowned over the shoulder of the maid he had in bed with him. He sent the girl toward the door with a flick of his fingers. Her eyes turned red and she sniffled, but neither Sandra nor her brother spared her even a morsel of pity. She gathered up her clothing and fled.

"Dearest sister…" Bari Fraser muttered. "Why aren't ye in Norris Sutherland's bed?"

"Because he's smitten by Daphne MacLeod," she snapped. "Which is why ye must ride out at first light."

Bari contemplated her for a moment. "Ye have a plan?"

Sandra smiled. "I do indeed, but ye need to be gone for it to be effective."

Sandra moved to the table where Bari's men had left his things. What she sought was the secretary's box that was guarded every moment it wasn't in her brother's keeping. She flipped it open without asking for permission. She shifted the paper aside and pressed on a section of the box most didn't know was there. It released what looked like the bottom of the box to reveal a secret compartment.

"We'll be hung if that counterfeit seal is ever discovered," her brother remarked from behind her. "Lord Home does nae suffer those who impersonate the king or his royal seal." He planted his hand down

in the middle of the parchment she was making ready
to write on. "I'll nae have ye risking me neck without
good reason."

Sandra offered him a smug smile. "Just a simple
letter summoning Norris to Edinburgh. We'll pay
some peasant to deliver it once we're away."

Bari pressed her. "What will that gain us?"

Sandra tried to brush his hand aside, but her brother
refused to move.

"Ye will receive a similar letter. Norris is good
friends with Broen MacNicols and will likely seek out
Deigh Tower tomorrow night. I need him away from
his slut so I can slip into his bed and bloody the sheets.
I expect ye to be properly outraged when I am discovered with me lover." She looked up and fluttered her
eyelashes. "Won't it be quite the coincidence that we
shall also be there? The MacNicols have no reason to
deny us shelter tonight."

"The man is pure Highlander. Slipping into his bed
will nae be simple," Bari cautioned.

"Leave the task of slipping a potion into his drink up
to me." She pulled the stopper out of the ink well and
dipped the quill into it. "I am much better at it than ye."

Bari lifted his hand and walked across the chamber.
"Ye are at that. Mother taught ye her craft very well.
Along with how to forge another's hand script. I will
miss ye when ye are wed."

"Me clan will always come first, and once I have
two sons to secure me place, Norris Sutherland will be
of no further use to us. I'll bury him and be a merry
widow, me sons securing me place." Sandra began to
pen the letter.

Bari poured himself a goblet full of expensive French wine. He admired it before draining it. His sister concentrated on her work, looking from time to time at the letter from Lord Home he kept in his secretary's box. When she finished, she pulled a signet seal from the secret compartment. It was the mirror image of Lord Home's. The man who had made it was such an artist, it had been a shame to have to slit his throat, but it was the only way to ensure he never spoke of the matter.

Sandra heated some wax and let it pool on the folded letter. When it was ready, she pressed the seal into it.

"Perfect," she announced. "Or at least it will be once I have Norris Sutherland for me husband."

"He'll likely refuse to wed ye, even if ye mange to soil his sheets and cry debauchery. Ye would nae be the first virgin he's disgraced."

Sandra replaced the seal in the box and closed the secret compartment. "I have considered that." She stood up and offered her brother a sweet smile. "It is the only reason I didn't poison his father's cup last night. That old man might be useful in forcing his son to honor me."

She reached up and pulled one of her hair ornaments free. With a delicate motion of her fingers, she opened one of the flowers to revel a compartment full of powder.

"Grandfather didn't much approve of our father bringing home an Italian wife from his campaigns, but I truly enjoy the gifts she passed on to me." Sandra shared a smile with her brother. "Now, enough wine, Brother. I have an earl to catch before ye shall have all the Sutherland retainers at yer command."

"Are ye happy to see them gone?" Norris asked.

Daphne jumped, earning a chuckle from Norris. He turned her back around and looked over her shoulder at the sight of Bari Fraser and his sister riding away from Dunrobin.

"I am," he confessed softly against her ear. "It will give me much more time to spend with ye."

He'd wrapped his arms around her, and she took a moment to stroke his hand, savoring the feeling of being able to touch him. But she couldn't pretend any longer that their time wasn't limited.

"Until yer father finds ye another bride." She sighed. "But that is as it should be. Ye should send me home now."

Her voice cracked, and tears threatened to slide down her cheeks. She tried to disengage herself from his embrace, but he held her close, his face buried in her hair.

"Is that what ye wish, Daphne? To leave me?"

"Nae." The denial simply slipped out before any rational thought might intercede. "But it is the right thing to do. I believe Asgree is correct about my being too thin. But I am gaining weight now, and I can nae take me own happiness at the expense of branding a child illegitimate. If it were only meself, I would stay as long as ye would have me near ye."

His arms tightened, and she heard him pull in a deep breath. His body shook. It was a tiny tremor but one that was unmistakable.

"I would have ye near me and more, lass, for I believe I love ye." He squeezed her once more before releasing her. She turned, shocked by his words but delighted beyond any feeling she'd ever known. He cupped her face, and his green eyes were full of affection.

"Forgive me for all but kidnapping ye, Daphne. I could nae make meself leave ye behind. Ye are a part of me."

"I told ye nae... only because I can nae take me happiness at the expense of the children I might bear ye."

Norris kissed her and then released her. "Another reason I adore ye, Daphne. I did nae think I could find meself thankful for Sandra Fraser's visit, and yet, I am, for it has shown me just what a gem ye are." His expression tightened. "And it has proven I have failed to take action, as well." He reached up and tugged on the corner of his bonnet. Her eyes widened at the respectful gesture.

Norris winked at her. "I have a matter to attend to, lass. Excuse me."

The moment he was gone, Isla squealed with delight. She danced across the solar, her skirts kicking up with her excitement.

"He's gone to tell his father he plans to wed ye!" Isla announced unceremoniously.

"Ye should nae say a thing like that, when he did not say such was his intention," Daphne admonished, but her tone lacked any true reprimand.

Because she was too full of joy. He loved her. If she heard nothing else her entire life, those three words were enough.

 ❧

"She is nae with child," Lytge Sutherland stated firmly from behind his desk. "Why are ye so set to wed her now that it's proven she's nae breeding?" The earl pointed a thick finger toward Gahan. "Ye should leave before ye get the notion to wed some penniless female because yer heart goes soft for her."

Norris leaned on the front of table, fighting to maintain his control. "Ye mean like the affection ye felt for his mother?"

"I still wed the bride me father contracted me to," Lytge insisted.

"And ye were so fond of each other, I was the only child from yer union," Norris remarked. "Do ye truly wish such a fate upon me, Father? I mean ye no disrespect, for I love ye, but Daphne MacLeod holds me heart, and I would see our children born legitimate."

Something flickered in Lytge's eyes for a moment, but it vanished before Norris identified it. For just a moment, he felt a tingle of suspicion chilling his neck. His father lifted his hand and waved it.

"Ye speak the truth, sure enough. Yer mother and I never agreed upon much, but I had hoped for more warmth in our marriage. It is possible, but fate was nae so kind to me."

"Love is different from affection, Father, and ye understand what I am talking about."

The earl glanced toward Gahan. His eyes grew misty. "I loved yer mother, it is true, but I never asked to wed her."

"Only because ye already had a wife," Norris argued.

"One who came with an impressive dowry," Lytge insisted.

"I earn ye plenty with me managing skills. Sutherland is not poor."

Someone knocked on the door, earning a growl from Norris.

"Enter!" Lytge bellowed.

The man who entered was thin. He pulled his bonnet off his head and bowed while holding up a letter. Gahan took it and scanned the seal.

"Lord Home," he announced gravely.

"Fine. Fine. Give the messenger something for his trouble," Lytge said.

Norris reached into the open box in front of his father and pulled out a few pieces of silver. The messenger's eyes lit up when Norris dropped the coins into his waiting palm. The man bobbed his head several times and backed out the door. From the table, Norris heard the parchment crinkling when his father unrolled it. His temper strained, but his personal matter would have to wait while his father read the message from Lord Home. The man was more of a king than the boy wearing Scotland's crown.

"Ye've been summoned to Court, to swear yer allegiance, Norris."

"Getting a sword put through me side at Sauchieburn was nae proof enough of me support?" Norris snapped while Gahan growled. They'd both nearly lost their lives five times over when the young king's supporters clashed with his royal father's forces.

"Apparently nae," Lytge groused. "And I am nae too pleased to have him summoning ye with winter creeping down from the north. But ye must go. He is the king, and without a king, we'd spend all our time fighting off the nearby clans."

Norris suddenly straightened and offered his father

a bow. "Then I'll make sure I'm gone within the hour." His father frowned, but Norris didn't give him a chance to voice his suspicions.

Gahan caught up to Norris in the hallway. "In a bit of a hurry, are nae ye?"

Norris offered his half brother a smug grin. "Of course. Fate has handed me the solution to me dilemma."

Gahan frowned. "Ye plan to seek permission from the king to wed fair Daphne?"

"Aye." Norris felt more relieved than he'd thought he might ever be. "The young king is pious and full of regret for the part he played in his father's death, for in spite of the fact that his father was a blackguard of the worst sort, the young king takes the commandments to heart."

"I hear the king is set to wear a chain against his skin during lent as penitence," Gahan remarked.

"Aye." Norris stopped before they crossed the doorway into the yard and leaned closer to his sibling. "The king will agree it is me duty to wed Daphne, for it was I who seduced her away from Broen and the match her father had made."

"I seem to recall her being a willing partner in that."

Norris inclined his head. "A fact she has never disputed, but I trust the king will be happy to give me his blessing when I tell him how it has troubled me. So much so that I went to fetch her."

"Ye did that sure enough," Gahan agreed.

"So now, I'm off to ask a king to bless me marriage and tell me father it would please him to see the deed done," Norris said, "all in the interest of following the Holy Book."

"Ye mean all in the interest of making sure ye do nae need to worry about having a shrew such as Sandra Fraser for a wife."

"That is simply a coincidence," Norris said softly.

"A bloody nice one."

Norris smirked and slapped his brother on the shoulder. "Is nae it? And here I've always been lectured on the wrath of heaven being unleashed upon me for me sinful ways."

Aye, he was arrogant, but he was also the happiest man on earth. And that was a fact.

❧

"Enough, Norris."

He growled playfully at her, refusing to release her until he'd kissed her once more. It was a slow parting, one that made her long for just another moment in his embrace.

"Ye are correct," he muttered, his breath still teasing her lips. "The sooner I leave, the sooner I shall return and wed ye."

"Ye really should nae—"

He pressed a kiss on top of her protest—it was a soft kiss, because her argument was weak.

"Ye really should nae sour me luck by forecasting failure, me fire fairy."

"I am no' an enchantress."

Norris spread his arms wide and bowed low as he backed toward the door of the solar. "Yes, ye are, and I plan to keep ye."

"Marauder."

She gained only a glimpse of his smug expression

before he was gone in a swish of Sutherland plaid. Aye, marauder was the correct word. Or perhaps Highlander. But she really couldn't say she objected to his ways. No, she enjoyed them full well.

&

Clarrisa MacNicols was no stranger to forcing a smile onto her lips when she was actually irritated with the person in front of her. No, she'd grown up a bastard child of the King of England and suffered plenty of relatives who planned to use her blood to further their causes. The War of the Roses had seen her torn between families willing to do anything to gain the throne of England. But Sandra Fraser was trying her patience.

"Ye are gracious beyond measure," Broen MacNicols murmured. He lifted her hand and pressed a kiss against the inside of her wrist. He pulled her close while their guests enjoyed the supper placed before them. "At least they will seek their beds soon enough, and we might do the same."

Her new husband's voice dipped with the last few words, sending heat into her cheeks. His keen gaze touched on the spots of color as he offered her a satisfied grin.

"You are incorrigible," she admonished him softly.

"I am exactly as ye like me, lass, untamed and yers to command."

Clarrisa laughed softly as the bells on the outer wall of Deigh Tower began to toll, announcing riders. They didn't ring fast enough to frighten her, but her husband stiffened, all traces of teasing vanishing. He was laird of the MacNicols and took the duty to heart. Broen was already halfway down the main aisle of the great hall before she finished muttering a quick prayer. His retainers dropped quick kisses on their sweethearts or wives and followed their laird. A castle was only as strong as the dedication of the men who manned her walls. The MacNicols retainers were as solid as steel.

Clarrisa turned back to the high table and her guests. Sandra and her brother had their heads close while they whispered. There was a light of victory shining in Sandra's eyes, which puzzled Clarrisa. As soon as Sandra noticed Clarrisa watching her, she straightened up and concealed her emotions behind a very polished expression. It was perfect and everything a noblewoman should appear to be, but Clarrisa recognized it for what it was. Deception.

Edme made her way down from where she'd been serving the high table, a pitcher held securely in her grasp. Sandra and her brother had dismissed the older woman as nothing but a servant, but Edme was also Broen's mother. She was the head of house at Deigh even if the fact that she had been Broen's father's mistress made it so she was not the mistress of the castle. Clarrisa gave her that respect, because she was no fool. Edme knew how to run the keep well, and her experience was beyond value.

"It seems our guests believe we are about to receive Norris Sutherland. Nae that they told me so, mind ye."

"Why would they know?" Clarrisa wondered.

Edme aimed a suspicious look at her, a feeling Clarrisa discovered she shared. That look of victory in Sandra's eyes did not herald good things if, in fact,

Six

Damn Norris's bastard half brother… Sandra Fraser struggled to mask her annoyance as Gahan continued to make it impossible for her to get anywhere near Norris's plate or goblet. The dark-haired hulk was infuriating in his diligence.

When she was mistress of Dunrobin, she would make sure he ended up wed to a shrew. That idea helped her cut through her frustration. What was important was her goal, and she had learned young to keep her mind on her prize. She mustn't allow anything to distract her from her purpose.

The MacNicols's staff was doing a fine job of serving the high table. The old woman who served as head of house directed her staff with a confident hand. Liveried maids carried plates of autumn harvest fruits. The head of house was overseeing the preparation of more food as Broen MacNicols stood up and called for cider.

Perfect. Sandra lifted her hand and laid the back of it against her forehead. She stood up and left the high table. No one really paid any attention. Except for her brother. Having noticed her hand signal—such a simple thing, but it had come in handy before, a prearranged motion to let him know when she needed him to slip away and have a private word with her—Bari loudly declared his need to make room for the coming cider. He exited the raised platform the high table was on by the stairs and walked down the main aisle.

Sandra slipped out the side door and looked behind her to make sure Gahan was still focused on Norris. He was.

She made her way softly down the corridors while making a mental note to make sure she got rid of Norris's bastard brother before she made herself a widow. She passed a storeroom, and her brother's face appeared in the doorway—only for a moment—before he stepped back to mask himself in the shadows. A quick look over her shoulder, and Sandra joined him.

"What do ye need of me?" he asked.

"That bastard guards Norris's back too well. The keg of cider Laird MacNicols just ordered is me only hope of slipping a sleeping draught into Norris's cup."

"We'll all end up consuming it."

Sandra shrugged. "It will nae kill—nae this concoction. The lot of ye will sleep soundly and wake up wondering how ye got to yer beds."

Her brother drew in a stiff breath. "I suppose I can play yer game. Ye are correct about that bastard Gahan. Ye'd think the man would realize how much he has to gain by his brother's death."

"He's a noble fool, just like Norris. Their chivalrous nature is their Achilles' heel. But it does make the Sutherlands the perfect choice for us. All we needs do is convince Norris our cause is just, and he will do our bidding easily."

"That's a character trait I plan to exploit at sunrise." Bari snickered softly. "How do ye plan to get at the cider?"

Sandra reached into her bodice and withdrew a small pillow. It could easily be mistaken for a scent sachet. She held it up with a smile that betrayed its true use.

"Put it into the barrel when I have the brewmaster's attention. When he carries it up to the hall, the motion will steep it well enough for our purpose."

"What of Norris's men?"

Sandra shook her head. "I've studied his habits. Such knowledge has nae been without its cost. There are a few maids at Dunrobin who enjoy more silver than their positions afford them. They assure me Norris likes to include his men in all his celebrations. Broen MacNicols is much the same with his generous nature. The men will have the cider as well, and fall asleep at their posts."

Bari clasped the bundle in his hand. "Then I suppose it is time for ye to distract the brewmaster, sweet little Sister."

❧

The brewmaster enjoyed his duties. He had only a few keys on his belt, but they unlocked the cellar doors. Once inside, he inhaled the scent of ripening spirits—something sure to place a smile on the face of even the sourest man. He placed a candle lantern near the shelf where the cider barrels were stored and contemplated the dates marked on their sides.

He pushed one hogshead barrel onto his two-wheeled cart and tipped it up. The cart made it simple enough to wheel through the doorway and out into the hallway. He took a moment to secure the door, for the contents were expensive, and he was charged with accounting for every last drop. His father had been brewmaster before him, and he'd been taught to always do his duty well. He pulled on the lock once he'd turned the key, making sure it was secure.

The hallway was lit with torches made from the dried stalks of barely. Lashed together and dipped in tar, they provided good light along the service hallways without using candles that would have been more expensive.

"Oh dear…" The brewmaster turned a corner to find the source of the soft exclamation. As he came face-to-face with the Laird Fraser's sister, a shiver raced across his skin. Her fair features were not what he was looking at. She had her skirts raised high, displaying one shapely leg all the way to her thigh. His mouth went dry when she stretched out her leg.

"My garter has come undone, and it seems me attendant is nowhere to be found. Was she back there with ye?"

"With me?" the brewmaster squeaked like an unbearded lad. "Well now…" He swallowed and tried to keep his eyes on her face. "No. I was about me duties."

The lady's eyes narrowed slightly, sending heat into his cock.

"I saw her looking at ye during supper, and truly, I do nae mind if she seeks out her desire, but I need assistance with me garter. If ye do nae want her discovered, perhaps ye might secure me stocking…"

She held out a ribbon. It shimmered with the help of the torch light, the ends gleaming because they were capped with pure gold. He wasn't an overly proud man, but there was part of him that enjoyed knowing the lady thought him striking enough to lure her servant away. He reached for the ribbon, not wanting to admit that no one intent on trysting had snuck into the cellar after him.

Blood rushed to his face as he lowered himself to one knee. The lady's skin was smooth and creamy above the top of her stocking. Beneath his kilt, his cock stirred. He cursed his fickle flesh but couldn't deny he was inhaling the sweet scent of her body with every breath.

Sweet bleeding Christ. He was shaking like a raw lad. He managed to slip the silk around the top of her calf and forced his fumbling fingers to tie the ribbon into a bow. It was uneven but held well enough, and he shivered when she let out a contented sigh.

"Ye have me gratitude, good sir. I would have been quite lost without ye."

The brewmaster looked up, and for a moment he lost track of time. The temptation to allow his hand to slip above the garter, to the creamy skin, was almost too great. His wife's face rose from his memory in time to save him.

He stumbled to his feet. "Good evening to ye, ma'am." He tugged on the corner of his bonnet, retrieved his cart, and wheeled the cider down the hallway.

A soft sound of applause came from around the

corner. Bari appeared and offered her a mocking bow. "Ye are more accomplished than I thought."

Sandra slowly smiled with triumph. "I am, dear Brother. Mother made sure of it."

While her brother had been learning to use a sword to gain the Frasers everything they might want or need, she had been tutored in the art of seduction—a woman's weapon, yet an effective one. And now, she was going to catch herself the heir to an earldom.

"Remember… do nae drink too much, or ye shall be useless. And do nae arrive too early, or it will be clear Norris had his wits dulled by something other than me."

Her brother frowned. "And just when would the perfect time be?"

"Do nae be such a child, Bari," Sandra groused. "The least ye might do is shoulder some part of this business yerself."

Her brother frowned, his pride clearly injured. "Ye're a bitch, Sandra. Pure and true." He reached out and smacked her, the sound loud in the tight confines of the hallway.

She gasped, outraged as she rubbed her cheek. "Ye'll mark me, ye toad!"

Bari smiled, a cold little curving of his lips. "Well now. Ye did want me assistance." He cupped her chin and raised her head so he might view the side of her face. "A good mark will help me convict Norris Sutherland of nae heeding yer warning to let ye be."

❧

"'Tis better," Asgree muttered. "Better that ye are nae with child yet. Ye need to gain some of yer strength back before giving the master a son. Yer courses will nae be upon ye long, either, mark me words. When the body is too thin, the blood will last but three days."

Daphne nodded, not certain what to say. While living at the convent, she'd steadily lost weight, but her thoughts had consumed her.

And now, her dowry still caused her difficulties. In spite of the fact that Lytge argued against her wedding Norris because she had no dowry, Daphne was grateful the fortune was missing. Norris loved her simply for herself, and she would not trade that knowledge for any amount of gold. Even if it did mean the maids in the bathhouse were eyeing her, some with happiness, others with suspicion. They leaned toward one another when they felt Asgree wasn't watching them, and whispered. The news of her courses arriving was spreading like fire, and the head of house was making sure it continued to do so by taking over bathing her when Isla had been doing a fine job. Gahan's sister stood one pace behind Asgree, worrying her lower lip as she tried to devise a way of slipping back to Daphne's side.

Yet her place was not secure. Daphne hated to doubt Norris, but the world was not kind. If the king did not agree they should wed, it was unlikely they would. Norris was set to become a prince among Scotland's nobles. Whom he wed was a subject for debate among the men who ran the country. Tender feelings would not be given much weight during those discussions.

Hopelessness closed around her, sending tears into her eyes. She drew in a deep breath to dispel them and reached for a comb. A sharp snap from the head of house's fingers, and a maid grabbed it before Daphne did. The girl stepped behind her to begin working it through Daphne's half-dry hair.

"I do nae need such attention. A warm bath was enough work."

Asgree shook her head. "It was heard plainly and by more than one that the master has set his mind to wedding ye. The staff needs to see ye being set above them."

"Ye mean the cook?"

There was a soft gasp in the back of the bathhouse that drew Asgree's attention. The maid responsible looked down at her work, but the head of house raised her voice to ensure her words were heard by all.

"The man is overly proud to be handing out slaps so easily. Ye are the daughter of a laird. It makes sense ye would know a thing or two about how to work in a stillroom."

"It was a misunderstanding." Daphne stood up, too nervous to sit any longer. "I should have made myself known to him. A good cook keeps a sharp eye on every detail he is charged with. Any laird's daughter would know such a thing."

"True enough," Asgree agreed.

Nonetheless, the head of house continued to direct her staff to serve Daphne. It was more trouble to avoid them than just to submit. She smiled when she realized Norris had employed the same tactics in securing her. It seemed Asgree was every bit as much of a marauder as the lord she served. The night before her seemed endless. And empty.

She scolded herself but still couldn't shake the

feelings of gloom. How was it possible to miss a man so much when she had known him for so short a time?

Ye've been longing for him since the first night ye lay with him…

That was solid truth if ever she'd admitted one to herself. Norris had never left her thoughts or her heart, even if she returned to MacLeod land as a daughter should. Yet she had not been as dutiful as her father might have liked.

She hugged herself and walked through the hallways leading away from the bathhouse. Two maids came into sight and stopped. They stared at her, indecision on their faces. Then one lowered herself, and her companion followed a moment later.

At the convent, she had been the lowest of the low. It felt awkward to have respect, even if she felt she'd done the correct thing in keeping Broen and Faolan from fighting over her. It had brought her to Norris… Something she'd never regret. Daphne lifted her chin and walked past the maids, intent on promising herself to never, ever allow herself to lament her choice. She wouldn't, for she was no longer a girl blindly following the instructions of her parents. Girlhood was behind her. That knowledge granted her the opportunity to embrace her confidence.

At the top of the tower, the sea stretched out before her. For the moment, the sight was one of endless opportunities. Ones she eagerly looked forward to embracing.

❧

Norris Sutherland did not weaken easily.

Sandra had to wait while the candles burned down

and Norris and Broen enjoyed their cider. For a bit, she worried the sleeping draught had lost its potency, but one by one, those sitting at the high table began to nod. Broen's wife rose and retired long before her husband.

Clarrisa MacNicols was a bastard of England's late King Edward IV. Of course the English woman weakened first. Norris was pure Highlander, as was Broen MacNicols. Sandra rose and followed her, leaving the men to more drinking but she didn't retire. Sandra made her way to one of the back hallways and watched the men through a doorway. The two men enjoyed more cider, but her single fear was washed away when they invited Gahan to join them once Laird MacNicols's wife had left the high table.

Bari made a good show of drinking and took his leave before his eyes glazed over. Sandra had to wait longer. At last, Broen shook his head and grinned at his guest.

"Forgive me, Norris, marriage has a way of making a man seek his bed earlier than he did before he wed."

"With a wife such as fair Clarrisa, 'tis a habit to be encouraged." Norris tossed the remains of cider in his goblet down his throat, stood up, and offered his hand to Broen. They clasped wrists and quit the high table. Broen went to a different tower for the night. Sandra pressed herself back into the shadows, following Norris and Gahan as the night wind rattled the window shutters.

She did not fear the night. In fact, she enjoyed creeping through the hallways. Her mother had warned her never to fear the darkness, for it was the cloak that might shield her when she needed to go undiscovered. Like tonight.

Norris climbed three flights of stairs, with Gahan and two retainers at his back. He clasped his brother on the shoulder, opened the door of a chamber, and entered it. Gahan followed, making her fret. It was possible the bastard might sleep in the chamber too. Time tormented her, refusing to flow smoothly while she waited. Sweat beaded on her forehead, and she fingered the fabric of her dress unconsciously.

The door opened at last, and Gahan appeared. He was slightly unsteady and only nodded to the two men still in the hallway before heading down the stairs to the chamber below. Sandra sank back into the hallway to avoid being seen by him.

The retainers did not last long. Sandra waited while they leaned against the wall, their heads nodding and their eyes closing. Soon, the sound of their even breathing confirmed that they had both succumbed.

She smiled and took a moment to savor the feeling of victory. Yet, it was not quite complete. Picking up her skirts, she held them tightly so they would not rustle as she climbed the stairs. A single lantern burned at the top of the stairs where the retainers were posted to guard their laird's door. Neither man moved as she brushed past them. The door was not barred, which would allow them to enter the chamber if their master needed them. She walked inside and pressed the door closed behind her.

Her heart accelerated. She could practically smell Norris—his vitality, the pure strength of the man. For a while, She and Bari had been torn between setting his sights on Norris or the Earl of Rothes, but George Leslie was well past his prime. Sandra could hear

Norris breathing softly and shivered with the anticipation of being beside him.

Oh, he would be furious with her, suspicious of her, but the sleeping draught would do its job well and leave him with naught to convict her of wrongdoing. In time, he'd settle down, and his nature would see him seeking her embrace. She planned to welcome him warmly—even hotly.

Working at her clothing, she shed her dress and stays, making sure to throw them about the room. She discarded her shoes, reached down to untie her garters, and pushed her stockings down her legs. Excitement kept her from feeling the cold, and she lifted the tail of her chemise without flinching at the temperature. Indeed, she stood proud and content in nothing but her skin as she stopped near the bed.

Norris was sprawled over its surface. The fire was only a bed of coals, but the ruby light illuminated his body well enough. She felt a tingle in her passage though regret that she would have no satisfaction from him tonight. The man was magnificent. It took a great deal of discipline to pull the pins from her hair and not reach out to finger his cock. It looked delicious…

Oh, she was no maiden, but Norris would never know it. She sat down on the bed, careful not to make the ropes creak. She did not trust Norris's wits to be dulled too greatly. The very last part of her plan was to pull a small chicken's bladder from its hiding place in her hair. The small sack was filled with blood, and she worked the thread loose that bound it. She made sure it splattered onto her thighs before marking the sheets.

For the final touch, she swallowed the empty bladder to ensure no one would find it in the morning. With a contented sigh, she lay back and indulged herself by dreaming of all the things she would do as mistress of Dunrobin. And all the delights Norris Sutherland would give her in bed...

❦

"Ye are going to let me pass!"

Norris opened his eyes and reached for his sword. Someone thumped a fist on the chamber door, and he was on his feet before Bari Fraser came storming in.

"I told ye no!" Norris's men grabbed Bari, holding the man in the doorway.

"There!" Bari bellowed. "Ye see? I demand satisfaction! How dare yer father act as though me sister is nae good enough for his precious son, and then ye take her to yer bed!"

"What are ye babbling about, man?" Norris demanded and set his sword back on the table near the bed. His head was throbbing. That didn't stop him from noticing the way his men were suddenly looking at the floor. He spun around to find Sandra Fraser gathering the bedding against her chest as the rising sun washed over her.

"He swore... he'd wed me... Bari..."

"What in the hell are ye doing in me bed, woman?" Norris demanded loud enough to shake the rafters.

Sandra's eyes widened, glistening with tears that began falling down her cheeks. "Ye promised... me..." She rose to her knees, looking like she was panicking as she searched for her clothing.

"She's nae wearing a stitch," Bari yelled. "What in the hell do ye think ye did with her in that bed? Do ye take me for a fool? Just because ye are higher born than me does nae give ye the right to ruin me sister after I came to ye seeking an alliance."

Gahan burst into the room, his sword in hand. He froze when he took in the scene. Norris tried to recall the moment he'd retired for the evening. He remembered nothing. Sandra was weeping softly—too softly, really. The sheets were stained sure enough, but he could not recall having had her.

"What is amiss?" Broen demanded from the doorway. His men were at his back, crowding the room.

"Retainers out!" Norris ordered. Broen's men looked to their laird before clearing the room. Norris's men were not happy about leaving, but they followed his command and took Bari's men along with them.

Norris grabbed his shirt and shrugged into it. "Ye retired before we did, Sandra. I recall that much very well."

"Aye, she did," Broen confirmed.

"How dare ye call me sister a liar?" Bari shouted, his face turning red. He pointed at the stained sheets. "The proof is undeniable."

"I did nae call her a liar," Norris barked. "I did ask her a question that I will hear the answer to, with or without ye here."

"I checked this chamber before leaving ye for the night," Gahan announced, "as I always do. No one was here. Ye should question the men at the door."

Sandra appeared wounded as she gathered up her

clothing. She made no attempt to dress, looking helpless with all her garments clutched against her body.

"Ye… brought me here… I was in the hallway, looking for me attendant, for I could nae sleep… and ye were below stairs and offered me cider to ease me belly…" She looked at the bed, appearing stunned. "Ye promised me we'd wed, that ye would settle accounts with me brother. That it was all but decided upon anyway. I trusted ye."

Norris was furious. It felt like a noose was knotted around his throat. He had never been a man to turn his back on honor, but he couldn't shake the feeling of panic digging into him. He walked over to the table holding his kilt. It was set at an angle so all he needed to do was lean back and grasp the ends of the belt set into the groove running down its center. Another thing he did not recall doing, but the wool was evenly pleated, confirming he had done it, as he always did, before going to sleep.

Responding to trouble in the middle of the night in naught but his shirt wasn't something he enjoyed. Still, he could not recall seeking out his bed. He kept the knowledge to himself, though, because Sandra began to lose her composure.

"Ye… ye ruined me if ye do nae keep yer promise to wed me!" Her hands were clenched into fists, and her face turned red. "Have ye no honor?"

"Mind yer words, Sandra. No one questions me honor. Especially nae a woman who knows full well I respect me father and would nae have promised ye marriage without discussing it with him. Ye know that well, as do ye, Laird Fraser, for I told ye both such at Dunrobin."

"Ye were soaked with cider last eve," Bari
accused. "I saw it well, but that does nae mean ye
can ruin me sister."

"Why do ye nae have someone watching over
yer sister during the dark hours?" Broen MacNicols
inquired softly. "Ye have men at yer back. Why was
she unattended?"

"A very good question," Gahan agreed. "There
were men at the door here. If ye came here with
Norris, they will have seen ye."

"They were sleeping…" Sandra shut her mouth,
and temper flickered in her eyes. "Curse the lot of ye!
Ye were all soaked with cider. It's well known ye share
everything with yer men. So 'tis yer doing that they were
sleeping. Ye owe me satisfaction." She turned toward her
brother. "And ye shall nae say a single word to me, Bari,
for ye told me negotiations were going well."

"The details were nae any of yer concern, woman,"
Bari snarled.

"Maybe so, but I had nae reason to suspect yer
promises were born inside a cider barrel. Ye gave me
yer word, and I expect ye to honor it." Sandra didn't
wait for an answer but swept from the room with her
rumpled dress trailing.

"She's right, I did nae tell her yer father was undecided in the matter. Women are troublesome when
they feel they have been rejected." Bari shook his
head. "But that does nae excuse ye, Norris Sutherland.
She says ye promised her. Ye must keep yer word.
The circumstances be damned."

Dunrobin

Isla knocked softly before entering her mistress's chamber. She kept her steps light and lifted one finger to caution the two maids following her to be silent.

Daphne was already up and standing in the window closest to the bed. The window was open, but Bacchus was not there. The falcon's absence was just one more glaring detail to remind her Norris was not at Dunrobin.

As if the long, sleepless night behind her was not proof enough.

"Forgive me for being tardy," Isla muttered as she lowered herself and the maids followed her example.

"Ye are hardly late, Isla. I simply could nae sleep."

Daphne turned back to watching the sunrise, desperately trying to disguise the loneliness that had woken her. Norris was the son of the Earl of Sutherland—if she hoped to have a future with him, she would have to suffer the times his duties separated them. If she were his wife, she would be expected to attend to her own duties. Not to be found weeping in the early morning because of a dream. Nightmare, actually.

Do nae dwell upon it…

Sound advice, yet her heart refused to listen. She couldn't even recall the details of the dream, only that it had felt like Norris was being ripped away from her.

Foolishness… Where was the strength that had seen her boldly refusing the match her father had made for her because she knew it was destructive? Her courage had not failed her when the winter had arrived and she

shivered on her pious bride of Christ's cot with little
to keep her warm.

She wiped her eyes and turned to face Isla. If Norris
could do his duty, she would too.

∽

"This reeks of deceit," Gahan muttered the moment
Bari Fraser left Norris's chamber. "I can nae recall
much from last night, and the men claim they have no
memory either."

"I suffer from the same ailment," Broen offered.

Norris finished dressing, his temper boiling danger-
ously. "I did nae have her, but I can nae swear to it,
because me memory is gone. There is nae enough cider
in this tower to make me blind to the shrew she is."

Nevertheless, the situation was damning. The
Frasers had allies. Not to wed Sandra would place
tension on the relationship the Sutherlands had with
those clans. Norris was no fool. To survive in the
Highlands, you needed your allies. If Bari called for a
feud, it was possible Norris would find himself fighting
a significant portion of his vassals.

What had seemed so simple the day before was
now taunting him with how impossible it might be
to wed Daphne.

God damn it to hell!

∽

"Everyone out!" Bari Fraser made sure his expression
was furious as he waited for the maids helping his sister
to leave the chamber. The door closed, and he walked
in a wide circle.

"I have already looked for peepholes," Sandra offered sweetly.

Bari stopped near her, leaning down to keep his words from drifting. "Such a crafty creature ye are."

"Did he swear to wed me?"

Bari shook his head, which drew a snarl from Sandra. He tapped her lightly on the cheek, directly on top of the bruise he'd given her the night before. The pain was brief but a subtle reminder her brother was arrogant. Like all men.

"Leave the details to the men." His eyes flashed with temper. "He'll wed ye, sure enough. His father will see to it once I make it clear I will nae stand for such an insult. I will continue on to Court with Norris, to make sure he does not secure permission to wed Daphne MacLeod from the king."

Sandra growled. "I did nae think of that. That little boy will no doubt think it a righting of wrongs if Norris has to wed the woman he had beneath the little puppy's own nose."

"Which would leave ye disgraced and us without the Sutherland forces at our back. Unless I am there to make sure the lad hears of how Norris promised ye the blessing of the Church."

"Curse that MacLeod slut! The king might decide upon her instead of me. I shall go with ye," Sandra said decisively.

"Ye will nae," Bari ordered. "Ye will ride up to Dunrobin and plead yer case with the earl. I do nae care for him having time alone with Daphne MacLeod. He might decide he favors her, which would make it a simple matter to see his son wed to her if it is what the king desires. The Sutherlands court royal favor too. I will make sure the king understands me rage will lead to a feud this summer if ye are nae honored. The king's advisers will no' want that. Our allies supported the young king, while the MacLeods fought against him. That will be to our advantage."

Her brother stepped back and studied her for a moment. "Now cry, Sister, and let the maids see how frightened ye are of yer brother."

Sandra sniffed. Her eyes widened, and within moments, tears were slowly falling down her cheeks.

Bari chuckled. "What a fine actress ye are. The earl will melt like butter when ye stand before him."

❧

Bari Fraser was waiting for Norris when he descended the stairs. His retainers looked ready to fight, while Norris felt his own men straining against the discipline he demanded of them. They were waiting on his order—barely. The moment was one Norris had spent many an hour avoiding—tensions between clans. In the Highlands, such unrest could easily result in a bloody summer of feuding.

Damn Sandra for starting trouble. She was everything he'd feared having in a bride. A woman who spent more time scheming than looking after the people who called her mistress. The sort of female who saw her position as nothing more than a possession she would squabble over like a child fighting for the last sweet cake on Twelfth Night.

Everything Daphne was not...

Bari tugged on the corner of his bonnet with a

swift jerk of his hand, which left no one wondering whether he was still furious or not. The man looked ready to kill.

"For all that ye are me overlord, I demand satisfaction."

"So ye have made it plain. But at the moment, I have been summoned by me overlord, the king. So ye will wait while I give him deference," Norris informed him.

"Ye can give me yer word ye will honor me sister. Such will no' interfere in yer duty to the king."

"What makes ye think I will give ye any such thing, when I know full well me father was not settled on the match with yer sister? Ye should have been honest with her." Norris's tone left little doubt he wasn't interested in arguing further. "The matter will wait until I return to Dunrobin."

Something flashed in Bari's eyes that looked like uncertainty. Suspicion returned to needle Norris, but he still had no proof.

"I will ride with ye to Edinburgh."

Norris stepped closer to Bari and waved his men back. The Fraser retainers backed away from their laird in response.

"Mind yer tone, man. I understand yer position, but ye will wait on me to complete me journey. Maybe that will give ye enough time to discover why yer men did nae know where their mistress was throughout the night. That's a bit of information I'd like to know meself. Ye've no right to be outraged if yer sister is accustomed to roaming the hallways at night. Trust me when I say no wife of mine will conduct herself like that. Even me illegitimate sister is nae allowed such behavior because it leads to fighting. So ye'll wait, because it's clear yer sister is either prone to slipping past her escorts, or yer men are no' as sharp as they should be. In either case, there will be discussion before any promises are made. The reason a Sutherland's word is worth something is because it is nae given unless we plan to keep it, and I know me place. Which for now, is to answer the summons of me king no matter what I must set aside to do it."

Bari reached up and tugged on his bonnet. "Fair enough."

But it wasn't fair. Norris shook hands briefly with Broen before leaving Deigh Tower. His men looked grim as they waited for him. To be sure, he agreed with them. There was nothing to be happy about.

≪≫

Dunrobin had been a long time without a proper mistress. The earl had a private secretary who kept some of the estate books in good order—but only those accounting for armor and gunpowder; things men thought of. The cook had a page who was crafty with numbers, and the lad kept a fair accounting of the goods used by the kitchen. That left several areas unaccounted for.

Daphne began with the cloth accounts. Everything from bed linens to staff livery needed to be recorded. There were stable boys who hadn't been given new shirts in two years. They wouldn't ask, for that would be an insinuation that the laird was not running a competent house.

It was something the lady of the house attended

to. One of the many duties that made her worthy of respect. When a man such as Norris negotiated for a bride, he was looking for a female who came educated in mathematics and languages, and was experienced in running a large household. Her days would be full of ensuring everyone had enough—be it shelter, clothing, or food. Overlooking even the lowest stable boy was unacceptable. The bond between laird and servant was ancient. The servant gave service, and the laird made sure they had all the essentials.

When the bells began to ring in the village in the afternoon, Daphne stretched her back and stood up from where she had been hunched over the table in the lady's solar. "Who is it?" she asked.

One of the maids Asgree had sent up that morning to attend her under Isla's command put the shirt she was sewing aside and looked out the window.

"Fraser colors, mistress."

The girl stumbled over the last word, but Daphne found it odd too. Not as odd as hearing who was riding through the gates.

"I believe I should greet them in person."

Isla frowned but followed Daphne down the stairs. Cam joined them too, and by the time they reached the ground floor, retainers were pushing open the doors. Sandra Fraser swept inside like a princess. Dust clung to her from the road, and she was wearing a dress too fine for travel.

"I would see the earl"—Sandra noticed Daphne and shot her a look full of impending victory—"for I seek justice for the wrong his son has done me."

A chill raced down Daphne's back. The nightmare

that had woken her suddenly played across her memory. She had been standing in the church while Norris took his vows with Sandra.

From the look in Sandra Fraser's eyes, it appeared the girl believed herself heading for marriage with the earl's son. The man Daphne loved.

❧

"Me son is nae here," Lytge declared in a steady voice from behind the large desk in his private chamber. The gray hair on his head seemed almost a camouflage, for his tone didn't lack strength. Sandra Fraser wasn't impressed with the high-backed chair he sat in, which had his family crest carved into the wood. No, the girl had marched right into his private space without lowering herself and begun to make her case.

"He used me after making promises he'd wed me," Sandra insisted. "I've come to demand justice from ye. Make him wed me before yer honor is sullied by his actions."

The earl studied her for a long moment. "Since ye just accused Norris of nae having the honor to keep his promise to wed ye, what makes ye believe he will honor me by taking ye to wife if I decide to request it of him? He is no lad."

"He always does what ye command," she muttered, disliking the look in the old man's eyes. "Every clan knows it too. Norris might be a rogue, but he gives ye respect and honor."

Lytge nodded. "Aye, me son is a rogue, and ye are nae the only woman inside Dunrobin who has lost her battle to refuse him. Why would I insist he wed ye, when I have nae insisted he take Daphne MacLeod to the church for the holy blessing? He spilled her virgin's blood after the king himself ordered her wed to Broen MacNicols."

"Daphne MacLeod?" Sandra sneered. "Her clan is disgraced, and she has nae a single piece of silver to her name. She brings naught to ye."

"I am more concerned with what she leaves behind, which is peace and happiness. Ye leave a trail of relief, because yer shrewish temperament drives me staff near insane."

Sandra gasped, her focus on her goal slipping from her grasp. The old man might be an earl, but he had gone too far to insult her.

"Why—"

The earl held up a hand, and his men moved toward her instantly, proving he had simply been granting her his time. It was a blunt reminder of how much power he held.

"Go on with ye, Sandra Fraser. Asgree will see ye have a chamber, and ye may wait on me son's return. That is all I offer ye for the moment. Yer brother knew full well I was undecided in the matter of me son wedding ye."

He waved her off, but for a moment, the urge to launch herself over the table and lock her hands around his throat was almost too much to contain. The retainers reached for her, and she jumped back out of their reach.

"Yer son was nae so cold upon the matter, I assure ye. I will be waiting, yer lairdship."

She lowered herself and left. Her temper boiled,

and the moment the old head of house left her alone, she threw herself onto the bed and beat it. By the time her rage was spent, two of the fine pillows were torn, their goose feathers floating gently through the air. Sandra didn't spare a second glance for the costly items she'd destroyed. She would have a dozen more pillows given to her and do whatever she wished with them. She would be mistress of Dunrobin—she would.

Maybe Lytge needed to be helped on his way to the afterlife before she might see her plan to fruition. Her temper slowly faded, and her confidence burned brightly once more. Yes, if the old man would not help her by ordering Norris to wed, perhaps he might still assist her by dying in such a manner as to make sure Daphne MacLeod was blamed for his death.

Two problems solved with a single solution. Yes, that cheered her up very nicely.

⚜

Norris pulled up his horse.

"What's the matter?" Gahan asked. He scanned the horizon and returned a questioning gaze to Norris, because there was nothing in sight.

"I feel like I'm going in the wrong direction." In fact, he was certain of it.

"Aye, I share that with ye," Gahan agreed. "There is something nae right about all of this."

Norris looked behind him, straining against his discipline. Duty had never been such a burden before. To be sure, there were Highland lairds who would tell the king to wait until spring for their oaths of loyalty, and he did want the king's blessing on his wedding to

Daphne. But something was pulling him back toward Dunrobin. The sensation had been building all day, and looking at the setting sun made his mouth go dry.

He felt as though he'd left something unprotected. He felt the pull stronger and stronger with each passing mile, and it was burning a hole in his gut. Damn his duty, for it damned him to journey on in spite of his suspicions.

Damn him...

❧

Sandra Fraser was waiting for Daphne when she went down to the bathhouse. "I told ye I'd have him for me husband. Ye might think yerself so grand with that brute Cam guarding yer door, but I warned ye what would happen once I was mistress of Dunrobin." Sandra flicked her fingers. "He'll be tossed into the gutter, like ye."

There was victory in Sandra's eyes. Daphne looked away, trying desperately to fend off the doubt that had been stalking her since Sandra arrived. "I suppose ye'll do as ye please."

"Oh yes, I always do what I please." Sandra came closer. "I want Norris for me husband, and he'll have to wed me now. Unlike ye, me clan is powerful, and he will nae risk having a feud over me soiled name. I will be mistress here, and ye will be gone."

Daphne backed away from the girl, because in that moment, Sandra looked insane. There was an unholy light shining in her eyes that sent a shiver down Daphne's back. Without a doubt, Sandra's heart was as dead as a stone. She was a law unto herself.

Despite her misgivings, Daphne lifted her chin. "It will nae be the first time I have made me own way in this world, and I promise ye one thing, Sandra, ye do nae control me ability to fend for meself."

Sandra apparently wasn't accustomed to having her victims fight back. Her face turned red, and she bared her teeth.

"Ye shall be what I say… Do ye hear? What I say!"

"No' if I am nae beneath Dunrobin's roof."

Sandra sputtered, granting Daphne a small sliver of satisfaction. It wasn't much, but she'd make do. The sun was sinking on the horizon, and she felt as if it was heralding the approach of death. Perhaps that was dramatic, but she couldn't deny the feeling in her belly that doom was looming over her. She felt its shadow and the touch of its icy breath on her neck.

Well… she'd endure.

Well enough.

As she always did.

So why are ye fighting off tears?

Because she loved Norris, and that idea brought calm to her at last. She smiled at Sandra before entering the great hall. Whatever happened, she would not live without knowing love. Small comfort, but comfort nonetheless.

෨෬

The tension in the great hall was palpable. The staff of Dunrobin whispered in the corners as they contemplated the high table. Lytge sat in the center chair at the table, the fine meal placed before him untouched. It didn't tempt him in the least, even though several of his favorite dishes were waiting on him. The cook stood off to one side, waiting to see if his work met with approval. Lytge ground his teeth with frustration. He didn't need to offend his staff.

"Ye have brought discord to me house," he muttered, not bothering to indicate which of his female guests the comment was directed at. "It pleases me not."

Daphne stood up, the page assigned to her chair having to hurry to pull the heavy X-framed piece of furniture out of her way.

"This fine meal should nae be wasted. Many are nae so fortunate." She lowered herself before leaving. Maybe it was the coward's way out, but she couldn't force a morsel down her throat, either. The opportunity to escape was too tempting. Sandra had not lied about her clan being strong. There was no reason to believe Lytge would not see the wisdom of insisting Norris wed her.

"I am so happy ye have sent her away," Sandra snapped. "She was spoiling me appetite, as well."

"Why are ye so sure Daphne was the cause of me discontentment?" The earl sent her a sidelong glance.

Lytge stood up, and the hall quieted as he did so. "Mistress MacLeod." Startled by the booming sound that came out of Lytge Sutherland, Daphne turned so fast her skirts rose up. He might look old, but there was plenty of strength left in his body. She lowered herself.

"I would have words with ye, in private."

He turned and headed for the doorway behind the high table. The room beyond it was a place few females ever ventured. She swallowed the lump that had formed in her throat and followed. She had been mistaken when she believed the hall full of tension while she still sat at the high table.

Because now it was tight enough to snap.

Every set of eyes was on her as she climbed the three steps to the high ground and then went around the table to follow the earl. His personal escort eyed her but allowed her to pass through the doorway into his private receiving chamber.

❧

The pages assigned to the high table took the opportunity to eat. The earl enjoyed long suppers, so it was a rare opportunity to stand closer to the fire and indulge themselves with personal conversation.

"He's going to send her back to her own clan, sure as can be."

"Ye do nae know that. I heard one of the upstairs maids claim the young master wants to wed her."

"He's off to Court and nae here to stop his father from dealing with her. She has no dowry. The Sutherlands always wed for position and gold. I wager he sends her home before his son returns."

"Mistress Fraser is sour-tempered."

"Aye, we'll have to suffer her, no doubt, since she has a dowry."

The cook began to ladle out hot stew, and all the pages turned to hold out their bowls. The musicians would play a fanfare when the earl returned, so they didn't bother to keep the high table in their sights.

Sandra smiled slowly, happy to be left unattended for a change. She reached for the earl's goblet and hid it in her lap. The tablecloth assisted her and, when no one noticed, she withdrew her flower hair ornament and began to smear its contents along the inside of the goblet.

∼∞∼

"Now then," the earl said as he sat down, "'tis time ye and I had a blunt discussion."

Lytge waved at his men. "Off with ye, lads." They hesitated in the doorway, their gazes traveling to her. The earl stood up with a growl. "Do ye nae think me capable of handling one wisp of a lass?"

His men tugged on the corners of their bonnets and quit the room.

"Somehow, I do nae think I will have the good fortune of having ye attempt to strangle me, even if I might hope for the pleasure of feeling ye wrap yer body around mine."

Her jaw dropped open in shock. Lytge beat the table with his amusement and walked over to the cupboard. He lifted a pitcher and filled two mugs, bringing them back to the table.

"Sit, lass."

The chairs behind his table were ornately carved and too heavy to move. A stool was pushed beneath the end of the table, obviously left there by one of his secretaries. Daphne pulled it out and sat down.

"If I'd invited young Sandra Fraser in here, she'd nae have missed the opportunity to sit herself down in one of me fine chairs. Ye may wager upon that fact for certain."

"This serves well enough."

He set one of the mugs in front of her and settled back into his chair. "I understand being tired of all the pomp and circumstance." He drew a sip from his mug. "There is a satisfaction in doing a thing or two for oneself. But outside this sanctum, I must make sure there is order, else we'd end up as naught but a snarling pack of wolves, all intent on killing one another for the most gain."

The earl drew another sip and watched her over the rim of his mug. "What are ye thinking, lass?" he demanded softly.

"That Norris learned a great deal from ye. Yer gaze is as sharp as his, and ye try to disguise how much ye do notice behind yer guise of entertaining and making merry. Yet ye are nae the aged man ye so often portray."

"And me son uses duty to me as his shield to keep the world from knowing just how much he does think before acting," Lytge offered gently.

"He does take his duty to ye to heart," she made sure she stared straight into the earl's eyes as she spoke.

Lytge chuckled and drained his mug. "Ye have strength and a spine of solid steel. I did wonder if ye were naught but a spoiled brat." He pointed at her. "Casting aside young Laird MacNicols might have been naught but a service to yer own petty preferences. It would nae have been the first time a laird's daughter decided she'd have what she wanted no matter the difficulties it caused others."

"I was thinking of the difficulties and naught else," she countered. "Broen MacNicols was growing closer to feuding with the Chisholms over the match. I refused to watch bloodshed because of my wedding."

The earl tilted his head to one side. "Aye, Faolan is as passionate as his father was. When it comes to women, they lose their heads." He placed the mug on the table and aimed a hard gaze at her. "What do ye want of me son?"

"To be near him." It was a simple answer but one that crossed her lips instantly. It was an emotional response, and logic had no control over it.

The earl grunted. "I noticed ye did nae say ye wish to wed him."

It was a baited comment, a test of her motives. Daphne slowly smiled, her confidence warming her. "If position was what I craved, I'd be Lady MacNicols. Twice I had the chance, and twice I chose to see the harm it would do. I understand how the world works, and I truly have no dowry, but I have something more important. Yer son's affection. That is all I desire."

For a moment, something flickered in his eyes. She realized he had Norris's green eyes, and they were full of a glimmer that touched her heart. He covered it quickly, clearing his throat as he stood up.

"Me appetite has returned. Let us taste some of the cook's fare before the man throws himself off the curtain wall."

"I doubt he'd do such a thing. The man does nae seem to lack confidence."

The earl raised an eyebrow at her as he came around the table. "He is a powder keg, is nae he? But the man can make even a Lent table appetizing. Ye have the spine to deal with him, but more importantly, ye have a clever enough wit to understand the value of nae crushing his spirit. That Fraser brat would crush him, simply for the sake of knowing she was being obeyed. 'Twould be a waste, I assure ye, and serving up bland fare would be the man's vengeance."

The earl brushed by her as he made his comment, but there was a note of amusement in his tone that snagged her attention.

"Ye are playing with me, Laird Sutherland."

He turned and winked at her, just as cocksure as Norris so often was. "As ye noticed, lass, I'm nae so old as I would let some believe. Nor am I as much of a miser. Me son's happiness is something I hold close to me heart. But this business with Sandra Fraser is nasty. It will take a bit of doing to clear it up."

The stone that had felt lodged on top of her heart for the better part of the day suddenly lifted away. It seemed impossible to have so much tension relieved by so simple a conversation, but it was. Lytge was laird of Dunrobin. His word was law.

None of that mattered to her. What warmed her heart and sent tears into her eyes was the way the man had winked at her. He approved of her. Coupled with the affection Norris had expressed for her, there was nothing else to long for. Life was perfect.

The musicians of Dunrobin lifted their instruments the moment the earl emerged from his private chambers. They filled the great hall with bursts of music as the people enjoying the evening meal stood in respect for their laird.

"Let us enjoy this fine meal, Mistress MacLeod."

Lytge sat down and didn't seem to notice the flurry

of activity behind him as his pages returned. His goblet was filled, and the maids began to bring the food back from where it had been warming in the kitchens. Once again, the cook appeared to watch his laird.

"Mistress Fraser has retired for the evening," Asgree informed the earl softly.

"How fortunate," he muttered low enough to keep his words from drifting too far. Daphne's eyes widened, which earned her another wink as he sampled the ale in his goblet and began to partake of the supper before him.

"Eat, lass! Ye look frail enough to blow away with the winter winds." He used his knife to deposit a serving of meat on her plate, laughing when she tried to protest. "Nonsense, it is nae too much. Sutherland is a demanding land. Ye will need strength here."

He waved at the musicians, and the hall filled with the sounds of the bagpipes and the clàrsach. Men at the lower tables began to keep time with the music, and some of the women rose to dance. Soon tables were moved aside so the younger girls might high step on their toes while their skirts twirled.

Daphne smiled and clapped in time. But she failed to completely forget Sandra Fraser was nearby, just waiting to do her best to destroy everything Daphne held dear.

❦

Deigh Tower was gloomy. Clarrisa frowned, trying not to curse her departed guests, but she failed. She sighed. There would be penance for certain later when she confessed her sins, but for the moment, she cursed Sandra Fraser for the mess the girl had made.

How had Sandra known it was Norris Sutherland arriving? The question needled Clarrisa throughout the day as she reflected on the previous night's events and had trouble recalling the moment she had fallen into bed. She was not normally prone to such lapses in memory, and when she considered she had partaken of only a single glass of cider, her mind refused to let the subject go. Her suspicions refused to allow her peace until she made her way to the back of the kitchens where the stillroom was. A large cabinet stood there, with numerous small drawers. It was the spice cabinet. Clarrisa gently pulled on each handle, making sure all the locks held. They did, confounding her, because it was the only place the more potent compounds were kept: compounds that might ease suffering and take an injured person into sleep in spite of pain; compounds that might make it difficult to recall the night before.

A loud sound drew her attention. She listened to it for a long moment before following it. The stone hallways of the tower made the sound echo. She'd lived at Deigh Tower only for half a year and was still learning the maze that made up its kitchens and storerooms. The sound drew her around a corner and then down another passageway until she smelled the scent of yeast from the cellar.

Clarrisa peered inside to see the brewmaster sound asleep in the corner. The man was leaning up against a wall, perched on a stool. She moved closer to him and snapped her fingers near the man's ear, but he snored on. In his hand was a mug of half-drunk cider, the barrel nearby. Suspicion rose back up inside her, for she recognized the scent of the cider. The man would never open a new barrel without permission; however, he might finish off one the laird would think empty after entertaining guests.

"Mistress?" Her head of house's voice came from somewhere down the passageways. "Mistress? Where are ye?"

Clarrisa moved back toward the door. "I am here… in the cellar."

Edme would send her husband's retainers looking for her if she failed to answer, because every castle had its spies. Clarrisa wasn't surprised when Edme appeared with two men close on her heels.

"If ye needed something from the brewmaster…" Edme's voice trailed off when she caught sight of the passed-out man in the corner.

"He will nae wake," Clarrisa said loud enough for her words to bounce between the stone walls. She lifted the mug cradled in his lap and sniffed the contents. "This is the cider from last evening."

Edme took the mug and sniffed it. She also tasted it before passing it to the men behind her. One of them knelt down and clapped his hands next to the brewmaster's ear. The man roused only partially before renewing his snoring.

"I've known this man since we were lads, and he never sleeps so soundly."

"I suspect foul play, as well." Clarrisa moved closer to the cask. "Pry off the top."

The man was happy to comply, even if his expression was dark. He pulled a tool from where it rested on the wall. Using a mallet, he hammered the steel rod under the lid until the wood splintered and the top came free. When he lifted the top away, they all peered into the barrel, but there was nothing but cider.

"Poor the contents into an empty barrel," Edme ordered. "Slowly."

There were only a few inches of cider left, and it took a brief moment for the small bundle of cloth to be discovered. Edme picked it up and placed it on the table used for smaller bottles of French wine. One of the men offered her a knife, and she used it to open the packet. She spread out the contents, inspecting them closely.

"A sleeping draught," she announced.

Clarrisa looked back at the brewmaster, frustrated by the fact that she could not wake the man. Every second he slept offered the culprit more time to escape.

"I needs speak with me husband. Place a man here, and tell me the moment the brewmaster awakens. We must know who had the opportunity to place that in the cider."

Truly, she already knew. A quick look at Edme, and Clarrisa realized the older woman agreed with her. Their opinions alone would not be enough to convict Sandra Fraser. Not in a world run by men, and Bari Fraser was a laird. Norris Sutherland had best say his prayers, for he needed divine deliverance.

⤳⤺

The cook in charge of the kitchens at Dunrobin looked satisfied—happy even—as Lytge wiped his lips on a linen napkin and nodded enthusiastically.

"The man is gifted, I tell ye, Daphne." He leaned closer to her. "Artists have the most unpredictable tempers."

"So I have heard."

The earl winked and drained his goblet. He let out a pleased sound before standing up to address his people. The hall went silent.

"A fine meal, Master Cook, one... I..."

He stopped and cleared his throat, but when he opened his mouth to continue, all that came forth was a strangled gasp for air. Lytge struggled to draw breath. His body shook as he failed to fill his lungs. He braced one hand against the tabletop and slowly collapsed. His men began rushing toward him; they couldn't help him. Lytge Sutherland fell to the floor, and as he suffocated, his face turned purple. Women screamed and men cursed. The head table was turned over and its dishes scattered down the stairs as more men tried to get close enough to the earl to aid him.

Daphne was pushed back. She wanted to help; every muscle in her body was straining with the need to offer assistance. However, there was no way past the solid wall of men surrounding Lytge.

"Ye did nae have to poison him..."

Daphne turned. Her mouth dropped open as she came face-to-face with Sandra. She had no idea where the girl had come from, but her complexion was red and her hands clenched into fists.

"Ye did nae have to poison my father-to-be! It is nae his fault ye have no dowry!"

"I did nae..."

Her words were overshadowed as Sandra continued to scream at her, and she wasn't alone. Other women pointed at her, rage contorting their features. Cam pushed her behind him. He and Isla seemed the only ones not intent on accusing her.

Despite the tumult, Daphne was more concerned with Lytge. His body contorted, twisting in agony, and his face turned as red as sunset. Men made the sign of the cross over themselves, and women began to pray. Once of his older captains looked up.

"Fetch a priest!"

Silence fell over the hall, allowing everyone to hear the sounds of the men running down the aisle toward the church. Each footfall felt like it pierced her heart.

Seven

LYTGE SUTHERLAND SURPRISED THEM ALL BY LIVING TO see the dawn. The priest still gave him last rites, because no one expected him to rise from his bed, except perhaps as a specter. His captains were grim faced as they debated what to do.

Daphne didn't sleep. Every time she closed her eyes, she saw the fingers pointing at her. She paced around the confines of the star chamber, freezing every time she heard the door move. It was impossible not to think retaliation might land upon her.

It ended up being only the wind, but she couldn't dismiss her fear. It was like a living thing inside her. It felt like a bird, flapping its wings frantically to be free. She paced some more, every moment expecting to hear the bells tolling the news of the earl's passing. Each hour felt like a year. And yet, part of her wanted to savor every moment, because she feared it might be her last. Many had taken Sandra's words to heart and looked at Daphne with hate. No one came with wood for the fire, and more retainers had arrived to guard her door.

Damn Sandra and her accusations…

Her temper flared up, keeping her warm, and she didn't bother to counsel herself to forgiveness. Sandra Fraser would receive no kindness from her. It would seem they had something in common at last. They hated each other. The emotion was so strong it threatened to consume her. Daphne warned herself to keep the blaze of hatred under control, because she would not become like Sandra. Norris was not a possession; he was the man she loved. Nonetheless, it was possible his own people might hang her before he returned. If Sandra had her way, Daphne would never see another sunset.

❧

"Enough of this indecision." Sandra Fraser walked boldly into the private chambers of the Earl of Sutherland. His captains were seated there and glared at her for interrupting. "Daphne MacLeod should be hung. Immediately," she announced. "A message needs to be sent to anyone who would harm a Sutherland."

There were eight men in the room, all of them wearing three feathers in the sides of their bonnets. Two were pointing up, the third down, declaring their status to the rest of the clan. Sandra refused to allow their rank to intimidate her. Her potion had failed her, so it was up to her to salvage the situation.

"Daphne MacLeod was alone with the earl—"

"So were ye," one of the captains remarked.

"But he did nae collapse after meeting with me," Sandra said, defending herself.

"That does nae absolve ye of being the one who poisoned him."

Sandra drew herself up as regal as a queen. "How dare ye! I had no reason to harm me future father-by-marriage. Daphne MacLeod is the one who needed to make sure Norris did nae have a father any longer. It's well known Norris respects his father. If his father were gone, she would have the chance to remain here and tempt Norris back into her bed. The MacLeods are destitute. Even a Sutherland bastard would help them bleed Sutherland dry."

Some of the captains glanced at one another, silently agreeing with her. Sandra walked slowly among them, keeping her steps even and enticing to dull their wits. She drew in a deep breath and ordered herself to relax. This was not the first time she had twisted men into doing her bidding.

"Daphne MacLeod has bled, and Norris knew it before he left." She turned and looked at them. "He told me how relieved he was to be rid of her hold on him. She doesn't want to return to her lands and the shame of being a soiled woman. The earl swore to me he was going to see her on her way this morning. That is why she poisoned him, and do nae think she will content herself with only one victim. One of ye will be next, or perhaps meself, if we do nae take action to protect ourselves."

"Perhaps… we should question her," one of the captains offered. "And any who might offer evidence in this matter."

"Aye."

"A sound action."

The captains agreed, and Sandra bit her lip to hide her displeasure. She needed more anger from them, more passion. Daphne needed to be gone before Norris returned, or all was lost for her.

~~~

The cook of Dunrobin had his bonnet completely off and was busy worrying the edge of it with his fingers. The great hall was deathly silent, something he'd heard only in the darkest hours of the night. Most of the benches were full. The day's tasks were left undone, because everyone wanted to hear what Daphne had to say. Hear her interrogation, actually.

She held her chin up and stood in front of the table where she'd had supper with Lytge the night before. The cook was on one end, while she stood to the left. Yes, in the sinister corner, already convicted it seemed.

"I found her in the stillroom, sure enough, and she never asked permission or made it known she was going in there," the cook said.

"Did ye have the keys?" one of the captains asked.

"I did, indeed, but we were preparing for a feast, so many of the cabinets were unlocked throughout the day."

There were whispers in the hall, and the oldest captain slashed his hand through the air. Silence returned immediately.

"Ye are dismissed. Return to the kitchens."

The next man called was one of the retainers whom Lytge had sent away from his private chamber the night before.

"The earl sent ye away?" the older captain asked.

"Aye, he did. He was in a dark humor," the retainer answered.

The whispers began again. This time, even a

slashing motion wasn't enough to quiet them quickly. Daphne could feel the noose tightening around her throat. She suddenly resented the years she would be deprived of. Nevertheless, she wasn't willing to quit.

"I did nae poison the earl," she stated in a clear voice.

The hall erupted into chaos. Men shouted, and women pointed at her.

"And why in the hell would she have, when I'd asked the lass to wed me before I left?"

People turned around so fast, several ended up sprawled on the floor. Benches toppled over, but Norris didn't pay any attention to it. He paused for a moment at the end of the aisle, shooting a furious look at his clan members.

"And why the hell are nae the lot of ye in church, where yer jabbering might do me father some good?"

Norris was furious, but he was the finest sight she'd ever seen. Daphne couldn't stop herself from moving toward him. One of the younger retainers set to guard her put his arm out to stop her. There was a snarl from Norris as he came down the aisle at a near run. "Get yer hands off me wife-to-be!"

The captains had risen, but Norris wasn't impressed with their show of respect.

The oldest captain spoke up. "Ye should nae shelter her. Even the laird's family is nae above justice when the crime is one of attempted murder."

A muscle on the side of Norris's jaw twitched, and she was sure she had never seen him so angry. He drew in a stiff breath and glared at his father's captains.

"I am not afraid of their questions," Daphne insisted. "For I have nothing to hide."

Norris lifted his hand. Everyone waited on his next words.

"If ye are going to investigate this matter, I am left wondering why me father's page is nae here?"

The captains looked startled; then one of the younger ones spoke. "We believe the earl was poisoned when he took Mistress MacLeod into his private chambers and dismissed his retainers."

"The definition of an investigation is that ye question everyone, nae just the person ye would like to find guilty of the crime," Norris growled. "Ye are finished here, and ye may thank Christ for the fact that Broen MacNicols sent a hawk to Faolan Chisholms with news that had me ride through the night to return home. There would have been hell to pay if ye harmed me bride."

The young captains ducked their chins in the face of Norris's displeasure, but the older captain still refused to bow. "If she truly is yer choice, ye must allow this investigation to continue, else there will never be an end to this matter."

Norris didn't like what the man had to say, but the whispers that rose up behind him could not be ignored. "Then it will proceed once I've had some time to make sure anyone who might have had a hand in this is nae overlooked."

Gahan suddenly appeared and shook his head. Norris sent a hard look at his father's captains. "Where is Sandra Fraser?"

Even Daphne was confused, for the girl had been standing nearby just a few moments ago. An icy touch settled on her nape, and she pointed to where Sandra had last been.

"Find her," Norris barked. Gahan directed Norris's men while the hall erupted into movement.

Daphne didn't get a chance to breathe a sigh of relief, because Norris caught her up against him, squeezing her so hard she couldn't draw breath. She didn't care. It was the most perfect embrace ever. He buried his head in her hair and inhaled.

"I'm so sorry, lass. I swear I will never leave ye so unprotected again."

She trembled, wanting nothing more than to remain in his arms, but the activity around them stole his attention. He stepped back and cupped her face. For a single moment, his expression softened.

"Forgive me, lass, but I can nae leave yer safety to chance." He rubbed her cheeks for just a moment before releasing her. "Gahan, make sure she is secure. I must see me father."

Gahan stepped up and actually gripped her arm. It wasn't his grip that hurt her, though; it was the sight of Norris walking away. The night of tension began to take its toll on her. She shivered, and her knees knocked as she tried to walk. The need to vomit almost overwhelmed her though there was nothing in her stomach. Gahan looked at her oddly and moved closer, intent on lifting her off her feet. She drew in a stiff breath and leveled her chin before he could carry out his intention. There was only one man she wanted cradling her.

Isla caught up to them, having been separated from her during the questioning. "They made her sleep in the star chamber again and refused her a meal this morning."

Gahan growled softly and looked at the men behind him. "Clear a path up to the lady's solar." He looked at his sister. "Three of ye escort me sister to the kitchen."

His tone was as solid as stone. His men responded instantly, clearing the stairs. No one protested when they opened the door to the solar and inclined their heads while she entered.

"Really… I am nae hungry, and the star chamber is a fine one."

Gahan reached up and tugged on the corner of his bonnet, but there was something burning in his eyes that didn't fit with the meek gesture. He waved the retainers back, and the door closed behind them.

"Yer place is here." His tone was soft but unyielding. "Only a guilty person would believe they should accept being pushed out of their place."

His words rang with a solid truth, one that made her lift her chin with pride. He offered her a nod before leaving her.

The moment she heard the doors close behind her in her chamber, her body won. Her muscles refused to hold her up any longer, and she sank down into a chair near the window.

She owed God more thanks than she would ever be able to voice.

❧

Sandra Fraser was frightened. No! She was never afraid! Girls who did not know how to manipulate the world into doing their bidding were victims of fear. She was confident; her mother had taught her how to be quick-witted and never allow a situation to overwhelm her.

Norris Sutherland would be hers! However, she needed to get rid of Daphne MacLeod; that much was clear. It was sad, actually, because she would have enjoyed breaking Daphne before throwing her into the gutter, but being the cause of her demise would also be satisfying.

Sandra hurried down the hallways, resisting the urge to duck into one of the storage rooms. She would only look guilty when she was found. There had to be a way to aim more suspicion at Daphne. Even if Norris didn't believe it, he would have to hand her over if there was too much evidence against her.

First, Sandra needed to make sure she wasn't caught with the remains of the poison. She ducked into the garderobe and pulled the little flower hair ornament from her hair. It was such a shame to lose it. Many artisans wouldn't even make them, because they feared being tortured when someone fell victim to the poison hidden inside of them. But she couldn't be caught with it. She held it out over the seat and pulled her arm back before releasing it. What if she became a victim herself?

Sandra opened the center of the flower and gauged the amount of poison left. She would have to be very careful. If she took only half a dose, it wouldn't kill her.

Yes... yes... The plan began to form quickly. She heard people in the hallway, confirming that Norris had ended Daphne's trial. She used her fingernail to scoop up some of the paste and pushed it into her mouth without hesitation. The second dose was hard to force down her throat, because she was already gagging. Nonetheless, she managed it and closed the flower before dropping it into the toilet.

It sank beneath the muck, giving her a moment of satisfaction. Then her body began to convulse. She fought the urge to vomit, needing to be weakened by the poison. It would be the only way to damn Daphne MacLeod. So she managed.

❧

His father had never looked worse. Norris stood near the bed and lowered himself to one knee to be closer. He could hear the soft rattle of his father's breath. It sounded dry and brittle, like a winter blizzard. Like death…

He refused to count his father dead while Lytge still drew breath. It wasn't easy to cultivate hope when he looked at the pasty-white skin of his sire's face. His lips were pale, and he was as still as death.

Norris shook his head. If he was going to think of death, it would be the demise he had planned for Sandra Fraser. There was no doubt in his mind who the culprit was. But there was doubt aplenty among his people…

He didn't want to doubt he could clear Daphne's name, but if his father died, it was very possible there would be no way to prove her innocence. It was also possible his father would side with his captains.

Norris growled and stood up. He would not be torn over the issue of hoping his father lived. If fate wanted to test him, so be it. He turned toward the door and the battle waiting for him. There was no way he would allow Daphne to be lost.

✑

"Grinding yer teeth will nae solve this puzzle." Norris shot Gahan a glare and shook his head when he noticed the dark circles ringing his brother's eyes. They were both exhausted.

"She's the guilty one. It's undisputable now that Clarrisa found that sleeping draught in the cider," Norris muttered. He was only repeating what he'd said several times already.

"Ye can bet the bitch will dispute it," Gahan snapped. "I imagine she will nae be quick to offer a confession on poisoning our father, either."

There was raw violence in his brother's tone and rage in his dark eyes. Norris paced back and forth in front of his father's private table in his sanctum.

"Those damned pages are nae going to make it easy for me to confirm that one of them left me father's goblet unattended on the high table."

"Nae," Gahan confirmed. "They are protecting one another."

Someone pounded on the door and threw it open before Norris gave permission. Asgree was flushed from running. She stumbled when she tried to lower herself, because she was in such a hurry. "We found... Sandra... She's been poisoned."

✑

His father's captains were already assembled outside the room Sandra Fraser had been taken to. Their faces were grim as they looked through the doorway at the flurry of activity near the bed. The oldest, Ronald, shot Norris a hard look and spoke up. "This is damning evidence. There is only one who would gain from both yer father and Mistress Fraser being dead."

"Ye're forgetting meself, Ronald." The other captains shook their heads, but Norris nodded. "Aye, meself. Ye heard that correctly. I want Daphne MacLeod for me wife, and Sandra Fraser knows it well."

Ronald looked back at the woman convulsing on the bed. "Ye can nae mean to suggest that she poisoned herself? No one would do such a thing."

"It makes sense when ye hear from Broen MacNicols that the cider we all enjoyed at Deigh Tower was laced with a sleeping draught. I was under its influence when Sandra snuck into me bed."

"Ye have proof of that?" Ronald asked.

"Proof the cider was tampered with," Norris responded. "Lady MacNicols found the evidence the next day, after the cider claimed another victim—the brewmaster. They sent a hawk to Chisholms's land to intercept me. Thank Christ the bird flew straight and true."

"That is nae proof it were Sandra Fraser who done the deed," Ronald argued, looking past the doorway at the woman suffering inside the chamber. Her moans were pitiful.

"She was the only one who claimed to have any memory after drinking that cider, and she somehow made it into me bed."

"It would nae be the first time a man woke up with a lass after raising a few mugs of cider."

Norris felt his temper nearing the breaking point. Ronald had the other captains agreeing with him.

Always dispense justice, Son, else ye'll be no more

than a tyrant… and men do nae truly follow tyrants. Nae when it matters, that is. Remember Sauchieburn. The king was a man who did nae give his subjects any respect. He treated them like cattle and, in the end, they left him to his deserved fate.

His father's words echoed in his mind, rising up from a memory that was branded deep into his subconscious. It wasn't his father's message that bothered him so much; it was the way his father's captains were looking at him with doubt.

"Now is nae the time or place. We needs hear from Lady MacNicols and their brewmaster to see if more light might be shed upon the matter. Once me father awakens, he can make it clear what he approves of and does nae wish."

Ronald nodded. "And if yer father does nae awaken?"

"He will," Norris announced. He turned and left his father's men, but not before he saw approval in their eyes. He just wished the sight brought him more confidence than it did. Instead, he walked away, struggling to fend off the doubt trying to destroy his happiness. How could he be so close to having life become the perfection he'd heard of only in ballads, only to have fate turn against him? He wanted to believe it would be resolved, but too many factors seemed set against him. For the first time in his life, he considered leaving Sutherland. The idea gained strength as he made his way up to the chamber Daphne was being held in. His father still lingered, tearing his emotions. However, the moment he opened the door and caught sight of Daphne, he knew without a doubt he'd leave everything behind if it was the only way to spare her life.

❧

Daphne could not sit and make lace. None of the books seemed able to hold her attention. The solar was filled with all manner of fine entertainments, and all she managed to do was pace. Around and around until at last she heard the door opening. Relief surged through her to be done with waiting.

Despite that relief, when the door opened, she trembled. Her breath caught in her throat, and she felt heat flushing her cheeks. For a moment, she stood frozen, simply content to stare at the man she'd missed so greatly. Norris filled the doorway and ducked to enter the solar. Fatigue was etched into his face, but what captivated her was the welcome she witnessed filling his eyes.

He held out his hand. "Come, lass. I've a mind to hide from the world. It has been most unkind as of late."

There was no careful thought, only pure enjoyment as she placed her hand into his. For a moment, his gaze was locked with hers, and there was an answering flicker of bliss in his green eyes.

He turned and pulled her out of the chamber. His retainers tugged on the corners of their bonnets and also stared at their clasped hands. A soft chuckle followed them up the stairs, making her blush hotter. Norris spun her loose once they entered his chamber. The windows were open, allowing the sound of the sea inside. There was no sign of Bacchus. Norris looked for the peregrine, frowning when he was sure the raptor was definitely not there.

"Are ye hoping for word from someone?"

Norris untied his sword and placed it on the rack

near his bed. She heard him make a low sound of frustration as he turned to look at her.

"Will ye run away with me, Daphne? Live common but free at me side?"

Sincerity shone in his eyes, and it twisted like a dagger through her heart.

"I would never take ye away from here. Ye are a part of this place, these people."

Nevertheless, she couldn't help but love him more for making the offer. Tears filled her eyes, and he growled softly, moving toward her and cupping her face. He leaned down to kiss one wet track and then the opposite one.

"Maybe I am a fairy after all."

He lifted his head, staring at her in obvious confusion.

"I destroy the men who are drawn to me."

Norris hooked her around the waist when she would have stepped away from him. She pressed a hand against his chest but wasn't really interested in fending him off. She ended up in his embrace, and as she inhaled the scent of his skin once more, it felt like happiness had completely surrounded her.

"Ye complete me, lass." He lifted her chin so their gazes met. "Ye brought me a gift I did nae even know I needed, and I refuse to allow Sandra Fraser to destroy it."

"Running away would do that." He shook his head, and she slid her hand along his jawline to stop him. "I am nae going to allow her to frighten me away. Only a guilty person would run."

Admiration shone in his eyes, flickering hotter and brighter until it was an emerald blaze. He tightened his arms around her and swung her up and off her feet, turning in a wide circle as her feet flew out like a child's. They laughed like youngsters, long and loudly, finally spinning to a stop near the bed. Norris placed a kiss against her mouth, softly and sweetly, before trailing more kisses down the column of her neck. She slid her hands up his chest to seek the buttons at the top of his doublet and gently loosen them. Need and desire built slowly, remaining hot as they refused to hurry. He petted her and stroked her skin as he helped shed her clothing. She pinched out the candles, seeking the darkness where only the ruby glow of the fire would illuminate the chamber. The window remained open and allowed the sound of the crashing waves into the room.

Daphne was only interested in discovering once again how warm her lover's skin was. She opened his collar and cuffs, and helped him set his kilt aside once his belt was loosened. She bent over and pulled off his boots, narrowing her eyes in mock scolding when he looked down her chemise.

He wouldn't allow her to disrobe. He cupped her face and held her steady for a kiss. It was everything she'd yearned for since his departure. The soft pressure before he boldly tasted her with a firm thrust of his tongue. She kissed him back, growing more desperate for a deep taste of him. Need twisted through her. This time it was harder, more necessary to her very survival.

He was right; the world was not kind, but his embrace was her haven. She stroked his chest, trying to absorb his strength as he trailed kisses down her throat.

"I do nae care who calls me weak… it was a torment being parted from ye, lass."

His voice was a mere whisper. A dark delight that complemented the moment.

He tumbled her into the bed, joining her, and they each tried to immerse themselves in the other. For the first time, the need for satisfaction was ignored in favor of savoring each other. Each touch was precious, and neither rushed toward climax.

It came at last. Daphne unsuccessfully fought back tears. Norris wiped them from her cheeks as he held her close.

"I will nae lose ye, Daphne. I swear it."

In spite of the fact that he whispered, she heard the determination in his tone. She tried to soak it up, but the harsh circumstances prevented her from being truly comforted.

"I love ye, Norris."

He growled softly and cupped her chin. When their gazes locked, his eyes were red from the light of the coals. "Do nae ye dare doubt that we shall prevail."

"Yet ye do," she accused softly. "Should nae I strive to be yer partner in all things? Is that nae the way of a common-born man and his wife? Do nae insist I stand by while ye shoulder all the burdens of our life. Lovers share all."

He chuckled softly and stroked her cheek gently. "And what do ye know of being a lover, lass?"

"That ye are learning just as I am, Norris Sutherland, because ye have never loved before, either."

He nodded slowly. "Aye, lass, ye are correct."

Aye... correct.

But perfect was a better word.

She just wished perfection were not such an unnatural

thing to find in the real world, because such thinking opened the door to the worry that had hounded her all day.

The world was not kind to lovers—not kind at all.

∽

Norris didn't want to sleep. He wanted to hold Daphne, stroke her skin and enjoy the sound of her breathing. But his body had other ideas. Despite that, he slipped into slumber, the days of hard riding taking their toll. The hours of the night passed too quickly. When he opened his eyes, the horizon was pink and gold.

There was a flap and flutter, and Bacchus glided in through the open window to perch on the curtain rod. The peregrine fixed him with its dark eyes and shook before settling.

"What was wrong last night is righted by dawn's light," Daphne muttered drowsily. She sat up, keeping an eye on the raptor as Norris stood up and untied the tiny leather sheath attached to its ankle.

Norris unrolled the strip of parchment and read the message. He nodded before moving off to begin dressing. Daphne struggled not to ask him what the message was. She bit her lip and mastered the urge to pry until she caught sight of the amusement lurking in his eyes.

"What did it say, ye marauder?"

He raised an eyebrow at her demand.

"And I recall very well the price of my curiosity. Since I plan to wed ye, unless yer captains want to hang me, tell me what it said."

Norris's amusement died instantly. "Me father's

damned captains will learn the error of their thinking today. Broen MacNicols is on his way with his brew-master. The man has something to add to this matter." He waved the scrap of paper in the air. "There are times I wish hawks were twice their size so they might carry more detailed messages. But it is glad news all the same."

Norris was confident. Daphne tried to let it soak into her, but she still felt chilled. Her dreams had been full of the condemning looks of the Sutherland people as they pointed and cursed her. A knock sounded, and Isla entered with Gahan close behind. Norris was once more the heir to Sutherland; even his time while dressing was not his own. Isla shepherded Daphne to the outer room, where two maids waited to help with dressing her.

For once, she was grateful for their help, because her mind was not on the matter at hand. No, she was lost in contemplation of the fact that she might never see the chamber she stood in again. Norris might wish it otherwise, but she refused to allow him to give up everything he was. She loved him too much for that. If his father's captains could not be appeased, she would leave him. Even if it killed her.

❦

"It must be public," Ronald argued. The older man was not intimidated by Norris's growling or the fact that Gahan stood at his brother's back, looking just as furious.

"If she is pronounced innocent in private, no one will trust ye—nae when it comes to anything to do with Daphne MacLeod. They will say ye are soft and maybe worse, that ye are in a hurry to inherit yer title. Sutherland has never been weak in the eyes of our neighbors and vassals. The appearance must be maintained."

Gahan grunted. "As much as I hate to agree, I do. The gossips are vicious."

They were, but Norris still resented the situation. There was no way to avoid it; he understood that much. Beyond the doorways of his father's private chambers, he could hear the people in the great hall. He was torn, because part of him wanted to hate them for being there. However, there was another side of him that marveled at their loyalty to his father. It was something his father had earned and, if he were fortunate enough, he would, as well. There suddenly came a rise in sound from the hall, a rumble of increased conversation. The two retainers at the door frowned, and one of them left to investigate. The man returned almost instantly. He tugged on the corner of his bonnet before speaking. "Mistress MacLeod stands ready."

Ronald and the other captains looked surprised. "Who brought her?"

"She came herself," Norris informed them. "She is no coward."

Ronald considered him for a long moment and then nodded approval. "Well done, then. Let us hear what the MacNicols's brewmaster has to say on this matter."

❧

"Be quiet... I tell ye!"

Norris had to fight to maintain his composure. Ronald was ruby faced as those watching continued to interrupt the proceedings. The older captain pounded on the high table with a fist until the hall quieted down again.

"Ye're dismissed," Ronald informed the brewmaster. The man bowed and fled.

Broen MacNicols stood up and addressed them from where he'd been sitting on the end of the high table. "The matter is clear. Sandra Fraser is the culprit."

One of the younger captains stood up to challenge Broen. "It is nae clear. I've a cousin on MacNicols land, and she told me ye stood before yer people and proclaimed Daphne MacLeod was like a sister to ye and ye would take issue with anyone who did her wrong."

Broen frowned. "That is true, but it does nae make me a laird who would force his servants to give false testimony when the crime is so high."

"The brewmaster knows well yer affection for Mistress MacLeod. It is possible he is trying to please ye."

"I am no' a liar!" The brewmaster had not fled far. He stood and propped his hands onto his hips. "'Tis just like an arrogant Sutherland to look down on us MacNicols because our laird is nae so high as yers!"

The hall erupted again, this time Sutherland men entered the aisle to face off with the brewmaster. MacNicols retainers hurried to back up their clansman, and the tension tightened.

What drew Norris's attention was the way Daphne paled. For the first time, fear entered her dark eyes, and it sickened him.

"Hold!" he shouted as Broen ordered his men to stand down.

The nature of a Highlander was volatile.

Daphne watched the two clans separate as their lairds commanded, but they glared at each other. It was the same thing she had seen when she'd been presented as Broen's betrothed. The celebration feasts had been tension filled and far from enjoyable. Leaving had been the only solution. She was cursed.

"Since ye have heard from the men, 'tis time ye hear from the women." The captains had to look around to see who spoke. Asgree's voice was low, and those yelling in the hall quieted in order to hear her.

The head of house moved in front of the captains and laid something on the table. Daphne stepped closer to see what it was and gasped. The small hair ornament was easy to recognize, because it was so unique.

"I had the privy where Sandra Fraser was found cleaned. That was in it. When ye open it, ye'll see the paste has a clear finger indention. That poison stains the skin dark mustard. Mistress Fraser's right index finger was stained when we found her. I was nae the only one who saw the stain." Several maids lined up, nodding their heads.

Norris picked up the flower pin and flicked open the center. Broen moved close enough to see it too, while the crowd shook their heads and grumbled. Ronald sat down, looking older than he had before.

Norris stood up and fixed the line of personal pages with a hard look. "When me father took Mistress MacLeod to his sanctum, who was still at the high table?"

"Mistress Fraser..."

Those who didn't answer nodded.

"Did ye remain at yer posts while he was gone?"

Most of the boys went pale. Their eyes widened,

and one of them found the courage to answer. "We…
went for supper… at the back of the hall."

"Who served ye?" Norris demanded.

The boys looked down at the hall, searching among
the faces of those watching, until a middle-aged
woman stood up. She lowered herself before moving
to the base of the stairs.

"I did, Laird. 'Tis the truth I served them when the
earl went to his chambers."

"Did any of them remain to watch me father's plate
and cup?"

She shook her head, sending a shocked ripple
through all those watching. Horror appeared on their
faces, and then shame. Most found a reason to look
away from Daphne.

"Ronald, have some of yer men remove Mistress
Fraser from the main tower. I would have her far away
from me father."

Every single one of his father's captains jumped up,
eager for the chance to escape.

"This matter is ended," Norris declared. Daphne
watched his people stand and lower themselves in
front of him. In that moment, he was the master of
Dunrobin, and she believed him a good one. He
needed a bride who brought him a strong alliance, not
one from a defeated clan. Broen was shaking Norris's
hand as men crowded around the high table to get a
closer look at the hairpin.

Daphne slipped away, just as she had before her
wedding to Broen. It was better this way… Her
heart ached, feeling as though it was being torn apart,
but she kept walking—through a hallway and on to

another before she made it to a doorway that led to
the yard. People were pouring out of the great hall,
making it simple for her to make her way across the
yard without being singled out. At least that was what
she thought.

People began to lower themselves. Full retainers
reached up to tug on the corner of their bonnets
as they cleared the path in front of her. The word
"mistress" began to surround her, and she was greeted
by one and all. No one was too hurried to ignore her.
It was humbling. She froze in her tracks, and tears
pricked her eyes.

Someone moved up behind her, clasping her
with strong arms she instinctively recognized. Norris
nuzzled her head, earning them giggles from the girls
and knowing looks from the older women.

"Where are ye going, me sweet?" His arms tightened just a bit, and he sighed against her ear. "All is
well now."

"No, it is nae. Ye need a wife who brings unity, nae
fighting among yer vassals."

"Look and listen, Daphne. Ye have won the
Sutherlands' hearts. No negotiated bride will ever
match yer achievement." His tone was thick with
approval, and it warmed her heart. Just like that, the
pain that had been threatening to kill her was gone,
her doubts dispersed in the wave of happiness that
washed through her.

"But… ye do have a problem when it comes to
taking wedding vows," Norris informed her, his
voice rising.

"I do nae have a difficulty," she argued. He released

her, and she turned to discover Broen MacNicols standing two feet behind Norris. Gahan and other retainers were there as well, drawing the attention of those who had begun to return to their workday. Even the men along the curtain wall looked down at them.

"Yes, ye do." Norris cocked his head and looked at Broen. "Did nae she slip away before her wedding to ye?"

Broen crossed his arms over his chest. "Aye, that's the truth, and I hear she let ye seduce her when the king had clearly told her she was to wed me. Which makes it twice she left without wedding me."

"Twice, aye, a hesitation problem to be sure." Norris smirked. Their retainers were enjoying their comments full well. Daphne blushed and then cursed her fickle feminine nature for being so vulnerable to their teasing.

"I was the only one acting with good sense," she protested.

Norris grinned at her, the expression warning her that she had stepped neatly into his trap. "Allowing me to seduce ye was good sense, I agree."

"Ye arrogant marauder…" she grumbled. "Is it nae enough that I have—"

"No, it is nae enough just yet, lass." A moment later he planted his feet wide and bent his knees before running into her at waist level. He straightened up, to the delight of those watching, with her hanging over his shoulder. He turned in a wide circle, ensuring that every man on the wall got the opportunity to witness the moment.

"I'm off to the church to wed me little fairy before she escapes, lads! I need a few witnesses."

People parted, allowing their laird to stride toward the church. The priests hurried to open both doors so Norris might continue on to the end of the aisle. He placed her back on her feet, and the dust from her skirts settled.

"Marauder…" she accused softly.

"Aye, I am that…" He sank to his knees and offered her his hand. "Yer marauder, if ye like."

She did like it. Daphne sank to her knees, clasping the hand of her lover as the priest moved in front of them. She loved it.

❧

The church bells rang out, informing everyone of their laird's wedding. Many came running to offer congratulations, but Asgree arrived and pushed her way to Norris. "Yer father is awake."

A cheer went up from those crowding around them. Norris kissed Daphne quickly; then he turned and ran toward the tower. His kilt bounced, and she might have mistaken him for a little boy being summoned by his father, if she discounted the sword strapped to his wide back.

No, he was a Highlander, a marauder… her husband. And a good son.

❧

His father looked weak. Norris forced himself to accept the fact that his father was growing older, while at the same time, he marveled at how the laird had defeated death.

"Ye think I know naught of love."

Norris was surprised by his father's words. The old man chuckled, and a fit of coughing overtook him. When he recovered, he grinned at his son, looking more lively than Norris could have hoped for.

"I'm nae ready to let Gabriel take me away just yet. But he does like a battle, so I let him think he was winning there for a bit."

Norris grinned. "Rather kind of ye."

"It was at that," Lytge agreed, "because it seems ye do nae understand me so well, me lad. Ye think me a harsh man when it comes to matters of the heart."

"Ye did nae seem very welcoming to Daphne," Norris replied. "Since we're in private, I do nae plan to start holding me tongue, since I never have before. Ye were blunt and overly harsh with her. I took her to me bed, knowing full well she was virgin. She is more than a lass I've dallied with—much more."

A gleam of approval entered the old man's eyes. "Oh, aye, I understand that well enough."

Norris cocked his head to the side, irritated with his father's jolly mood. "Do ye? And when were ye planning on sharing that bit of information with me?"

His father grinned, as arrogant and cocksure as ever. "I was nae. Ye are me son and would nae have listened to an old man if he told ye how much ye looked like a new foal following behind its mother. So damned dependent on her for yer life."

"I am nae dependent—" Norris shut his mouth with a click of his teeth. His father chuckled again and pointed a bony finger at him.

"Oh, ye are, and 'tis a fact that I envy ye that feeling. But I had to be sure the lass was worthy of it, ye understand." He nodded, his expression becoming somber. "Oh, yer mother, she played me well, she did. Smiled and fluttered her eyelashes and made me think I had her heart just as she had mine. The truth of the matter was she loved me title." Disappointment flickered in his eyes. "But she was nae unkind, and she gave ye to me and raised ye with love. I confess I envied ye her love." He slapped the surface of the bed, determination gleaming in his eyes. "So I wanted to make sure ye did nae stumble into the same trap."

"She's still penniless."

His father chuckled again. "Are ye thinking to test me, lad?"

"Aye, I do believe I am, Father."

"Well, ye tested me when ye left to seek the king's permission to force me to yield to yer wish to wed her."

Norris shook his head slightly. "Ye knew that, did ye?"

His father nodded. "I knew it because it's what I would have done. It stung, just a bit, I'll admit. I understand it's just an old man's pride, trying to get involved in something I have nae right to be involved in. I did nae care very much for the fact that me own sire took such a dislike to Gahan's mother. She was the lass who held me heart, but yer grandfather refused to allow her to live at Dunrobin. He thought yer mother would be more welcoming to me if that were so—and I did try, Son."

"I recall that well, in spite of how young I was. Forgive me, for ye are correct. I was set on gaining the king's blessing, because I knew ye'd accept it. For that, I am sorry, because we have never been dishonest with each other. But it matters naught to me if she is penniless. I've wed her and am sorry only that ye did nae get the chance to give us yer blessing."

His father chuckled. It started him to coughing again, but he didn't seem to mind. "Ye had it, me son, have no doubt of that. She had the strength to stand beside ye when everyone was quick to turn away."

"Aye, I've noticed that meself."

Lytge winked. "She's nae penniless, but I wanted to see if ye'd have her in spite of the gold her father settled on her."

Norris shook his head, suddenly understanding the amusement in his father's eyes. "Ye've known where her dowry was the entire time," he muttered slowly. "Ye crafty fox."

"Ye forget sometimes that ye learned every trick ye know from me, lad. Gahan too. Ye're me sons, and I have made sure to raise ye both, nae leave it to some power-hungry bastard who thinks to earn himself a comfortable place by endearing ye to him. Leave that practice to the English nobles." He reached out and clasped Norris's forearm. "Ye are me son, the most precious thing God has ever given me. I wanted ye to have a woman who loved ye with all her heart, for that is another gift I once dreamed of having. Well, I ensured ye'd get both by keeping the knowledge to meself. Besides, ye never asked me if I knew anything of the lass's dowry."

"No, I did nae." Norris chuckled. "Ye got me there, pure and simple. But ye were her father's overlord."

Lytge nodded. "And as such, I sent me own men to safeguard that treasure on its way to Broen MacNicols. When the lass put him in his place and I heard the rumors of her father siding with the Royalists, I made sure to put that gold some place it would nae be carried off by raiders."

"Yer own coffers."

His father smirked.

It was brilliant, but it sent a chill down his spine. "She might have died over yer keeping that secret. Ronald was thinking to hang her."

"Well, I did nae know that Fraser bitch was going to poison me. There's the reward I get for letting Gahan watch yer back, when I should have kept the man for meself," he groused. "And do nae cross yer arms over yer chest like that, me lad. Ye'll nae brood over the matter. I was making sure the lass was nae after yer title, and ensuring ye were nae simply amused by the idea of having something ye thought I would nae approve of. Ye youngsters are bedazzled by the forbidden, and ye, me lad, are a proud one. It would nae have been the first time ye bedded a lass ye knew I'd disapprove of, just to remind me that yer respect for me ended at yer bedchamber door. Yet rightfully so."

Relief poured over him, and Norris suddenly laughed. "I love ye."

His father nodded. "Aye, and I treasure it. Now get that lass to bed, because I want the comfort of grandchildren in me old age."

Norris stood and tugged on the corner of his bonnet. "I'll do me best."

Lytge watched with pride the man his son had grown into leave his bedchamber. He was certain Norris would prevail, but he was also sure Daphne would give him a bloody hard time claiming that victory.

He cursed Sandra Fraser again for laying him in a sick bed where he wouldn't be able to watch the battle.

◦⁀◦

"What of Sandra?" Gahan had waited until they had left their father's chamber before asking.

Norris turned to his brother. "I believe I've discovered what they say about love to be true. It's turned me soft, Brother—at least when it comes to vengeance. I'm more interested in cherishing life."

Gahan slowly smiled. "Then I suppose the matter falls to me, as the next-eldest son."

"Only if ye want the duty. For meself, I do nae care. Me father can have her hung once he recovers. It is his right. We'll have to appeal to the king if we want to prove Bari had any knowledge of it. Nonetheless, I plan to make sure the man knows he is never welcome beneath me roof again."

"Oh… he's welcome to come here… no promise on how he leaves," Gahan growled softly and shot Norris an exasperated look. "Here I am, plotting vengeance, and ye can nae wait to get to yer lady's side."

Norris nodded. He reached out and clasped his brother on the shoulder. "I pray ye feel the same someday."

Gahan watched his brother begin climbing the stairs to the upper floors in the main tower. He waited until two retainers fell into step behind their laird's son before he turned and walked toward the oldest tower in Dunrobin. The stone walls were rougher there, the archer slits like large crosses, allowing the sunlight to hit the opposite wall in glowing signs of the cross. Fitting…

The wind whistled, almost moaning through the

hallways and tugged at the edges of his kilt. The stairs were narrow, and some of the edges crumbling. The door at the top was narrow, too, but the retainer there opened the lock and pushed it inward for him.

"I was never here," Gahan muttered and made sure Sandra heard him.

She sat up, reaching for the retainer. "Do nae leave me with him!"

The door slammed shut, and Sandra glared at it for a moment before she picked up the thin pillow the cot-like bed afforded her.

"Ye'll nae find it simple to smother me with this thing." She threw it at him, and it landed with a soft sound against the bare stone floor.

Gahan studied her for a moment. Her chemise was fine linen with black-work embroidery around the neckline. It was a stark contrast to the bed. Little more than a cot, it was sturdy but lacking in luxury.

"A hundred years ago, this was the only tower at Dunrobin."

"I do nae care. It is a hovel. The dungeon is likely better afforded."

Gahan's eyes narrowed. "Something ye can easily judge for yerself."

She sat up on her knees, pressing her hands on top of her thighs so her chemise was pulled tight across her breasts.

"Are ye sure, Gahan? Maybe ye should consider becoming me savior instead of me executioner. Why let Norris have everything, when ye can take it?" She licked her lower lip and leaned forward. "I could be very grateful."

Gahan grinned, and victory flickered in her eyes. She leaned farther forward to give a look down her chemise. He kept his attention on her eyes. He moved closer, until he was only a single step from her. Sandra reached out, seeking the edge of his kilt, when he tossed her flower hair ornament onto the sheet beside her.

"Done," he muttered as he stepped back. "Ye can show yer gratitude by relieving us of the chore of ending yer life."

Sandra picked up the hairpin, and her face drained of color.

"I refilled it with something a little less exotic, but deadly nonetheless."

He turned, and she launched herself at him. Gahan turned back, lifting his foot so that he kicked her in the center of her chest. With a muffled cry, she ended up sprawled on the stone floor.

"Me father will have ye hung unless ye do the deed yerself. I find meself unwilling to suffer touching ye. So those are yer choices."

"Gahan… Gahan!"

Gahan never looked back. He watched the retainer lock the door and left. It was a better death than she deserved.

※

Bari Fraser heard his peregrine cry and waited for the animal to land. It glided to a stop in the wide window opening of the master's chamber at Seabhac Tower. The animal knew it was home, chirping happily as Bari relieved it of its leather pouch. Seabhac was

Gaelic for raptor, and the land had been known for its birds for over a century.

He tossed the bird a piece of fish from a bowl on his table and unrolled the message. When Bari let out a howl of rage, the bird was startled and took the fish across to another tower to eat. *Damn the Sutherlands to hell!*

Sandra was dead. His spy at Dunrobin could be trusted, but it still took time for the news to sink in. Once it did, he growled again, cursing Lytge with every fiber of his being.

The earl was to blame. Bari shook and wiped at the tears that spilled from his eyes. He would have his vengeance. He sat down to write a message. Lytge Sutherland had taken his sister, so he would make sure the man lost something of equal value. A bastard son was the same as a legitimate daughter.

Bari wrote quickly and placed the message into the pouch, but he didn't whistle for the peregrine that had brought it. Instead, he went down to the mews, searching among them for a bird trained to fly to Matheson land. His rage continued to boil as he set the peregrine on its way. With Sutherland retainers, he'd have grabbed up Matheson land and made it Fraser. Now, he would have to call on Achaius Matheson as an ally. Another thing Lytge would pay for, and Bari intended to make sure the cut was deep. The old earl had only three living children, two sons. Bari was going to make sure Gahan Sutherland died by his own hand. Sandra deserved as much.

He laughed, throwing his head back and startling the birds.

"Brother? Are ye well?"

Bari snarled and delivered a sharp slap to the young woman busy tending to the birds. She flinched but didn't make a sound.

"I have told ye never… never call me brother!" he raged at her. Anyone else would have backed away from him, but Moira stood steady, her blue eyes fixed on him. "Ye are me half sister!" He made a slashing motion with his hand. "Yer mother was common born. Sandra was me sister, nae ye! Get back to work!"

"Why do ye say Sandra 'was' yer sister?"

"Because she is dead at the hands of the bastard Sutherlands, and I will have vengeance!"

Moira sighed softly as her brother left the mews. She far preferred the company of the birds to that of her sibling. Oh yes—half sibling. Strange, but she somehow didn't think Bari would appreciate how much comfort that little bit of knowledge brought her. Which was what made it so very amusing!

Well, she'd never get the chance to tell him. Bari did his best to ignore her, as if she were the lowest servant on his land. It was better that way, better that he hadn't yet tried to wed her to another person he had no intention of keeping his promise to. Bari Fraser was not a man of his word, and his neighbors knew it. Half sibling was certainly enough for her.

Enough of a curse!

❦

"So, me fine husband, is the window going to remain open through the snowstorms?" Daphne trailed her fingers through the hair on Norris's chest. Alone at last, sated for the moment, she indulged herself in savoring the feeling of having him hold her. Bacchus was perched in the corner, eyeing her as though the raptor understood her question.

"If ye continue to call me husband, ye will likely get me to agree to anything ye ask of me."

Daphne lifted her head, still slightly amazed to see Norris in bed with her. How had everything settled out so well? *Does it matter?*

Her husband grinned and pressed her head down onto his chest again.

Nae, it does not...

"I love ye, Daphne MacLeod."

That was what mattered! Indeed it was.

To Conquer a Highlander

Highland Hellcat

Highland Heat

The Highlander's Prize

From

To Conquer a Highlander

Scotland 1437, McLeren land

FIRE COULD BE A WELCOME SIGHT TO A MAN WHEN he'd been riding a long time and the sun had set, leaving him surrounded by darkness. But the sight of flames on the horizon could also be the most horrifying thing any laird ever set his eyes on.

Torin McLeren wanted to close his eyes in the hopes that the orange flames illuminating the night might not be there when he opened them again. He could smell the smoke on the night air now but didn't have the luxury of allowing the horror to turn his stomach. He was laird, and protecting his holdings was his duty.

Digging his spurs into his horse, he headed toward the inferno. Wails began to drown out the hissing flames. Laments carried on the night wind as wives and mothers mourned bitterly. The scent of blood rose above the smoke, the flickering orange light illuminating the fallen bodies of his clansmen. He stared at the carnage, stunned by the number of dead and wounded. He might be a Highlander and no stranger to battle, but this was a village, not a piece of land disputed and fought over by nobles. This was McLeren land and had been for more than a century.

A horror straight out of hell surrounded him. Mercy hadn't been present here—he'd seen less carnage after fighting the English. The slaughter was almost too much to believe or accept. His horse balked at his command to ride forward, the stallion rearing up as the heat from the blaze became hot against its hide. Torin cursed and slid from the saddle. Every muscle in his body tightened, rage slowly coming to a boil inside him. Hands reached out to him, grasping fingers seeking him as the only hope of righting the wrong that had been inflicted on them.

His temper burned hotter than the fire consuming the keep in front of him. They suffered raids from time to time, but this was something else entirely. It was war. The number of bodies lying where they had fallen was a wrong that could not be ignored. Nor should it be. These were his people, McLerens who trusted in his leadership and his sword arm for protection.

"Justice…"

One single word but it echoed across the fallen bodies of men wearing the same plaid he did. Every retainer left to keep the peace was lying dead, but they had died as Highlanders. The ground was littered with the unmoving forms of their attackers. His gaze settled on one body, the still form leaking dark blood onto his land, the kilt drawing his interest. Lowering his frame onto one knee, Torin fingered the colors of his enemy. The fire lit the scarlet and blue colors of the McBoyd clan. His neighbor and apparently now his enemy.

McBoyds? It didn't make sense. These were common people. Good folk who labored hard to feed their families. Every McLeren retainer stationed there knew and accepted that they might have to fight for their clan, but that did not explain the number of slain villagers. There was no reason for such a slaughter. No excuse he would ever swallow or accept. McLerens did not fear the night, be they common born or not. While he was laird, they would not live in fear.

"There will be justice. I swear it." His voice carried authority, but to those weeping over their lost family, it also gave comfort. Torin stood still only for a moment, his retainers backing him up before he turned and remounted his horse. He felt more at home in the saddle, more confident. His father had raised him to lead the McLerens in good times and bad. He would not disappoint him or a single McLeren watching him now.

"Well now, let us see what the McBoyds have to say for themselves, lads."

Torin turned his stallion into the night without a care for the clouds that kept the moonlight from illuminating the rocky terrain. He was a Highlander, after all. Let the other things in the dark fear him.

From

HIGHLAND HELLCAT

"COME, MY BEAUTY, WE SHALL SEE IF WE CAN IMPRESS anyone tonight with our skill."

Brina patted the mare on the side of the neck, and the animal gave a toss of its silken mane. She smothered a laugh before it betrayed to those around just how much she was looking forward to riding out of her father's castle. She gained the back of the mare, and the animal let out a louder sound of excitement. Brina clasped the animal with her thighs and leaned low over its neck.

"I agree, my beauty. Standing still is very boring."

Brina kept her voice low and gave the mare its freedom. The animal made a path toward the gate, gaining speed rapidly.

Brina allowed her laughter to escape just as she and the mare crossed beneath the heavy iron gate that was still raised.

"Don't be out too long… Dusk is nearly fallen…" the Chattan retainer set to guarding the main entrance to Chattan Castle called after her, but Brina did not even turn her head to acknowledge the man.

Being promised to the church did have some advantages after all. Her undyed robe fluttered out behind her because the garment was simple and lacked any details that might flatter her figure. There were only two small tapes that buttoned toward the back of it in order to keep the fabric from being too cumbersome.

"Faster…"

The mare seemed to understand her and took to the rocky terrain with eagerness. The wind was crisp, almost too chilly for the autumn. Brina leaned down low and smiled as she moved in unison with the horse. The light was rapidly fading, but the approaching night didn't cause her a bit of worry.

She was a bride of Christ, the simple gown that she wore more powerful even than the fact that her father was laird of the Chattan. No one would trifle with her, even after day faded into night.

But that security came with a price, just as all things in life did. She straightened up as the mare neared the thicket, and she spied her father's man waiting on her.

Bran had served as a retainer for many years, and he was old enough to be her sire. He frowned at her as she slid from the back of the mare.

"Ye ride too fast."

Brina rubbed the neck of the horse for a moment, biting back the first words that came to her lips.

"What does it matter, Bran? I am promised to the church, not betrothed like my sisters. No one cares if I ride astride."

If she had been born first or second to Robert Chattan, there would be many who argued against her riding astride, because most midwives agreed that doing so would make a woman barren.

Bran grunted. "It's the speed that ye ride with that most would consider too spirited for a future nun."

Brina failed to mask her smile. "But I shall be a Highland nun, not one of those English ones who are frightened of their own shadows."

Her father's retainer grinned. "Aye, ye are that all right, and I pity those who forget it once ye are at the abbey and training to become the mother superior."

Bran turned and made his way into the thicket. Brina followed him while reaching around to pull her small bow over her head. The wood felt familiar in her grip. It was a satisfying feeling, one for which she might thank her impending future as well. Her sisters had not been taught to use any weapons. They were both promised to powerful men, and the skills of hunting would be something that those Highlanders might find offensive to their pride.

She snorted. Going to the church suited her well indeed, for she had no stomach for the nature of men. She could use the bow as well as any of them.

"At least I know that ye will nae go hungry." Bran studied the way she held the bow, and nodded with approval. "Those other nuns will likely follow ye even more devoutly because ye can put supper on the table along with saying yer prayers."

"I plan to do much more than pray."

From

HIGHLAND HEAT

1439

SPRING WAS BLOWING ON THE BREEZE.

Deirdre lifted her face and inhaled. Closing her eyes and smiling, she caught a hint of heather in the air.

But that caused a memory to stir from the dark corner of her mind where she had banished it. It rose up, reminding her of a spring two years ago when a man had courted her with pieces of heather and soft words of flattery.

False words.

"Ye have been angry for too long, Deirdre."

Deirdre turned her head slightly and discovered her sister Kaie standing nearby.

"And ye walk too silently; being humble doesn't mean ye need try and act as though ye are nae even here in this life."

Kaie smiled but corrected herself quickly, smoothing her expression until it was once again simply plain. "That is my point exactly, Deirdre. Ye take offense at everything around ye. I am content. That should nae be a reason for ye to snap at me."

Her sister wore the undyed robe of a nun. Her hair was covered now, but Deirdre had watched as it was cut short when Kaie took her novice vows. Her own hair was still long. She had it braided and the tail caught up so that it didn't swing behind her. The convent wouldn't hear any vows from her, not for several more years to come.

"But ye are nae happy living among us, Deirdre, and that is a sad thing, for those living in God's house should be here because they want to be."

"Well, I like it better than living with our father, and since he sent my dowry to the church, it is only fitting that I sleep beneath this roof."

Kaie drew in a stiff breath. "Ye are being too harsh. Father did his duty in arranging a match for us all. It is only fair that he would be cross to discover that ye had taken a lover."

Melor Douglas. The man she'd defied everything to hold, because she believed his words of love.

Deirdre sighed. "True, but ye are very pleased to be here and not with Roan McLeod as his wife. Father arranged that match for ye as well, and yet you defied his choice by asking Roan McLeod to release ye. There are more than a few who would call that disrespectful to our sire."

Her sister paled, and Deirdre instantly felt guilty for ruining her happiness.

"I'm sorry, Kaie. That was unkind of me to say."

Her sister drew in a deep breath. "Ye most likely think me timid, but I was drawn to this convent. Every night when I closed my eyes, I dreamed of it, unlike ye…"

Kaie's eyes had begun to glow with passion as she spoke of her devotion, but she snapped her mouth shut when she realized what she was saying.

Deirdre scoffed at her attempt to soften the truth. "Unlike me and my choice to take Melor Douglas as my lover."

It was harsh but true, and Deirdre preferred to hear it, however blunt it might be.

"He lied to ye. Ye went to him believing ye'd be his wife."

"Ye do nae need to make excuses for me, Kaie. I made my choice, and I will nae increase my sins by adding dishonesty to them. Everyone knows, anyway. It seems all I ever hear about here, how I am unworthy of the veil ye wear so contentedly." Deirdre shrugged. "At least no one shall be able to claim I am intent on hiding my actions behind unspoken words and unanswered questions."

Her sister laughed. A soft, sad little sound that sent heat into Deirdre's cheeks, because Kaie was sweet and she didn't need to be discussing such a scarlet subject.

"Ye have ever been bold, Deirdre. I believe ye should have been born a son for all the courage ye have burning inside ye. For ye are correct, I am content, and there is no place I would rather be but here. Living a simple life. Roan McLeod was a kind soul to allow me to become a bride of Christ instead of his wife. Wedding me would have given him a strong alliance with our clan."

From

The Highlander's Prize

Scottish Lowlands, 1487

"KEEP YER FACE HIDDEN."

Clarrisa jerked back as one of the men escorting her hit the fabric covering the top of the wagon she rode inside of. An imprint of his fist was clearly visible for a moment.

"Best keep back, my dove. These Scots are foul-tempered creatures, to be sure. We've left civilization behind us in England." There was a note of longing in Maud's voice Clarrisa tried to ignore. She couldn't afford to be melancholy. Her uncle's word had been given, so she would be staying in Scotland, no matter her feelings on the matter.

Better to avoid thinking about how she felt; better to try to believe her future would be bright.

"The world is in a dark humor," Clarrisa muttered. Her companion lifted the gold cross hanging from her girdle chain and kissed it. "I fear we need a better plan than waiting for divine help, Maud."

Maud's eyes widened. Faster than a flash, she reached over and tugged one of Clarrisa's long braids. Pain shot across her scalp before the older woman sent to chaperone her released her hair. "You'll mind your tongue, girl. Just because you're royal-blooded doesn't give you cause to be doubting that the good Lord has a hand in where you're heading. You're still bastard-born, so you'll keep to your place."

Clarrisa moved to the other side of the wagon and peeked out again. She knew well who she was. No one ever let her forget, not for as long as she could recall. Still, even legitimate daughters were expected to be obedient, so she truly had no right to be discontented.

So she would hope the future the horses were pulling her toward was a good one.

The night was dark, thick clouds covering the moon's light. The trees looked sinister, and the wind sounded mournful as it rustled the branches. But Clarrisa didn't reach for the cross hanging from her own waist. No, she'd place her faith in her wits and refuse to be frightened. That much was within her power. It gave her a sense of balance and allowed her to smile. Yes, her future would hold good things, because she would be wise enough to keep her demeanor kind. A shrew never prospered.

"Far past time for you to accept your lot with more humbleness," Maud mumbled, sounding almost as uninterested as Clarrisa felt. "You should be grateful for this opportunity to better your lot. Not many bastards are given such opportunities."

Clarrisa didn't respond to Maud's reminder that she was illegitimate. There wasn't any point. Depending on who wore the crown of England, her lineage was a blessing or a curse.

"If you give the Scottish king a son—"

"It will be bastard-born, since I have heard no offer of marriage," Clarrisa insisted.

Maud made a low sound of disapproval and pointed an aged finger at her. "Royal-blooded babes do not have to suffer the same burdens the rest of us do. In spite of the lack of blessing from the church your mother suffered, you are on your way to a bright future. Besides, this is Scotland. He'll wed you quickly if you produce a male child. He simply doesn't have to marry you first, because you are illegitimate. Set your mind to giving him a son, and your future will be bright."

Clarrisa doubted Maud's words. She lifted the edge of the wagon cover again and stared at the man nearest her. His plaid was belted around his waist, with a length of it pulled up and over his right shoulder. The fabric made a good cushion for the sword strapped to his wide back.

Maybe he was a Scotsman, but the sword made him look like any other man she had ever known. They lived for fighting. Power was the only thing they craved. Her blood was nothing more than another way to secure what the king of Scotland hungered for.

Blessing? Not for her, it wouldn't be.